To Alan.
Hope you en~

C000178267

ABOUT THE AUTHOR

Dave Rigby, who lives in West Yorkshire, started writing after he retired nine years ago.

His first book, *Darkstone*, was published in 2015. *Shoreline*, the first Harry Vos Investigation, followed in 2016.

Redline is the second of the Harry Vos books.

Redline

A Harry Vos Investigation

Dave Rigby

Copyright © 2018 Dave Rigby

The moral right of the author has been asserted.

Apart from any fair dealing for the purposes of research or private study,
or criticism or review, as permitted under the Copyright, Designs and Patents
Act 1988, this publication may only be reproduced, stored or transmitted, in
any form or by any means, with the prior permission in writing of the
publishers, or in the case of reprographic reproduction in accordance with
the terms of licences issued by the Copyright Licensing Agency. Enquiries
concerning reproduction outside those terms should be sent to the publishers.

This is a work of fiction. Names, characters, businesses, places, events
and incidents are either the products of the author's imagination
or used in a fictitious manner. Any resemblance to actual persons,
living or dead, or actual events is purely coincidental.

Matador
9 Priory Business Park,
Wistow Road, Kibworth Beauchamp,
Leicestershire. LE8 0RX
Tel: 0116 279 2299
Email: books@troubador.co.uk
Web: www.troubador.co.uk/matador
Twitter: @matadorbooks

ISBN 978 1789013 436

British Library Cataloguing in Publication Data.
A catalogue record for this book is available from the British Library.

Printed and bound by CPI Group (UK) Ltd, Croydon, CR0 4YY
Typeset in 11pt Minion Pro by Troubador Publishing Ltd, Leicester, UK

Matador is an imprint of Troubador Publishing Ltd

Cover Image: Sint-Anna Tunnel, Antwerp

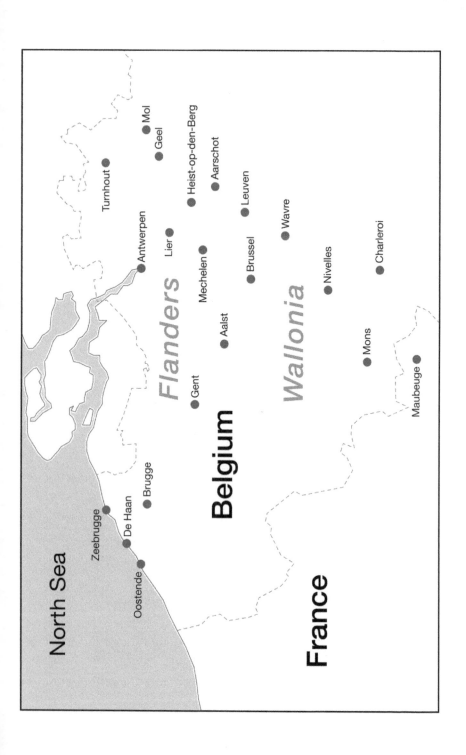

< are you sure?
< yes, he's a real threat to us
< you know what to do?
< of course

A spring morning

In his befuddled state, his front light out of action, Yannick lost control of his ancient bicycle and swerved off the narrow track. Landing awkwardly in a riverside ditch, he passed out immediately.

When he finally came to, in the early bright light of a spring morning, head throbbing, it took a while before he realised he wasn't alone in the ditch. Someone else was lying beneath him. Maybe his companion had been similarly affected by drink. But neither his questioning nor his repeated prodding produced any response. Only then did the awful truth creep over him: he'd spent the night sleeping on top of a dead man.

Yannick struggled desperately to raise himself without becoming entangled in the man's limbs. Finally upright, he staggered away from the body, brushing his clothes with his hands, as if trying to remove some form of contamination. The rhythmic thrum of the blades of a wind turbine was the only sound he could hear. There were no houses to be seen. Instinctively he'd always tried to avoid contact with the police, but he knew this was different: he'd have to tell them about the body. Without a phone – he'd never been one for new-fangled devices – there was no choice but to try and find somewhere to make a call.

When the buckled front wheel of the bike refused to turn, Yannick cursed, attempted to get his aching legs into action and tried to ignore the continuing pain in his head. His progress on foot along the track was slow. Eventually he reached a narrow road which crossed the river. A farmhouse on higher ground caught his attention and he stumbled along a rutted track towards it.

A man dressed in overalls called out to him, wanting to know what he was doing on his land. Yannick told him about the body, but his explanation was garbled and rambling and it took a while before the farmer was able to work out what had happened. Eventually he submitted to his unexpected visitor's insistent pleas and called the police. They stood together silently in the early morning sun, smoking the farmer's cigarettes until the police car arrived. Yannick led them to where the body was lying in the ditch by the river.

Chief Inspector Antoine told his officer to secure the site. The dead man was dressed for walking in the wet – a good quality waterproof which had seen better days, over-trousers and a decent pair of boots. It looked as if he'd been lying face-down in the isolated ditch for a good while. Although his pockets were empty, his rucksack, which was found in a nearby hedgerow, contained a map of the local area, notebook and pen, a torch, a pair of binoculars, the long-decayed remains of a sandwich and a flask of black coffee. There was also a plastic wallet containing three thousand euros.

When they searched his pockets more thoroughly, they found a train ticket stuck in an inner lining – a return from Brussels to Charleroi.

The case was assigned to Antoine.

One

Despite searching high and low in the bungalow, Paul Demotte had been unable to find his father's wartime gun and notebook. He was worried. The gun wasn't licensed and, from the little he knew about it, he suspected the notebook contained compromising details about some of his father's wartime activities. The old man had been moved into a care home and the keys to his bungalow were due to be handed back to the landlord. Rather than running the risk of the missing items being discovered by a new tenant, Demotte had decided to hire Harry Vos, a private investigator, to carry out a thorough search.

It was an early morning visit. As Vos pushed open the front door to the bungalow, he was overcome by the smell. A quick scout around revealed the sources of the stench – rotting food on the kitchen table and an unflushed toilet. The whole place was damp and airless, full of ageing furniture and bric-a-brac. While Vos sorted the toilet out, Katerine Verlinden, who'd accompanied him out of curiosity, removed the food from the table, wrapped it in carrier bags she found under the sink and threw the decaying mess into the dustbin outside the back door.

They'd brought along a flask of coffee and bacon sandwiches wrapped in greaseproof paper, but a single glance between them was enough to decide to abandon the idea of having a breakfast picnic in such a damp, stinking and oddly creepy place.

Still, there was a job to do and they searched methodically through each room, emptying cupboards, rolling back carpets and lifting loose floorboards. The roof space was restricted and Katerine struggled to haul herself up there and make her way around it. But all their efforts were in vain. There was no sign of the gun or the notebook.

"What now, Harry?" Katerine asked.

"Well, Demotte mentioned his brother-in-law. He lives just over there," Vos said, pointing through the window. "Perhaps I should pay him a call, see if he knows anything. Mind you, I don't think there's any love lost between the pair of them."

"Alright dear. I think I'll head off to work and try to get the smell of this place out of my nose." They went their separate ways in the grey light, Katerine to give a lecture on Congolese artefacts, Vos only as far as the house across the road.

He knocked loudly on the front door of the mid-terraced house and waited, leaning on his stick, taking in the neglected garden and the peeling paintwork.

Eventually the door was opened by a middle-aged man wearing jogging bottoms, an over-sized, grubby t-shirt advertising Tongerlo beer and a baseball cap. It looked as if his clothing had only just been thrown on and the man rubbed his eyes then yawned without covering his mouth. Vos couldn't help thinking of the old soap adverts which featured *body odour*. He took an instant dislike to the man, but tried not to show it.

"I've been watching you snooping around in the bungalow. My brother-in-law said something about it. What do you want?" Another yawn. Was it rudeness or boredom, or perhaps a bit of both? Vos explained he just wanted a brief word.

"Can I come in? It won't take long." The man stood aside reluctantly and Vos hovered in the hallway before being ushered into the front living room. There were empty bottles everywhere and a few unopened. Chairs were piled high with newspapers and a small dog was asleep in the corner by the TV. Vos realised he'd have to move the papers from one of the chairs himself before he could sit down.

"As you know, your brother-in-law asked me to search over there. I've been looking for two items belonging to his father – your wife's father as well of course. I haven't been able to find them and wondered if you could help me track them down."

The man hesitated and looked down at a small pile of plates, roughly stacked on the old carpet, congealed food squeezed over the edges. Vos could tell from his shiftiness that he knew about the gun and the notebook and saw no point in prolonging things.

"Have you still got the gun?" The man looked affronted by the abruptness of the question, but when Vos stared back at him, his resistance melted away.

"I took it for safe-keeping," he muttered. "You don't want to leave something like that around."

"What – and you didn't think to tell your brother-in-law? You could have saved him and me the trouble of searching." There was no answer. "Have you tried to sell it?" No reaction again. "Well if you can retrieve it from its new hidey-hole, I'll take it to its rightful owner."

"Wait a minute. I'm not giving it to you. He's my relative not yours!" Vos wasn't surprised by his reaction.

"In that case I'll have to let him know what you've done. Or maybe I should just tell the police you're holding an unlicensed gun!"

Vos flinched when the man rose to his feet and stood over him, but then relaxed when he noticed the bulges of fat under his t-shirt and heard his breathlessness.

"Just get me the gun and while you're at it, bring me the notebook as well."

The man slouched off to the back of the house. Through the front window, Vos saw a woman walking up the garden path, then heard the front door opening and closing. As soon as she walked into the living room, the bleached-blonde, cigarette in the corner of her mouth, asked Vos what he was doing there. Before he had chance to reply, the man returned, carrying a cardboard shoebox. His wife made a grab for the box but he managed to evade her.

"You should have sold the damn thing already. We need the fucking cash for Christ's sake!" He looked scared but handed the box over to Vos, who lifted the lid, checked the contents and walked out of the house.

The Vectra started first time. He still couldn't get used to it and smiled as he set off on the road back to Heist-op-den-Berg.

Two

Paul Demotte was not best pleased when he learnt that his brother-in-law had removed the gun and the notebook from the bungalow. But he was furious when, after handing over the notebook, Vos told him what he'd done with the gun.

"You see, the police have a weapons amnesty just now, so it seemed the right thing to do – to hand it in. I mean, with your father in an old folks' home, he'll have no use for it, will he? And you'd told me the gun was unregistered so it would have just caused trouble." Vos tried not to sound too righteous about it.

"I don't care about any damn amnesty. The gun wasn't yours to hand in!" Demotte shouted. Unsurprisingly he refused to pay Vos anything. But there was nothing else he could do about it. A complaint to the police would not have been a wise step.

Without telling his client, Vos had photocopied the notebook before handing it over. He'd wanted to read it straight away, but it had been written in some sort of code. When he phoned Katerine to ask whether there might be someone at the university who could decipher it, she told him she'd check. He faxed the photocopy of the notebook through to her office.

It didn't take her long to find a colleague who cracked codes for fun and he had no trouble with the notebook. That was the great thing about working at the uni, Katerine told Vos. Experts in most subjects were available, almost on tap. You just had to know the right way to approach them.

+ + +

She delivered the decoded version of the notebook to Vos in person. As he cooked, she read extracts from it out loud. The entries started in 1944 when Demotte senior had been in the Ardennes area of Wallonia. It was clear he'd been involved in some heavy action.

"Have you met him?" Katerine asked.

"No – just his son, and his son-in-law of course. I think I mentioned he now lives in a care home here in Heist. It's strange, but because he's in a home, I've been thinking of him as just a frail, harmless old man. What you've read out so far puts him in a very different light. I'd like to find out more about what was going on back then." Katerine said she couldn't see why he wanted to know any more.

As Vos drained the spaghetti, she looked through the various cards propped up on the mantelpiece. He glanced up, colander in hand and saw she was reading from an invitation.

"Would you like to go to that?" he asked. Katerine read out loud from the card: "...*we have great pleasure in inviting Harry Vos plus one to our wedding on June 17th at...*"

"Who are the happy couple?"

"The son of one of my cousins and his fiancée. I don't see much of him and I've never met her, so I was a little surprised to get the invitation. You could be my plus one."

"I'll have to get something to wear," she said. Vos took it as a yes.

+ + +

The Vectra's recently fitted new engine was purring. Aarschot, Leuven, Wavre, Nivelles and Mons. They were in no hurry. Katerine asked whether he'd finished reading the notebook. He said he had and found it fascinating if rather disturbing. On the surface, it looked as if old Demotte had been active in the resistance from 1944 but Vos felt there was something that didn't quite ring true about a number of the entries. He hadn't mentioned it to Katerine, but he hoped to get the chance to do a little research about Demotte's activities. Maybe one of the older Wallonian relatives attending the wedding would be able to throw some light on things.

Their hotel was in Mons town centre, close to the Marché aux Herbes. For dinner, they found a small restaurant down a side street. Although there was only one dish on the menu – tarte flambée, an Alsace favourite – there were fifteen variations to choose from. After over-indulging, they walked arm-in-arm in the twilight back to the hotel.

At breakfast they were all touchy-feely, much to the young waiter's obvious embarrassment. Katerine went back to their room to start getting ready for the wedding, leaving Vos at the table with his third cup of coffee and the local paper. His legs were stretched out to the side of the table and he felt pleasantly content.

His attention was caught by an article about 'Charlie'. The man had been found dead, close to a tributary of the river Sambre, not far from Charleroi. As yet, the police had been unable to identify him. None of the few belongings they'd found had given any firm clue as to who he was or where he was from. A journalist had christened him *Charlie* simply because he'd been found near Charleroi and the name had stuck. Vos was intrigued. He walked slowly across to the breakfast buffet, poured himself another coffee and decided that a little more to eat would be a good idea. In his experience, weddings generally involved an awful lot of standing around and a long, long wait for food.

He re-read the article and chuckled when he saw the name of the investigating officer – Bernard Antoine.

Katerine scrubbed up well, as Vos' mother would have put it. But then she had ready access to the Antwerp fashion quarter.

He was in his suit – his only suit – which at least still fitted him reasonably well. He was pleased he could even manage to do up the top button of the trousers.

The wedding service more or less passed him by and he spent the time studying the detail of the stained glass windows and surveying his fellow guests. Although there were many people he didn't recognise, there was a reassuring sprinkling of cousins and their ever-expanding families.

Seeing these members of his mother's side of the family triggered thoughts of his grandfather, who'd lived and died a miner in Charleroi. As a young boy, Vos had spent chunks of his summer holidays in his grandparents' small terraced house, his grandmother, taking every opportunity to teach him French, telling him that the language was far superior to his guttural Flemish. He'd been a quick learner. Apart from the French lessons, what stuck in his mind was her permanent headscarf, her rough-skinned hands and her ready supply of boiled sweets.

Grandfather was a gruff man, normally very serious. But he would occasionally slip out of his formal, reserved skin and play the fool with the young Harry. He could remember trips to the fairground and the baths. Swimming lessons had been short and stern affairs but they'd finally succeeded in getting him to risk taking his feet off the bottom of the shallow end of the pool. Grandfather had rewarded the completion of his first width with a pair of swimming goggles.

Once the service was over, Vos had to tear himself away from his childhood memories and rejoin Katerine and the rest of the world. Everyone moved on to the reception in a swish hotel, just off the road to Maubeuge.

He refused the offer of a small glass of fizzy wine from a circulating tray and sloped off to buy what he thought of as a proper drink.

"Bernard! I hoped I might find you at the bar – didn't see you in the church." He shook his cousin's hand vigorously.

"Harry – how are you? No, I couldn't make the actual service, held up at work. Not that I really minded, to be honest. I'm not one for churches. It must be a few years since we last met – a funeral no doubt. It's nice to have a wedding for a change." His phone started to ring. "Sorry – just excuse me for a second. There's no escape … 'Antoine. Yes, you need to do it right away. It can't wait until tomorrow. Yes – make sure you do!'" He ended the call. "Can't get the staff you know." His look of preoccupation slowly melted away. For a man who must be coming up to retirement, Vos thought his cousin had aged well, silver-grey hair and goatee, an athletic looking frame with only a hint of a beer belly.

They spent time catching up on family gossip, draining their glasses simultaneously. Vos bought refills and they retired to a pair of comfortable chairs hidden away in a small recess.

"I've just been reading about the man they've nicknamed Charlie," Vos said, keen to find out more. "Do you have any leads yet?"

"Join the queue, Harry! Everybody wants to know about him," Antoine said, grinning ruefully. "But we haven't really got anywhere. Neither his clothes nor his few belongings are in any way unusual, so we can't really use any of those items as a starting point. The money's interesting, but so far we've got no idea why he had that much cash on him. His prints aren't known to us and his DNA's not on our database. Nobody's recognised the e-fit yet, but, given that his face wasn't all there, this one's even more of an approximation than they usually are." Vos was startled. There'd been nothing about that in the paper.

"So, was he assaulted?" Vos asked, more and more drawn in as the conversation progressed.

"Not by a human." Vos stared at his cousin. "Probably a mixture of animals, insects and the weather at work. He'd been there on the ground, face-down for a few months. Are you here on your own, by the way?"

Vos realised that he'd more or less abandoned Katerine in a place where she knew nobody. Yet the recess was a pleasant escape and he had Antoine to himself. She'd be OK for a while yet, wouldn't she? He explained how he and Katerine had met and skirted round the ups and downs of their relationship.

"Well, Segolene and I are still together," Antoine said, somewhat abruptly. "Sorry, that came out more negatively than I meant it to. I'm the one at fault – always have been. She keeps us going. I don't know how she puts up with it. My job I mean. Do you still dabble in PI work?"

Vos wanted to protest. The people-smuggling case hadn't seemed like dabbling to him and it had become far more risky than he'd ever anticipated. But he didn't want to sound petulant, particularly as he was after a favour from his cousin.

"Yes, I've been quite busy, one way or another. To tell you the truth I wouldn't mind finding out a bit more about the Charlie case – nothing that's under wraps of course – but maybe just a run through the detail. Would that be possible?"

Antoine's first instinct was to turn down the request, thinking it would be an unnecessary distraction. But then he reflected that firstly, he had a staffing shortage and secondly, a colleague in Brussels had told him about the success of Vos' investigations in a recent case that the police themselves had steered well clear of. From what Antoine had heard, his cousin might be an amateur, but he was also doggedly persistent and not lacking in imagination – just the kind of qualities he could do with on the case and it wouldn't cost him a cent. On top of that he thought he could control Vos' involvement, whereas drafting in extra professional expertise would not only further stretch his already limited budget, but also run the risk of him losing control.

He laid out the ground rules for his cousin's involvement.

+ + +

Vos needn't have worried about Katerine being stuck on her own. He found her talking to Segolene Antoine as if they'd known each other for years. She didn't appear to have noticed his prolonged absence and told him that they'd been invited to the Antoines' for dinner the next day. It was a pleasant surprise that the seemingly random events of the day had come together so neatly.

During the wedding breakfast, he spoke to those relatives within earshot, conversations about people he barely remembered, old scores which had never really been settled and new babies that had recently arrived on the family scene. The woman on his right, whose name he couldn't remember, mentioned Albert, his mother's brother. There'd been an awful argument between the two siblings decades previously and they hadn't spoken to each other since. Vos had never really liked the man but thought it a shame that the estrangement had become permanent.

"I assume he is still alive," Vos said, then thinking this sounded a little insensitive, he hurried on to add, "given that I've not heard anything to the contrary." He wasn't sure if this made his opening comment any less insensitive but the woman didn't seem to take any offence. Maybe other people had the same view of Albert – a cantankerous old man whose main hobby had always seemed to be baiting other people.

"Yes he's alive and kicking – 93 now. He was interviewed in the local paper about the battle in La Roche, you know, The Bulge. He likes to tell anyone who'll listen how he single-handedly held off the Germans there."

La Roche, Vos recalled, was one of the places mentioned in Demotte senior's notebook. Maybe Albert could assist him in his research. But he'd have to try and make sure that word of any meeting with the old man didn't somehow get back to his mother.

Apparently Albert was still living on his own. Although he'd moved into an old folks' home a couple of years back, he'd been more or less thrown out for antagonising all his fellow residents and had returned to his own house which, luckily, had remained unsold.

Vos decided he'd visit Albert the following morning. Katerine said she'd be happy to go on ahead to Charleroi with the Antoines.

+ + +

Albert's house, close to the Mons Memorial Museum, was set in a large garden. The front was given over to trees and large shrubs rather than the usual suburban flowerbeds. The shuttered front windows gave the house an appearance of deep repose. Vos leant on his stick briefly before lifting the polished brass knocker and hammering it against the front door, more in hope than expectation of an answer. The door remained stubbornly closed. Not to be defeated, Vos walked around the side of the house and opened a wrought iron gate that led to the back garden. His uncle was sitting with his eyes closed on a garden chair lined with cushions, a tortoiseshell cat on his lap.

Vos had a sudden memory of himself as a five year old watching a much younger version of Albert adding a dead butterfly to an already extensive collection, his face a study in absolute concentration. He wondered if the collection was still around somewhere in the house, or perhaps in one or other of the dilapidated garden sheds.

He was reluctant to rouse the man, who looked calm and relaxed, suspecting that this outward show of peace could turn into wakeful annoyance in an instant. Still, he told himself, he wanted information and probably had only this one chance to get it.

When he coughed rather theatrically the old man stirred but did not wake. It was only on the third cough that Albert opened his eyes. He stared at Vos for a long while before speaking.

"Ah, it's Harry, isn't it? The family nose gave you away! To what do I owe this pleasure? It must be a while." This was completely unexpected, certainly not the uncle he knew and disliked. Was it possible he'd mellowed? "How's my dear sister?" Was there a trace of sarcasm in the voice or was he imagining it? "Come take a seat and we can have a little catch up. Over forty years if I'm not mistaken!"

Vos pulled a bottle of Courvoisier from his bag and held it in front of Albert.

"Shall I get the glasses, the good ones?" he asked. The old man nodded. Vos found the glasses exactly where he'd last put them all those years ago. He poured two generous measures and carried them into the garden. Albert fixed his eyes on the glasses and licked his lips in anticipation.

He tipped up his glass and emptied it in one, smacking his lips as he did so. Vos sat down on an adjacent chair. Unfortunately it was cushionless and the worn wickerwork stuck into his behind in several places. He put on his best stoical face, sipped his cognac and watched as his uncle pulled a ready-rolled cigarette from a silver case and lit up. They talked a little about the old days. But Vos didn't want to spend too long playing catch up with his uncle and at an opportune pause in the conversation, he removed the photocopied sheets of Demotte's decoded notebook from his bag.

"Here's a tale you'll be interested in, Albert." Vos realised he'd never called him Albert before. It had been *Uncle* or sometimes *Uncle Albert* but never just his first name. It felt like a daring thing to do, but for goodness sake, he was in his mid-sixties and perhaps this liberty could be justified. In any event, his uncle didn't react.

Vos read out loud from the notebook, choosing tasters to get his uncle going about his own experiences of 1944. It didn't take long before the old man started talking, with an almost dream-like look on his face. He told Vos about how he'd been stuck with his unit in a beech copse just outside La Roche-en-Ardenne, German troops shelling them, certain that he'd end his days there. And then Allied troops had appeared out of nowhere. At first it was as if he was relating these experiences as a detached observer with a fine eye for detail, rather than a participant in a bloody battle. But suddenly he lost this detachment, the roll-up fell from his grasp onto the lawn and he fell back exhausted against the cushions. Vos was shocked by this rapid change in his demeanour and immediately regretted his own irresponsibility in disturbing these memories.

But, just as suddenly, Albert recovered. He asked to see the notebook, fished a pair of John Lennon glasses from the top pocket of his white jacket and studied it intently for a while.

"Who did you get this from?" he asked, almost gruffly. Vos explained. "Well it doesn't add up. The man couldn't have done all these things. It's hard to tell, mind, because he's quite careful in what he writes. As far as I can work it out, at first he seems to be in cahoots with the local administration and they were collaborators. Later it looks as if he was with the resistance – maybe the Armée Secrète – who were linked to the Government in Exile, you know. He's off sabotaging railway lines with them and goodness knows what else. I really don't know what's going on here. He's certainly a good storyteller. Can I keep these papers for a day or two? I'd like to go through them in more detail. By the way, what's your interest in this document?" Vos wasn't sure how to answer his uncle's question. He felt he should give some reason why he'd initially kept a copy of the notebook.

"It's recently become something of an interest of mine – what the resistance got up to, particularly in '44. So the chance to be able to read about it first hand – well it was too good to miss." He made this up on the spot and hoped Albert wouldn't probe him about the extent of his knowledge. "That's what started me off, but now – well I'm keen to know more about what was really going on and a bit concerned, to be honest, especially after what you've told me. Please keep the papers for a few days. I'll come back and pick them up and maybe we can have another discussion."

"I'll look forward to it. When you come, you must stay for dinner." When Vos said he didn't want his uncle to go to any trouble, Albert insisted it would be a pleasure.

As Vos rose to leave, his uncle held out the brandy bottle.

"No, no! It's a present for you. It's the least I could do after forty years," Vos said. Albert smiled.

"How's that sister of mine?" he asked again, still smiling. "Tell her I've been thinking about her. It's true – just the last few days. I don't know why, maybe guilt for having shut her out of my life for so long." Vos was thrown by these candid comments.

"Thank you, Albert. I will tell her. You'll know she was widowed, wasn't well for a number of years, but now, I'm glad to say she's a lot better, lives with a friend of hers – a Mr Wouters – which has worked out very well." Vos recalled all his previous doubts and forebodings about Jan Wouters, but he had to admit that his mother really had found a new lease of life. He just wished they'd do the decent thing and get married.

"Good for her!" Albert said. Vos wondered whether the old man would ever stop smiling, now he'd discovered how to.

+ + +

He was pleased he'd stopped himself downing a second cognac. *One for the road* Albert had suggested. The traffic on the N90 to Charleroi was manageable. Antoine had given him directions to his house but, as usual, Vos found it impossible to hold the steering wheel, read his own scrawled notes, watch for road signs and keep an eye open for other vehicles. So his progress was interrupted several times by the need to pull off the road to check and recheck his notes. The route took him past ruined industrial buildings and a huge steel pipe that threaded its way along the side of the road. But there were also modern premises and cranes towering over new developments in the town centre.

When he finally reached the house, he found Katerine and the Antoines sitting in the garden well through a bottle of wine. They ate dinner outside taking full advantage of the warm evening and the merciful absence of biting insects.

+ + +

After seeing Katerine off on the early morning train to Brussels, Vos made his way to Antoine's office. The detective had cooked up a cover story about his cousin having some specialist information that might be useful in the Charlie case. A couple of people put their head round Antoine's office door, but neither of them questioned Vos' presence.

They chewed over how Charlie might have reached the Sambre valley. The train ticket they'd found in his pocket would have got him as far as Charleroi, but how had he travelled on from there? If it had been by bus, surely the driver would have come forward by now, or he'd have been picked up on CCTV at the bus station. Vos reckoned he might have walked. It was a fair step, but less than twenty kilometres and he'd been wearing walking boots. Or perhaps he'd hitch-hiked, picked up by a driver just passing through the area who'd missed the subsequent publicity surrounding Charlie's death.

He read through the file and studied Charlie's few belongings which were sealed in transparent evidence bags. There was very little to go on. The only items that caught his eye were the walking boots. They looked exactly like his own pair. Antoine removed them from the bag and Vos held them carefully with gloved hands.

It was clear there'd been a small label on the leather tongue of each boot, which had been cut off. There were no other identifying marks. He was sure they were the same make of boots as his own – *Beacon* – or something like that. It was the stitching that was distinctive. The salesman had told him it was the 'welt' that gave them their distinctive look – though he'd never got round to checking what the word meant. He'd bought them from a specialist shop in London whilst visiting his daughter Kim. The salesman had insisted on carefully measuring each of his feet. The metal foot gauge had felt really cold on his bare feet. Although the boots had been expensive he'd thought it was worth investing in a good pair. And he'd promised himself that he'd look after them – a promise that hadn't been kept.

He mentioned his thoughts about the boots to Antoine, adding, on the spur of the moment, that as he was already planning a visit to London, he'd have an opportunity to make some enquiries with the man who'd sold him his own pair.

"I remember him saying that the firm had only three outlets so there's a fair chance Charlie bought his boots from the same branch as me. He couldn't have bought them online," Vos added, as an afterthought, "because they only sell their boots to customers who've had their feet measured in the shop. He was very particular about that – the man in the shop I mean."

Antoine told him his enquiry could be useful and that he certainly couldn't afford the cost of one of his men travelling to England, what with all the budget cuts.

"But, as I'm sure I don't need to remind you, Harry, you won't be taking the full weight of the Belgian police service with you. You'll be there as a civilian with a hunch."

Vos looked at the other bagged pieces of evidence and studied the photographs that had been taken of the body and the scene of crime. He forced himself to look at the photo of Charlie's damaged face. So that was what happened to you when you were in the ground – or, more accurately, lying face down on the ground. Even allowing for the nature of the changes wrought by decay, Vos couldn't help feeling that the e-fit wasn't particularly helpful. Maybe that was one reason why there'd been no response from any members of the public so far.

The description of Charlie was brief. *'Male, Caucasian, height 1.8 metres, weight 70 kilos, hair colour black, eye colour not known, birthmark on left inner thigh.'* Not many people would have known about that last item, Vos mused.

Being a bit of a sucker for maps, he felt he couldn't leave without a quick look at the one found in Charlie's rucksack. It was an ordinary large-scale map of the area around the Sambre, southwest of Charleroi. A line had been drawn in red around a small part of the area. Antoine told him that they'd not been able to establish anything particular about the land marked on the map – except that it included the location where Charlie's body had been found. One of his men had questioned the local landowner but this had produced nothing of interest.

They were still no wiser about why he'd had three thousand euros on him. On the assumption that he might have been killed, it seemed to rule out robbery as a motive.

Antoine bought lunch at a small café near the train station where they ran through possible causes of death. There were no signs of injury to the body. He'd had a slight heart condition but it was unlikely to have been a contributory cause of death. A single needle mark indicated some kind of medical treatment or possibly drug use. There was slight evidence of a possible allergic reaction. However the fact that the body had been exposed to the weather, the earth and the hostile attentions of insects and animals for months meant that any conclusions drawn from a toxicological analysis had to be speculative.

Charlie didn't appear on any local CCTV footage that had been trawled to date – not even at the train station. Nobody had come forward with any information. Vos had provided the first glimmer of hope.

"When will you be going to London then, Harry?" Vos had no idea. It had been an off-the-cuff comment. But then he'd been saying for ages that he must visit his daughter again. He'd half-promised to take Katerine on his next trip there. And now he had to go. He was on the case.

He told Antoine it would be within the next few days. His cousin looked pleased and poured him another glass of wine.

+ + +

The river was not particularly wide at the point where Charlie's body had been found. It was a tributary, which joined the Sambre a few kilometres downstream. Vos poked about in the riverbank undergrowth, inspected the ditch and the adjacent birch copse, hoping to find something that might have been missed in previous searches. There was nothing. It was a pleasant spot, sunlight dappling through the trees, the water flowing slowly by, no sounds of passing traffic. If he'd been able to forget why he was there, Vos would have enjoyed the rural tranquility.

Maes

Christ! What next? Whatever you give him, Mertens always wants more.

The boss never looks you in the eye. He'll look over your shoulder or out of the window or down at his laptop, but never at you directly. Perhaps he's worried about betraying himself, but then you'd never describe him as being short of confidence.

He explains about my next task. That's what he always calls them, as if it's something like fixing the vacuum cleaner or making sure there's enough food in the freezer. I mean, I wouldn't expect him to use the word mission, but some nod in the direction of the complexity of our activities would be nice.

After he's outlined the 'task', I tell him I don't fully understand. This isn't true of course. But I don't want any ambiguity. I want him to go through it again – which, to give him his due, he does. Then he hands me a folder which contains all I need to get the job done.

Outside, I'm on my own again. That's the way I prefer it. All the crap that's talked about working in teams! Other people just get in the way and you end up making compromises which threaten the goal or put you at risk, or both.

+ + +

As it happens I haven't got far to go to start work – N12 to Turnhout, then it's less than 20k to Dessel. I've heard of it, but I didn't know about the nuclear detail until Mertens' briefing. My first call is a farm of 15 hectares. The place is rundown, a young boy in wellington boots looks totally pissed off as he tries to move half a dozen poor-looking beasts into a small pen. The dog doesn't help and the heifers seem oblivious to instructions from either the canine or the small human, who tells me his father is in the milking parlour. At least I've got my

*choice of footwear right, to cope with the slurry flow that's being urged
by a water jet across the pitted concrete floor of the lean-to building.
Mr Peeters, it says on my list, a man struggling to keep things going,
farm too small to be viable as a full-time concern, bank likely to
foreclose on his loan in the near future. I've never asked Mertens how
he unearths this kind of information, but it's essential to have this
kind of background knowledge so I can work out where to pitch the
opening offer – which in this case will also be my closing offer.*

*Peeters is expecting me. I spoke to him on the phone, told him
why I wanted to see him and a little about me – a bit of money to
spare, interested in buying some land, no problem if it's marginal,
just want to keep a few animals. Hobby farmer.*

*He's suspicious at first, as I expected. There's been no interest in
his land for years. It's poor quality and the nuclear waste facility is
not far down the road. Why would anyone want to buy his place?*

*We sit in the small farmhouse, the kitchen a haven of cleanliness,
our boots on the mat by the door. Mrs Peeters, who provides us with
mugs of strong coffee, seems more wary of her husband than she is
of me. He dismisses her from the room and I begin to talk. I love
talking and I can be very persuasive. When I mention the figure, I
can tell he's half-tempted to ask for more. But only half-tempted.
Offer too much and people get suspicious. Maybe the land is worth
more than they'd assumed and then they start thinking it might be
worth hanging on to check out other potential buyers.*

But it's always the cash 'bonus' that convinces them.

*I pull out a roll of notes from my jacket pocket and remove the
elastic band. A taster! Two thousand euros in cash and most people
will bite. As I spread the notes out on the plastic tablecloth I can
tell he's hooked. I reassure him. This is over and above what I'll pay
him to buy the farm, it won't be mentioned, won't go through any
books and he won't need to sign anything. It's just between me and
him. The only thing I need from him is his silence – for tax reasons
I explain. He nods his assent.*

The notes are safely in his pocket. He pours out two glasses of gin from a newly-opened bottle. Perhaps it's only for special occasions and there haven't been any of those. We clink glasses. It's clear that he can't believe his good fortune.

Six weeks later I tell Mertens the purchase is complete. By then I've got three other properties in the pipeline.

He hasn't told me anything about how the land will be used, but I've done my own research. There's been some speculation about an expansion of the waste facility, but nothing's gone public. After all it's nuclear waste we're talking about here. As the buyer, I exist only for as long as it's takes to complete the deal. A back to back sale from me to GreenEarth takes place immediately. They're registered in Luxembourg, with a local lawyer the sole named trustee – no other company information is publicly available.

It's taken me a while to unearth this information. It's good to know more than they think you know.

Three

After the third time of trying but failing to speak to Kim directly, Vos decided that he'd make the trip to London whether or not his daughter ever bothered to get in touch. His next call was to Katerine. Would she want to go with him? Was she free to have a break or were there continuing academic demands over the summer months?

Her phone continued to ring and he held on expectantly. Finally she answered, told him she was with someone, but that she'd call him back. He thought she sounded awkward and he started worrying immediately who the 'someone' might be. Ever since she'd told him about the *thing* that she and Jalloh had together, a few years ago, he'd half-convinced himself that the *thing* might be back on. But he had no evidence for this whatsoever.

When his phone finally rang it wasn't Katerine.

"Uncle – guess what?" It was Ryck with one of his daft questions. He hadn't heard from his nephew for a while. They'd spent so much time together on the people-smuggling case that Vos had come to see the two of them as a team. But things had changed since.

"I'm off to college!" Ryck had obviously waited long enough for an initial response from his uncle and decided to race on. "This autumn, nursing, specialising in learning disabilities hopefully. It was talking to one of the nurses at Uncle Pieter's place that set me off thinking." How could this be? As far as Vos could remember, Ryck had left school at sixteen with very little in the way of academic qualifications. How could he be on his way to college? "MSES," Ryck continued, clearly able to read Vos' thoughts. "Mature Students Entry System."

"That's great news, Ryck." Vos wasn't really sure about this. In his view, Ryck had a habit of starting but not finishing and he was unsure whether he could really be described as mature. "What are you going to do for money?" Ever practical, Vos had focused in on the likely problems.

"That's the great thing. I've got a bursary. And you know the garage in Berchem?" Of course Vos knew. It was *his* garage after all. "Well I've got some work with them." Why would they have taken Ryck on? What did he know about car mechanics? "Jan – the bald one – he's got some health problem and has to take it a bit easier, so I can work there for about fifteen hours a week, at times that suit me, more or less."

"So, the college is in Antwerp then?"

"Yes of course. Where else would I go?" Vos could think of several alternatives, but he let it go. "Can I come round and show you the course details?" Vos had to admit, the lad was certainly enthusiastic. "I'll bring Magda as well and the baby if that's OK." Vos was taken aback and had to remind his nephew that he didn't know anything about a Magda – or a baby. That story took another ten minutes to tell.

No sooner had he finished the call than Katerine was on the line. Whoever the *someone* was, they'd gone. She sounded her usual self and told him that London would be good. She had a colleague there who was doing research on cultural signifiers. They could meet up whilst Vos pursued his own enquiries. Katerine admitted she was nervous about meeting Kim and he told her he felt exactly the same.

It was only when he checked on the internet that he found out what a cultural signifier was. Why couldn't academics use ordinary language?

+ + +

It wasn't a peak-time Eurostar service and there were plenty of empty seats. Vos, struggling to keep his eyes open, supped his coffee and glanced at his paper. He'd been pleasantly surprised when Mr Wouters and his mother had agreed to dog-sit. So Barto, his adopted Irish wolfhound, was having a break as well. Vos still wasn't sure whether to keep the dog, feeling he might be too much of an encumbrance. With a bit of luck the old couple might decide they didn't want to give him back.

Ryck's visit had gone well. Magda, his girlfriend, had seemed very pleasant. Sun, a toddler rather than a baby, had sat on her mother's knee looking around inquisitively. A large bag of parental paraphernalia had dominated the kitchen table. Ryck had explained that he wasn't Sun's father, that Magda lived in Antwerp and that the three of them were going to share her small house.

For reasons Vos couldn't quite recall, Katerine was due to join him on the Eurostar at Lille. He fretted the whole time about whether she'd be there and what it would signify if she wasn't. At least it took his mind off Kim. He'd finally managed to catch her on the phone. She was still with Anders – her current boyfriend – which was a good sign. He also worked in the City.

Vos had booked a hotel room in London. Without discussing the matter, both he and his daughter knew that staying under the same roof together would not be a good idea. As the train pulled into Lille, Vos rose from his seat, left his bag and his stick on the luggage rack and joined the end of the queue of passengers lining up to disembark. Katerine knew his seat number, but he felt restless and was unable to sit back and wait for her to board the train.

There was no sign of her and he immediately assumed the worst. Why couldn't she just tell him if there was a problem? Tiredness crept over him once again as he returned to his seat.

Half-asleep, he had a vision of a place by the water. Water everywhere – and boats too. Harlingen of course! A face in front of him, his other grandfather, Grandfather Vos, a fisherman: beard, dark shaggy hair, hard as nails and with few redeeming features. He'd always tried to avoid his grandfather and kept close to his grandmother. Chalk and cheese, she was kindly, always had a good word for him and the occasional treat. Their faces gradually faded from view to be replaced by track-side gantries and English buildings flashing by.

At St. Pancras his spirits lifted. He never failed to be impressed by the station building and Katerine was suddenly there by his side.

"Sorry, love. I caught an earlier train. Tried to text but I think your phone must be on the blink." They walked slowly, arm-in-arm, down to the underground, eliciting sharp stares and muttered comments from hard-eyed, impatient commuters.

+ + +

It was a real turn up. Kim had booked a restaurant – a posh one – and was insisting that she would pay, telling her father that her bonus had been reasonable. Anders said he thought twenty thousand was better than reasonable and Vos cringed, waiting for the inevitable eruption. But Kim just smiled at her boyfriend and patted him on the arm. Vos had to admit that the food was superb even if the portions were a little small. It was some sort of tasting menu and he lost count of the number of courses after the fourth. The two K's were ever so formally polite initially, but then relaxed into ordinary conversation. Anders was unlike any of Kim's previous boyfriends. Vos actually liked him and he seemed to have a way of defusing the occasional conversational landmines that threatened the surface peace.

The foursome parted on friendly terms with a loose arrangement to meet up again. In the taxi back to their hotel, Katerine said she thought Kim needed Anders more than he needed her and she hoped it would last. Vos wondered, not for the first time, if his daughter had ever really recovered from the death of her mother.

Back at the hotel as they prepared for bed, Katerine suddenly asked him about his intentions. He misunderstood, thinking she meant his immediate intentions which he'd thought were fairly clear. He stuttered over his response, until she cut in.

"No – you fool. I didn't mean the next few minutes, I meant the next few years, or hopefully longer." Vos knew he should have thought about this. He'd been meaning to, but kept putting it off. Out on walks with Barto, he'd tell himself to forget about his plans for the garden or his worries about his mother and concentrate on Katerine. But, try as he might, his butterfly mind always floated off somewhere else.

They sat on the end of the bed, both looking towards the curtains, rather than at each other. He knew that this was a significant moment. They'd known each other long enough to think seriously about being serious. But he liked the idea of not tying things down, not because he wanted something else, but because he valued the informality of their relationship and didn't want to risk stifling it or boxing it in. Nor did he relish the idea of a big expensive wedding with lots of guests. But he was aware that this was probably not how Katerine saw things and doubted that it would be a sensible move to try to postpone the discussion until the morning.

Not for the first time, he was saved by his phone. Katerine raised her eyebrows but he answered it anyway, walked into the ensuite shower room and closed the door. The caller was hesitant, as if he hadn't quite convinced himself whether he should be making a call to a private eye. Mr Waarschoot was calling about his wife who'd started acting out of character, as he put it. They'd always done things together but recently that had changed and his wife was away from home a lot. He wanted Vos to make a few discreet enquiries. It wasn't that he didn't trust her. He was just worried about her. Vos thought he sounded genuine enough.

As he was beginning to feel uncomfortable perched on the lid of the toilet seat, he got up, but found he couldn't stop himself automatically pressing the flush. It took a while before he was able to continue the conversation with Waarschoot, the noise of the filling cistern competing with the clatter of an ageing bathroom extract fan. Eventually he managed to conclude the call with the promise of a meet-up once he was back home.

Stepping out of the suddenly silent ensuite, he was relieved to see that Katerine had fallen asleep. He slid into bed beside her and pulled up the bedclothes, only to push them down again once he discovered he was far too hot. He had a list of things to think about. 1. What to do about Barto? 2. Who would he get to help him in the garden now that Ryck was decamping to Antwerp? 3. What to do with the gun? 4. When was he going to start thinking about his future with Katerine? He knew it was the wrong time of night to be thinking about any of these problems but he couldn't help himself. As his thoughts went round and round he pictured a kind of mental spin dryer and it was this image that eventually sent him to sleep.

+ + +

Barry's Boots was just off Covent Garden. Vos recognised the man behind the counter; the same man who had sold him his own pair about eighteen months previously.

"I'm Terry, by the way. If I remember rightly, you were eleven on the left and eleven and a half on the right." It was an unusual way to open a conversation, but a quick check of his records proved he was right.

Vos explained the purpose of this second visit, telling him about the discovery of the dead man and the nickname he'd acquired. Terry glanced at the photograph of Charlie's boots and confirmed, as Vos had thought, that they were indeed a pair of *Beacons*. He took a moment to explain that the each of the company's boot styles was named after a Welsh mountain range.

"It's a bit of a long shot I know," Vos said, trying to move things on, "but I wondered if you could help me to find out which branch he might have bought his boots from. I seem to remember you saying there were only three. Is that right?"

Terry confirmed that *Barry's Boots* had only the three outlets – London and the two Welsh shops in Cardiff and Crickhowell. He added that Barry himself was something of a TV personality, with his niche programme *Barry's Walks*.

"So unless this Charlie, as you call him, visited Wales when he was over here, then he would have bought his boots from this very branch," Terry said.

Vos showed him photograph number two, the e-fit of Charlie. Terry rubbed his chin and thought for a while.

"I'm normally pretty good with faces. There's something about this one but I can't quite place him." His phone rang and he spent a couple of minutes attempting to calm down an irate customer. When the call ended, he suddenly called out "Tattoo!" Vos, puzzled, asked him to explain. "I remember him now. He'd just had some tattoo removal work done – the name of the woman he'd just broken up with, I think it was. Kept on complaining about how much it hurt. Spoke good English. He was buying the boots as a present to himself to help compensate. Wait a mo and I'll look him up. Must be nearly a year ago I reckon, smallish feet, two nines if I remember rightly."

He turned his attention to his computer and after a couple of minutes punched the air.

"Told you – two nines! He paid in cash so I don't have a name or any card details. I had him down as Mr Belgium so it looks like he's your man. The tattoo removal might be a lead for you. I'm sure he'd only just had it done, like he'd literally just come from there. Didn't stop moaning about it, said it felt like someone had poured hot oil on his skin – an image I couldn't easily forget. Here, I could have a quick shufty on the internet if you like, check out any tattoo parlours round here."

Vos said that would be very helpful and wondered what a shufty was.

Several clicks later Terry had the addresses of two parlours both within half a mile of his shop.

Armed with this information and two pairs of walking socks, which he didn't really need, Vos made his way to *Sick Ink* where, after a brief conversation with a very unpleasant man, he managed to establish that Charlie had not been a customer. *EezyTattooz* was a very different kind of place. Even Vos thought it was cool – despite the name. The proprietor couldn't have been more helpful. He didn't recognise the e-fit, but when Vos told him his man was from Belgium it rang a bell.

"We had this conversation about German heavy metal. He was really in to it. I gave him his first removal session and told him he'd need several more."

"It can't be done too quick you know – each session needs to be spaced out over several weeks. Said he didn't want no anaesthetic and then complained about the pain. Very common that is. A bit of a macho thing. Think they can take it. Anyway he paid up OK. Cash it was. No doubt he'd have gone to a local parlour back home to get the removal job completed, so that might be one way of trying to find out who he was."

"I don't suppose you can remember what the tattoo looked like?" Vos said, hoping for a bit more.

"Sorry – should have said straight away, guvnor. It was on his arm, the name *Edith* – same as my old lady. Named after Piaf she was. Her mother was a real fan but you don't hear those songs these days." Vos thought this was real progress and another lead to follow up. "Don't suppose I could interest you in having a tat done, could I?" Vos had never understood the attraction, all that pain to go through for something you'd probably want to get rid of after five minutes. He shook his head and thanked the man for his help.

Feeling like some fresh air, he ambled through the side streets. Outside a bank a small, placard-waving crowd had gathered. He asked one of the demonstrators what the protest was about and was informed that they were protesting that the bank was funding a fracking company. The woman had to remind him what fracking was and why there were objections. As far as he could recall, it had been banned by the Belgian government. A leaflet was thrust into his hand, full of details about their cause, which he stuffed into his trouser pocket. Two side streets later, he emerged onto the Embankment, walked to the middle of Waterloo Bridge and gazed at the passing river traffic. A catamaran sped upstream in the direction of the Houses of Parliament and he thought it would be nice if he and Katerine could take a boat trip sometime.

His mind drifted back to their early morning conversation about the future. He hadn't been able to delay it any longer. It had been surprisingly productive and they'd agreed to spend more time at each other's place. She'd spend her weekends at his and he'd spend a couple of weekdays at hers. Katerine hadn't fancied a daily commute from Heist to Antwerp and he didn't think he could manage being in an apartment – even a pleasant one – for more than two days at a time. And spending time in Antwerp would mean he could still have some contact with Ryck. They both knew it wasn't a permanent solution but it was an arrangement that was worth trying.

When they met for dinner, he could tell Katerine was on edge and was immediately worried that she was having second thoughts about their plan for split-site living. But then she told him that she'd had a call from Kim – a long one. He wasn't aware they'd even exchanged numbers.

"The thing is," Katerine said, sounding awkward, "your daughter's pregnant." Vos was dumbfounded. It was the last thing he'd have guessed. Kim had always been resolute about not wanting children. Obviously it must have been an accident and he knew she wouldn't handle any of it well.

"I fear the worst," he said. His daughter had always lived her adult life as if on the edge of a precipice. As yet she'd just about managed to keep her balance, but he was very worried that this might send her tumbling. It didn't take long for the resentment to bubble up inside him. Why had she confided in Katerine and not him? After all they'd only just met each other. But he knew the answer all too well. Kim had spoken to her because there'd be no strings, no baggage and no family relationships to trip over.

"I don't think you should be so fearful," Katerine said. "She's being quite mature about it." This was a first, he thought, but said nothing. "She says she wants to keep the baby but she's scared that when she tells Anders it'll drive him away. Apparently he was very relieved when she told him right at that start of their relationship that she didn't want kids. Kim says he's good for her, so that's one reason she doesn't want to lose him. But there's also the practicality of paying the mortgage on her apartment which she told me is rather large. She doesn't think she can afford to be off work at all, if she ends up on her own with a baby."

Vos found it so difficult to imagine Kim as a mother. He could recall a host of comments she'd made over the years about other people's children, even about her own nephews. Could she really change? He needed to concentrate: Katerine was still telling him about the conversation with his daughter. At first Kim had been adamant that nothing should be said to her father about the pregnancy, but Katerine had managed to talk her round on that one. And she'd been able to persuade Kim to let Anders know.

"In fact, she should be telling him round about now. Let's hope it goes well. Perhaps we better choose something from this menu." Vos ran through the list of mains and decided on steak. He didn't have it very often and enjoyed it even more as a result. They swapped information on progress, him on walking boot shops and tattoo parlours and her on cultural signifiers.

Vos was pleased with what he'd found out about Charlie – the tattoo and the ex-girlfriend. But apart from the train ticket, which had a Brussels departure, there was no real clue as to where the man had lived. And nothing was yet known about what he'd done for a living.

When he'd spoken to Bernard on the phone, Vos had managed to convince him to start a trawl of tattoo parlours. He kept his fingers crossed that it would prove fruitful.

< so it was him – a fucking inside job
< yes, covered his tracks well, that's why it took so long to find out
< shit, that means he knows about…
< of course
< he'll have to go

Walking the dog

The Jack Russell disappeared into the bushes, in pursuit of a particularly interesting scent. His owner walked on, glued to her phone, the conversation with her best friend now well past the twenty minute mark. The dog reappeared and ran ahead of her. When he veered too close to the road, her shout brought him to heel. She put him on the lead and finished her call.

Rounding a bend, she caught sight of two vehicles, one slewed across rough ground at the edge of the road, the second parked in an adjacent lay-by. Two men were dragging something across the verge into the long grass. She grabbed the dog in her arms and hid in a group of pine trees, praying he wouldn't start barking. It took only a dreadful second or two for her to realise that the object being moved was a body.

"That's far enough. Go through his pockets and find the cash. We'll need his car keys, phone and wallet as well," one of the men said in a low voice.

"And the site map. How can a man have so many pockets?"

She watched as the two men went through the dead man's clothes.

"About fucking time too! Let's go before somebody sees us."

They ran to the two cars and screeched away. Forcing herself forward through the long grass, the woman froze when she saw the shape just beyond her feet. Immediately the dog started barking. The phone shook in her hands as she called the police.

+ + +

Chief Inspector Franke found it tiring, moving his large frame across the rough ground. Once she'd calmed down, the woman had been most helpful. He'd been impressed how she'd been able to recall the registration number of one of the cars. Her description of the two men was limited, but they'd looked similar – possibly brothers she'd thought. Despite her best attempts to silence him, the dog had barked throughout the interview.

Franke thought it likely that the victim had parked up in the lay-by, walked towards the rough ground at the side of the road and had then been hit by the attackers' car. Hit, move, rob and run rather than a straightforward hit and run. Perhaps they'd shifted the body in order to delay its discovery. And from what the witness had said, they'd known in advance about the cash and the site map.

Franke told one of his officers to drive the woman and her dog home.

Sitting in his car, he finished writing his notes then sighed, partly out of sadness for the victim and partly in anticipation of the additional workload he'd just inherited. He could barely cope as it was. One officer had left the previous week, another was on long-term sick leave and a third was off on secondment in Brussels – something hush-hush he'd been told. Despite already being grossly overworked, he knew the case would end up on his desk.

Maes

Not my first visit to the UK by any means, but the first time I've worked here. It's the same kind of work I do back home and I speak the lingo well enough. I'm picking up on a north–south divide, just like we have at home. I like the northern moors, so different from the Ardennes and the good news from our point of view is that there's shale gas just below me. The area's run down, there's not much money about and the soil's poor, but ironically, it's fertile ground for us.

I'm met with suspicion at my first stop, which isn't surprising. Initially I get a… we don't like strangers round here … look. Things change – they usually do – when I pull the cash from my pocket. Judging by the number of empty beer bottles littering the kitchen floor, I think I can guess how this money will be spent, but that's none of my business.

My next stop is rather different. Somehow, the owner of the site has got wind of the fracking potential, even though there's been no announcement. And he's someone with principles. It makes my job much more difficult. I need to know just how strong his principles are. The last thing I want to do is to waste my time if he's not for turning.

He shows me a file, full of anti-fracking press cuttings from other parts of the country. Then he tells me there's absolutely no way he's going to sell if the land ends up being fracked. It's a matter of prin…Yes, I know all about it and it's obvious he's no use to me. Of course I can't say anything about our fracking plans so I make up an excuse and leave. Back in the car I study the map, to get an idea of how this 'failure' – because that's how Mertens will see it – will affect the programme. But the land is in the bottom south-east corner of the proposed development, so it's not crucial and I have a reserve option. All is not lost!

There's a lengthy drive along narrow lanes to my 'Plan B' site. A small stone-built cottage perches above a river which seems to have too much water in it. I recall seeing on the TV how bad the local weather has been recently, with flooding not far from here. It takes a while to discover that the owner is underneath a tractor, one which has seen better days and he struggles to wriggle free from his prone position. Getting to his feet seems to be an equally difficult process. Although his hand is smeared with oil, I shake it anyway as I introduce myself. He's a man of few words and those he does utter are in an accent so strong that I can barely follow him. Still, at least he's not hostile. It's plain he thinks life is bloody awful, particularly since his wife left him. From the way he talks about it, I assume she's only just gone, but it turns out she went several years ago.

I'm sure he'll bite. Why would anyone want to stay and farm in this backwater? The geological maps are very positive and there'd be no objections from neighbours as there aren't any. We sit in his van. I go through my usual spiel and pull the roll of notes out of my coat pocket. It works a treat. He then surprises me by telling me he'll use the money from the sale to go off to some Mediterranean island – something he's always wanted to do, although he's never been out of the UK before.

It's time to go home.

+ + +

Leaving the Channel Tunnel behind, I get a call from Mertens. I'm on my guard immediately. It's unusual for him to call when I'm in the field and it's not good news. One of the other operatives – we never use names – has been found dead, a hit and run. Mertens tells me he needs me back pronto.

I hope it was just a hit and run and not anything more sinister. I've been threatened before now. Not everyone likes what we do – and they'd like it even less if they knew what we really get up to.

Four

Antoine had been in contact with Vos again, sounding upbeat. They'd identified a tattoo parlour in Mons which had done some removal work on a man resembling Charlie. The clincher was that he'd mentioned that the tattoo had been of his former girlfriend, Edith. However payment had been in cash and they didn't have a name or an address for him. Local CCTV footage was being checked.

Vos was on his way to Lier to visit the man with the disappearing wife. It took him a while before he managed to find the house, which, beyond a long garden, backed onto a railway line. Their conversation in the conservatory was regularly punctuated by both the noise of trains on the line and his new client's flowing commentary on the type, origin and destination of each one.

Waarschoot's initial hesitancy to talk about his wife soon disappeared. He was frustrated by her frequent absences and was at a loss to understand her recent changes in behaviour. This time she'd said she'd be away staying with a friend, but the weekend had already turned into a week and he'd no idea when she'd return. It wasn't the first time this kind of thing had happened. Her phone was switched off and she very seldom responded to his messages. Vos said he could understand how this was worrying, but was sure there'd be a simple explanation, keeping to himself the thought that most people would assume she was having an affair.

Mr Waarschoot showed him a photograph of his wife and played the one recent voicemail message she'd left. Vos thought that she sounded distant, but not like someone who was in any kind of trouble. He took the necessary details from Waarschoot and said he'd start work on the case within a couple of days.

It wasn't far to Antwerp, but traffic was slow. Vos was pleased that his mother and Mr Wouters had asked him if they could hang on to Barto for a while longer. As far as he was concerned they could hang on to the dog permanently, but he thought it would be better to build up to this gradually.

He was looking forward to staying at Katerine's and seeing Ryck and his new family again. Cutting across town to her apartment, using back streets he'd known since his childhood, he found the visitor parking space free – just as she'd told him it would be. He put the permit she'd given him in place on the dashboard. Once inside the apartment, he stood for a while in the living room breathing in her lingering scent, before unpacking his two suitcases. He hadn't been sure how much to bring. Living in two homes at once was a new experience and as he didn't have that many clothes to start with, he had a feeling that whatever he needed at any one time would turn out to be in the other place.

The café he found was only five minutes' walk away. There was a single table outside where he could soak up the sun and sip his espresso. He was surprised when a middle-aged woman invaded what he'd marked out as his territory, although he had to admit that the second chair was free and he didn't need the whole of the tabletop for his single cup and saucer. As soon as her waffle arrived, she tore at it with her fingers and dipped a piece of it into the quickly melting ice-cream, before tossing it onto the floor for her small dog to consume greedily and noisily. This process was repeated several times – Vos becoming more and more uncomfortable with the performance. The final straw came when the woman reached across and, without a word, took his neatly folded serviette and used it to wipe the dog's mouth. Vos fled to the sanctuary of an inside table, where he soon found he was too hot. Eventually the woman left *his* table and he was able to resume his rightful position outside.

Order restored and with a second espresso in front of him, he flicked through the pages of the Gazet Van Antwerpen, but found nothing that really caught his attention. The *Charlie* story didn't appear to have made it as far as Antwerp. He was distracted by the sight of a lad walking along the pavement towards him, mid-teens, sullen expression – and a face that caught his eye for some reason. The youth walked on past the café, a phone clamped to his right ear. Vos was about to return to his newspaper when he had a sudden vision of that night, on the cobblestones, down by the docks – what was it, fifty years ago? The boy he'd hit, the boy he'd done time for, the incident that in many ways had changed his life. Then it struck him, the youth walking on down the street, gabbling into his phone must be related – that's why his face had seemed so familiar. Maybe a grandson? He'd be about the right age.

Leaving a five euro note on the table, Vos picked up his stick and followed the youth as he turned the corner at the end of the street. Luckily there were a few other people about, so Vos didn't feel too conspicuous. What was he doing though? So what if this lad was the grandson? There was nothing he could do about it. But he carried on walking all the same, keeping a safe distance behind, sweating in the warmth of the sun. His leg didn't hold him back. It had been better of late, but that was usually the case in the summer.

After a few minutes, the youth turned onto a residential street and stopped in front of a terraced house. He pulled a key out of his pocket, opened the door to number 27 and disappeared inside, leaving Vos with a decision to make.

+ + +

The text from Kim was brief.

Told Anders about the baby. Haven't seen him since.

Katerine wondered whether she'd done the right thing when she'd encouraged Kim to tell her boyfriend about the pregnancy, but he'd have to have known sooner or later. She picked her way around Vos' suitcases and guessed he'd be in a local café or a bar. He seemed to have left all the contents of his pockets on the dressing table – loose change, keys, used tissues and a neatly folded leaflet. It was written in English and was all about fracking.

She'd been a supporter of the campaign to persuade the Belgian government to ban it. However she'd read that there'd been some recent uncertainty about the strength of this commitment and the fracking lobby was powerful. The leaflet went into some detail and there were photos of demonstrations against a number of sites in England. She recognised the logo on one of the banners, two intertwined Gs – the Green Guards. She hadn't realised they were active in England as well.

Halfway through her preparations for dinner, Vos returned to the apartment looking hot and bothered. He wouldn't explain why he was in this state and she knew she'd get nowhere by asking him questions. After a suitable gap and a refreshing cold beer each, she told him about his daughter's text.

"That's more or less what I expected," he said. "I knew he was too good to be true. What on earth will she do now?"

"Why don't you ask her?" Katerine responded, expecting him to turn down the suggestion. But he surprised her by ringing Kim immediately, only to be frustrated by being diverted to voicemail.

The meal was pleasant. With the window open, evening birdsong provided the background music. The pasta dish disappeared quickly, along with a bottle of red. Curled up on the sofa, the hum of the dishwasher in the kitchen just audible,

Katerine felt pleasantly relaxed. Vos chose this moment to tell her about the chain of events which led to his conviction and subsequent imprisonment, when he was in his teens – facts she'd known about, without being aware of all the background. He moved through the story slowly and finished by telling her about the youth he'd encountered that afternoon.

She was immediately worried that he might have done something foolish.

"No, I just knocked on the door," he said, as if it was the most natural thing to do. "It wasn't the lad who answered, but a woman who I took to be his mother – some of the same family features. I asked her if she knew of someone called Schopges living on the street. It was the first name that came into my head. She said she didn't – of course. We chatted for a bit. I talked about my mother and what a worry older people were and she mentioned her father, who still lives in the same house he'd bought as a young man. I was so tempted to ask her where it was, but that might have sounded more than a little suspicious so I left it at that. I don't know whether her father is the man I'm after. His name's Tillens. My father kept the press cuttings of the trial and I've still got them now. They printed everybody's name in those days, even if you were underage."

Katerine could tell this was still a delicate issue for him and she'd need to tread carefully around it. But she didn't want him to start off down a road to vengeance, especially after all these years.

"I'll check their house on the electoral register. Their names might give me an indication as to whether I'm on the right track." Katerine asked him why he needed to be on any track. What was done was done, surely. Vos replied that he'd never been able to forget about what had happened all those years ago. Any further discussion was interrupted by the arrival of Ryck, Magda and little Sun.

Bottles were opened and glasses filled as they drank to Ryck's new life as a student. Vos found he got on surprisingly well with Magda, although he couldn't understand how anyone could call a child Sun. She worked in therapies, helping people to *find their inner balance* as she put it. Sitting cross-legged on the floor with Sun balanced on her lap, she looked very comfortable. Although Ryck was similarly seated, he looked more than a little uncomfortable.

Vos reminisced with his nephew about the people-smuggling case and considered telling him about Charlie, but then thought better of it. It would be an unnecessary distraction for the new Ryck – student and family man.

+ + +

Back in his own house, Vos reflected that the two days at Katerine's had gone well. He didn't think he'd have a problem settling in to his new, part-time, second home. This upbeat view was helped by the fact that even in a short space of time, he'd managed to build up a local circuit: a newspaper shop, a regular café with espresso just how he liked it and a garden chair underneath the apple trees, perfect for an afternoon snooze.

Mrs Waarschoot was proving to be elusive. Vos had visited two of her friends, but neither of them had seen her recently. He had a feeling that each of them was holding something back. The only useful thing he'd managed to pick up was the name of an old flame, who'd apparently been in touch with her recently. Maybe his initial thoughts about an affair might turn out to be correct.

Now though, he was weeding, a job he hated. No longer able to bend easily, his rate of progress in removing the damn things seemed to decline by the week. Gardening assistance would soon become a necessity. Defeated, his back aching, he retired to the deckchair on the patio and a cold lemonade. He came to with a jolt. Imagining he'd only closed his eyes for a few minutes, he checked his watch and found an hour had passed.

There were three messages on his phone.

The first was from Antoine. Without giving any details he said he had good news and bad news. The second was from – well he wasn't sure who it was from. He didn't recognise the number and the text said only *Can we talk –A?* The final message was from his former adversary, Leo Rodenbach, who confirmed he'd be willing to check the 'merchandise' as he called it. Vos was relieved that the voicemail hadn't included the word 'gun'.

This was a bit too much to cope with all at once and Vos decided he needed a coffee. A new place, *The Kat*, had just opened in Heist. It took him about twenty minutes to walk there. Having forgotten to bring his hat, the sun had taken advantage, beating down especially hard on his bald patch. A shaded table on the pavement was free and he settled into a seat, phone at the ready. Unusually he felt like a cappuccino and he sipped at this, having first downed a large glass of water.

Antoine told him that the good news was about the tattooist they'd found in Mons. As well as confirming he'd done a couple of removal sessions for the man known as Charlie, he'd added that his customer had come across as something of an environmentalist. So that provided another avenue of enquiry that could be used to try and establish his identity. Antoine's bad news was that because of a recent terrorist incident locally, he'd had to transfer men off the job. Could Vos help out – unofficially of course?

Vos knew that his cousin would have already guessed the answer to that question. The bad news was good news for him. When he asked Antoine to forward a copy of the interview with the tattooist, there was only a slight hesitation before his request was agreed to.

Unfortunately they'd drawn a blank with CCTV footage for the area around the tattoo parlour. There were only two cameras and they'd both been out of action at the time.

His next call, to the mysterious 'A', went to voicemail – a standard pre-recorded message in English. He asked the caller to try again. He had better luck with his call to Leo Rodenbach. He'd just docked in Antwerp and would drop in at the house that evening to give his opinion on the 'merchandise'.

Demotte had believed his story of the amnesty, but far from handing the weapon over to the police, Vos had kept hold of it, hiding it on a soot-coated ledge in the sitting room chimney flue. He wasn't at all sure why he'd hung on to the weapon, but something about it fascinated him. Apart from a toy cowboy gun, which had been his pride and joy, he'd never had anything to do with firearms. He'd asked Rodenbach if he could examine the gun and let him know what type it was. Vos reflected on the way the relationship between himself and the people-smuggler had changed over time, from mutual antagonism to a grudging shared respect.

+ + +

His visitor was on time, bottle in hand.

"Good to see you're making a habit of bringing a drink with you, Leo." The man had only been to the house once before and had brought along a similar gift on that occasion. Rodenbach wasted no time asking about the gun. Vos passed it to him and watched as his guest handled it carefully, checked it over and then took it to pieces.

"I'm glad to see it's not loaded. Sometimes these old things still have a bullet or two in the chamber." Vos didn't admit that he hadn't bothered to check whether or not the gun was loaded. "It's a 1910," Rodenbach said, sipping Camus cognac from one of Vos' shot glasses, "an FN, made in Belgium of course. Did you know that this model was used in both world wars and guess what, it was a 1910 that did for the Archduke!"

Vos was impressed with both Rodenbach's knowledge of history and his ability to take apart and reassemble the 1910.

"So, tell me Harry, what's your interest in this weapon? Don't tell me you're getting tooled up for a job!"

The question took him aback. What was he doing with the gun?

"No, no Leo, nothing like that. A client hired me to find his father's old wartime gun – which I did. For some reason I took against the client and was buggered if I was going to give the weapon to him. So, I told him I'd handed it over to the police under one of their periodic amnesties. Except I didn't, I kept it. There's a wartime notebook that goes with the weapon. From the details in the book, it looks as if the owner of the gun – the father – may have used it in ways he shouldn't. I'm worried he may have been involved in war crimes. The gun might become a useful piece of evidence." Vos realised he hadn't really thought this through before, but that it made sense.

Rodenbach rubbed his chin then took a sip from his glass before responding.

"I would doubt that very much. But you never know."

Glasses were topped up and the conversation moved on.

Vos decided another conversation with Uncle Albert might prove useful.

Maes

Vervloet is the name of the guy who's died. And I knew him!

Even though we're not supposed to have any social contact with other operatives, I'd met him a couple of times. He seemed OK but didn't have the right attitude as far as I was concerned. You can't afford to have any doubts about 'ethics' or whatever you want to call it, in this game.

Mertens tells me to clear out Vervloet's apartment right away – not the furniture, that will be removed separately. My job is to go through his personal belongings in case there's anything 'compromising' as Mertens puts it. So, that's why the family's not doing it.

It feels odd sifting through bits of another person's life. I look at everything before shoving it into a box. All seems OK until I come across a report with 'confidential' stamped all over it.

It's about nuclear waste, seems to go way over the top pointing out the dangers. Why did Vervloet have this? Apart from Fukushima which you couldn't avoid, I've always ignored this kind of stuff. Buying up potential sites for nuclear waste is part of our bread and butter so we can't afford to be picky. But reading this report sets me thinking.

Once I've dropped off Vervloet's personal things at the storage depot, I give the key and the report to Mertens. He actually thanks me, calls me "Mr Reliable".

There's this small nagging voice in my head telling me that maybe V's death wasn't an accident. If he had that kind of report, what else might he have been up to? Still, the police won't go looking for work. Hit and run, couldn't trace the driver, job done. The Company will do its own investigation to make sure there's nothing else to it. After all, according to Mertens, Vervloet was working when he was killed. But I'm sure if they find anything, they'll only release the information that suits them. If there's been anything dodgy going on, they'll cover it up and remove the evidence.

Mertens' parting shot is that I'll be working on a site clearance job next. My favourite!

Five

It was the headline on the front page of the Gazet Van Antwerpen.

BODY FOUND NEAR MOL.

Police are investigating after the body of a man was found on waste ground, next to a road, a few kilometres from the town of Mol. "It would appear that the man was involved in a hit and run accident," said Turnhout-based Chief Inspector Franke. "We are trying to ascertain what happened. The victim had no ID, the immediate area is fairly isolated and there is no CCTV coverage locally. In order to assist in establishing the identity of the victim we would ask the public to contact us, on the number below, if they recognise the e-fit or have any other information which may be of help in our enquiries."

Vos reached for his phone.

"Bernard? Hi – good morning. Guess what I've just found in the newspaper?" He read out the relevant details. "Another body without ID. It's probably nothing, but might be worth checking out. Any chance of you having a quick word with your oppo? Thanks – that would be helpful. Talk to you later."

That was the only similarity though – a body with no ID. He was probably clutching at straws. The journalist hadn't speculated on a link, but that was understandable. Charlie might have been big news in Wallonia, but that didn't mean the story had been picked up to any extent in Flanders. Aside from the language differences, they were almost two separate countries – or at least that's the way a lot of people saw it. Vos wasn't one of them, but then he had strong family ties with both 'countries'. He hoped Antoine would be able to arrange for him to speak to Franke directly.

Before that, he had business to attend to in Mons.

+ + +

At first sight, trains to Mons appeared to be missing from the departure board at Brussels Zuid station. Vos kicked himself when he remembered he should also be looking for the Flemish name for the place – Bergen.

The journey took less than an hour. Mons Grande Place was more of an ellipse than a square and all the better for it, he thought. Kids ran in and out of the fountains, getting completely soaked and screaming with delight.

Vos sat at the café table, soaking up the warmth, half in and half out of the shade, a glass of Grimbergen in his hand and an unopened newspaper at his elbow. He'd visited the Memorial Museum that morning and seen the black and white photos of the occupying troops, tanks and armoured cars filling the Grande Place during the second world war, not a fountain in sight.

He'd finally got through to the mysterious 'A' and felt a fool for not guessing that it was Kim's boyfriend Anders. His disappearance had only been temporary. He'd needed some time to think things through on his own and work out how best to support her. Having finally overcome his embarrassment about contacting her father on such a sensitive matter, he was phoning for some advice.

Vos had been at a loss as to how to respond to this request, but finally managed to mumble some vague generalities, before cautiously asking Anders what his reaction was to the pregnancy. It turned out that he was looking forward to the idea of becoming a father, but was having difficulty in getting Kim to believe him. She was convinced he was just playing along and that in reality he would disappear when it suited him. Vos was sure that anything he said to his daughter might only make things worse, but felt he had to try. He could hear his mother telling him to get on with it through one ear and Katerine whispering the same message through the other.

But instead of phoning Kim, he ordered another Grimbergen and watched as a man in a long black apron set up tables and chairs outside the café opposite, taking particular care with laying and smoothing the tablecloths and positioning the cutlery and the glasses just so.

Vos felt he must have appeared to be just like any other older male tourist gazing out over the square, but he doubted whether any of the others had a gun inside his rucksack.

As he recalled Leo Rodenbach's comments about the heightened state of security in the country, he began to get nervous. What sort of excuse would he have if he were to be caught with the damn thing?

Having left the pleasures of the Grande Place behind, he called in at the tattoo parlour, not expecting to pick up anything new about Charlie, but wanting to get a feel for the place. A muted TV was showing a group of Tour de France, riders struggling up a steep hill, support vehicles in over-close pursuit. Vos waited until the parlour's only customer had left before explaining the purpose of his visit. Apart from introducing himself as Kris, the proprietor was initially reluctant to say anything else. He'd already told the police all he knew and besides Vos had no authority and no ID. But he softened a little when Vos commented on

the Smashing Pumpkins posters that covered the parlour walls,
explaining that he'd been to and enjoyed one of their gigs. The
reality was he'd driven his son Eddie and his mate to the gig in
Brussels and had spent the entire time standing at the back of
the venue waiting for the deafening music to stop. After a while,
Kris seemed to forget about his earlier reservations and opened
up in his slow, deliberate way, confirming what Vos already knew.
Unexpectedly, though, he added a little gem, something he'd
only just remembered. Charlie had lived in the Marolles area of
Brussels. Vos shook Kris by the hand, slapped him on the back
and left him standing somewhat bemused in the shop doorway.

Mons train station was undergoing a complete rebuild. New
concrete staircases emerged from the ground unconnected to
anything above. Further back, the new station building itself was
taking shape, waiting for a connecting bridge to link it up to the
newly sprouting stairways. The site had the look of some huge,
avant-garde art installation.

Vos hurried down the temporary ramp, his stick clicking
noisily on the metallic surface. The train was on time and he
settled into his seat for the short journey to Binche, hoping that
his visit to a friend of Mrs W.'s might throw some light on her
current whereabouts. He'd been in two minds about whether to
make the short trip but as he was in the area anyway, thought it
was worth it.

But when he reached the house it was shuttered and there
was no response to his knocking. A neighbour leaned across the
party fence and asked him what he wanted. She seemed satisfied
with his response and informed him that the owner had just gone
on a walking holiday and wouldn't be back for a while. When
Vos attempted to find out a little more about the occupant of
the empty house, the neighbour appeared not to have heard and
started a lengthy story about the problems she'd been having with
the local council. Vos struggled to bring the monologue to an

end. As he was about to leave he risked asking a final question and mentioned the name Ann Waarschoot. This time the woman heard him, stated bluntly that she'd rather not pass comment and disappeared suddenly back into her house.

Dozing off on the return journey, he almost missed Mons. Only the jolting of the train as it pulled into the station woke him – the perils of afternoon drinking, he told himself. He took the bus to Albert's house, refreshing himself from a bottle of water purchased from the station shop.

Albert welcomed him. As soon as the kitchen door was opened the aroma reminded Vos that he was famished. He'd forgotten to eat lunch.

"Cassoulet! I hope you like it," Albert said as they shook hands. "It's always been a speciality of mine. And I've opened a good Bordeaux. What have you bought, Harry?" Vos hoped the bottle of Edradour would pass muster. It was his favourite malt. He pulled the bottle out of his rucksack first and then unwrapped the gun.

Albert stared at both items on the kitchen table and smiled.

"You know how to amuse an old man." He picked up the gun. "Ah – a 1910! This is one of the earlier ones. Where did you get it?" Vos told him it was Demotte's, how it had been hidden away along with the wartime notebook and how he'd failed to hand it over to its owner.

Albert admonished him with a 'tut-tut' before turning his gaze back to the gun. "There were a lot of these about in the war, but this one has an unusual marking – look, just here. Which reminds me, I read through the copy of the notebook you left me and I've done a little research since." Vos asked how he'd carried this out. "On the internet of course – how else! It's surprising what you can find out. Anyway I think your man Demotte writes a good story. How much of it is true though? That's the question. There are inconsistencies and inaccuracies, which isn't unusual for a wartime journal, but it rings warning bells with me. Towards the end of the war, some soldiers, realising how things were going to work out, decided to reinvent their wartime lives, burying the things that would show them in a bad light and making up experiences that would look good. Of course there was so much confusion at the time that many were able to get away with it. I reckon your Demotte could be one of these and that maybe he was really in the Legion Wallonie. You know about the Legion?" Vos nodded. He remembered his father talking about the collaborators who'd assisted the Nazis. "I need to do some more work on it. He could have been in one of their splinter groups. There are a couple of people I need to speak to."

Vos' interest in Demotte senior's story had started out as a bit of curiosity, but he'd become increasingly intrigued. He'd put to one side his dislike for Demotte junior, his ex-client, wanting to concentrate on the bigger picture – what had the old man really been up to and had this involved activities which ultimately might have to be exposed publicly?

Albert filled two wine glasses and Vos carried them into the garden. Now was the time to ask the question he'd wanted to know the answer to for so long – what had caused the fall out between Albert and his sister? His uncle took a mouthful of wine and savoured it for a while.

"I was wondering when you'd get round to asking me. It's all a very long time ago now. I was still a teenager – although we didn't use that word then. I met Miriam at a dance and thought she was the most wonderful woman I'd ever seen. In those days your mother and I were quite close. I thought I could trust her with my confidences and I told her about Miriam. To my great disappointment, she told Mother and that was what put the cat amongst the pigeons. I had no idea, but Miriam's father had been a jailbird and not a pleasant man by all accounts. Mother's view was that the family was tainted and that I should have nothing to do with them." Albert took another mouthful of wine and again held it a long while before gradually swallowing. Albert's cigarette lay smouldering on a saucer on the rickety garden table.

"Anyway I was banned from seeing Miriam and when I refused to agree to this I was sent away to live with an aunt. That was that – the relationship which had barely started was over. By the time I came back a few years later she had married – a solid enough chap, but not one to set the world alight. That was my view of him anyway. I never forgave Mother and because of that my sister never forgave me."

Vos had never heard any of this sad tale before. His mother had always refused to talk about her brother. He topped up the glasses and lit a small cigar, an occasional indulgence.

"Did you ever see Miriam again?"

"Of course! I saw her only yesterday." Vos couldn't follow this. His mind was still in the 1930's when these events had taken place and suddenly his uncle was talking about *yesterday*. "Her husband died a few years ago and several weeks after his death, I bumped into Miriam in the market. Talk about fate! We've seen each other regularly ever since. So you see – you should never give up."

"Could I meet her?" Vos asked cautiously.

"Naturally – next time you're here. Now I think the cassoulet should be about ready."

+ + +

On the train to Charleroi the following morning, Vos wondered if it had been wise to leave the gun with his uncle. But Albert had dismissed his concerns telling him that if the worst happened, he'd tell them it was his, that he'd hung on to it since the war.

Vos jotted a few things down in his notebook, not wanting to forget what his uncle had told him. After the cassoulet had been polished off and the wine glasses drained, they'd started on the Edradour. Albert had told him about his recent contact with some of his former resistance comrades. A lot of the men had died and of those who were still alive, many didn't go anywhere near a computer – but there were some who were online more than they were off it. After decades of tight-lipped silence about what had happened during the war, they'd found they couldn't talk or write enough about it.

Antoine was in his office eating a sandwich when Vos arrived. He pulled a face, screwed up the remains and threw them in the bin.

"Hi Harry. I don't know why I buy those things. They're disgusting. How are you?"

"Good, thanks, and all the better for discovering that our Charlie lived in Marolles." Antoine looked pleased. "That gives me something solid to go on – although it is rather a big area."

The two men speculated about Charlie for a while, before Antoine mentioned the recent development near Mol.

"I spoke to Chief Inspector Franke in Turnhout. Interesting! He told me the press release for the case was changed by the high-ups. They cut out reference to three facts. Firstly, that the body had been dragged from its original location and hidden in undergrowth, secondly that the two men involved removed a phone, a wallet and some cash – we don't know how much – from the body and finally that there'd been a witness to all this." Antoine paused to work loose a small piece of meat from between two of his front teeth. "I can't get rid of this awful taste." He drank noisily from a large plastic water bottle before continuing. "Whether this case has any link to Charlie's I wouldn't know. There is the lack of ID similarity, but the dead man's documents were probably inside his stolen wallet."

Antoine poured sludgy-looking coffee into two small cups and placed a large tin in the middle of the table. Vos removed the lid, selected a biscuit, broke a piece off and dunked it in his cup.

"I hope you're going to tell me that you're still under-resourced for this case, that you're up to your eyes in anti-terrorist work and that you've persuaded Franke to give me an audience."

"I couldn't have put it better myself," Antoine replied. "Luckily he seems to regard the rules about as flexibly as I do. By the way – how's Uncle Albert?"

Vos gave his cousin a brief summary of the previous evening's discussion, omitting any reference to the gun. It didn't do to push family loyalty too far.

Maes

I'm still thinking about Vervloet, wondering if it really was a straightforward hit and run or whether there was more to it than that. It's all a bit unsettling. Still, as I'm working on the site clearance job – nothing too controversial – I should be safe enough from eco-nutters for the time being.

It's a redevelopment scheme, an area of old apartment blocks just beyond the Boulevard Baudouin in Brussels, well past their sell-by-date. The owner wants the tenants out. There's three of us working on it. We need to get the blocks emptied, whatever way we can and there's some cash to help oil the wheels. So far it's gone OK. One block's nearly done, the second is about halfway there and the final one we're just starting on. But – and there's usually a but in our game – somebody's been stirring things up recently and there's talk of legal action and tenants' rights. We have to nip this in the bud.

Money's the answer – it always is. We'll need to up the offer. The thing is the Company's got a double interest in this scheme. First, we get paid by the landlord for getting the blocks emptied. Second, the company he's selling to is another branch of our network – not that he knows this. Once it's in their ownership, the site will be sold on to a big multinational – a new HQ for them. So there's a lot of money swilling round and plenty of it coming our way.

Mertens hasn't told me any of this. I've found it out for myself, with a little help from a mate of mine. I'd probably be out on my ear if the boss knew what I was up to. But in my book it's all about survival, the need to keep one step ahead.

Until I started checking out this kind of detail, I'd no real idea about what the Company gets up to behind the scenes. Backhanders, straightforward bribery, tax avoidance, bending or breaking the law if they reckon they can get away with it.

A lot of the network we're a part of is hidden away. It's multinational, powerful, rich and pretty well unknown out there in the real world. Or maybe they think they're the real world – who knows.

Six

When Vos was ushered in, Franke was sitting at a desk piled high with files and loose papers, with no sign of a computer. As he introduced himself, the detective finished off a paper tray of frites, licked his lips noisily and wiped his greasy hands meticulously on a napkin. Vos mentioned Antoine's name. Franke nodded. Turning to his left, he picked up a file from the top of one of the piles and flicked through it, talking as he did so.

"You'll know that the press described it as a hit and run. What the reports didn't mention was that after the collision, two men moved the body into the undergrowth and stripped the dead man of his possessions, then drove off in both cars. A very helpful witness told us this and also managed to give us the reg number of what we assume was the assailant's car. There's been no mention of any of this in the press reports either. I think Antoine's told you some of this already. Of course the car was stolen and we've got nowhere with tracing the two guys involved. Unfortunately the witness didn't get the number of the dead man's car. With no ID and no belongings, we literally didn't have a clue as to who he was – until this morning."

"So what happened this morning?" Vos asked.

"We had an anonymous phone call. Turned out it was from a pay phone in the Marolles area of Brussels." Vos was suddenly all ears – the same area that Charlie had lived in. Maybe just a coincidence but... "The caller told us that the dead man was named Vervloet, even gave us his address and said his death might be connected to waste disposal – nuclear waste that is. You know about the storage just down the road from here?" Vos nodded. "Our call-handler was unable to get any more detail as the informant hung up straight away. Female, Flemish speaker, accent hard to place, youngish from the sound of it."

"Is there any useful information on file?" Vos asked, glancing at the green folder that Franke was holding.

"Oh no, this file has nothing to do with Andries Vervloet. His file's been removed." When Vos asked him how this had happened, Franke hesitated.

"Look, I should have asked you a few questions right from the start. Don't get me wrong, Antoine vouched for you, said you're a PI – although you don't seem like one to me – but he's obviously going out on a limb letting you nosy around, just like I'm doing now. So what's the score?" The question wasn't asked aggressively but Vos knew he had to justify his involvement. He explained how it had started, about Antoine's lack of resources, about his own previous experience and what had happened with the people-smuggling case. That seemed to reassure Franke.

"Well as I was saying, Vervloet's file was seized. Bloody special unit from Antwerp swooped in – they specialise in environmental activism. I don't know how, but they'd already picked up on a possible nuclear waste connection and took what little we had. We had to route the press release via them and of course they doctored it. The powers that be get nervous when there's even a hint of a problem, so they'll want to keep the public story nice and simple. Car hits man, man dies, car drives off. Still, given that our mystery phone-caller also mentioned a possible nuclear waste link, there might be something in it. Now – here's another thing I shouldn't be telling you. A man called Dirken is in charge of the Antwerp unit. They're based in the old cloth warehouse just off Noorderlaan – you know where I mean?" Vos said he did.

Franke waved a fresh water bottle in Vos' direction but the offer was declined.

"Look, I shouldn't be revealing any of this, but I get pissed off with their attitude. You might want to see if you can get anything out of them, though you'll need to be clever to get to see Dirken. If by some miracle you do – well I'd love it. But I'll tell you now, if they confirm a nuclear waste connection, they'll sit on the case to avoid any complications."

Vos was unsure about how he might use this information. His current hunch was that there might be some kind of link between Vervloet's death and Charlie's but he had no real evidence. Having got this far though, he thought he might as well try and find out a bit more. He asked Franke about the local politics surrounding the nuclear waste issue.

"Well, a lot of people are in favour of the storage because it means jobs and more money circulating locally, but there's also a bunch of persistent campaigners who are keen to expose what they see as a threat to the environment. These antis are generally OK," Franke said, "but there are one or two nutters out there as well, the so-called non-violent direct action brigade, Green Guards and the like. Truth be told, some of them love a punch-up. So if we're looking for motive – if Vervloet had some connection to nuclear waste – he could have got on the wrong side of one of these guys. On the other hand he could be an anti himself, in which case he'd have come up against some powerful vested interests. There's big money to be made in that game so the stakes can be high."

Vos wondered whether it would be worth checking out if there was a nuclear waste connection to Charlie's death.

Franke gave him a photo of Vervloet, a summary sheet of the very limited information he had on the man and the location of the pay phone from where the anonymous call had been made.

"For God's sake, don't let anyone know that you've got this stuff – more than my job's worth and all that. But good luck."

+ + +

As the rain battered against the windscreen, Vos had difficulty seeing clearly and had to slow down to try and improve his vision. The E34 to Antwerp was busy and not everyone followed his example, idiots continuing to race along the outside lane as if the weather was normal. He wondered whether Vervloet might turn out to be a distraction. But he wanted to take it a bit further before deciding whether to call it a day. Vervloet's apartment was in Borsbeek on the outskirts of Antwerp, in a quiet cul-de-sac.

There was no answer to his knocking on the front door of the ground floor apartment. The gate at the side of the block was unlocked and the path led to a small garden area. The lock on the French windows provided little resistance against Vos' rarely used breaking and entering kit. It wasn't a wise thing to do – forcing entry into private property. But, not for the first time, impetuosity got the better of him.

Once inside, he closed and relocked the doors. The apartment was empty – completely empty. Someone had done a very professional job clearing things out and he doubted very much it would have been Vervloet's family. In his experience, families normally took considerably longer to move out the deceased's belongings.

It was a real sense of anticlimax. He wasn't sure what exactly he'd hoped to find in the apartment but the emptiness was almost eerie. There was no sense in hanging around. The lock on the front door was a Yale so he was able to leave the apartment easily.

A row of mailboxes lined one wall in the shared hallway. He thought it was worth checking the box for number 7. Simple enough to prise open, the box was stuffed with junk mail, but in amongst this was an interesting-looking envelope, which he slid into his jacket pocket. Whoever had done the clear out had missed this little item. Back in the car, when he checked the postmark date, he realised that the envelope must have been delivered just that day. After the disappointment of the empty apartment, he was more than pleased to find the envelope contained a report on nuclear waste storage written by a Doctor Poortmans. It was some kind of audit of potential future storage options. This was more like it! He was still doubtful of any link to Charlie's case, but Vervloet's case had suddenly taken on a significance of its own.

Vos had one further call to make before driving to Katerine's. She'd been very firm with him about his pursuit of Tillens, the much older version of the boy he'd hit all those years ago. She'd told him that it was bad enough he'd wasted his time finding out where Tillens lived and was emphatic that no good could come of confronting him. Vos had tried to convince her that it wouldn't be a confrontation but it was just something he had to do.

Tillens lived in the Hoboken area of the city. Vos parked a couple of streets away and walked to the house. The man who opened the door looked ill – seriously ill and Vos was thrown. He could hardly inflict some kind of delayed revenge – however mild – on someone suffering in this way. A coughing fit was followed by an apology and then a polite question. *Could he help?* Was it Tillens? Vos couldn't be sure.

"Look…I'm sorry to bother you but…" Vos had no idea how to continue. It dawned on him that his recently rekindled obsession with what had happened so long ago was a pointless waste of time and mental energy. Part of him wanted to talk to the man, find out what was wrong with him, make some kind of link. But deep down he knew he couldn't really do this. "I was looking for a Mr Laenen, but I don't have a house number. Would you by any chance know…?"

Of course Tillens wasn't able to help him track down a fiction. When Vos confessed all to Katerine that evening she told him in no uncertain terms what she thought of his actions, but then she softened. After all, he'd not in the end done anything reckless and he promised her it was the end of the matter.

Her concerns resurfaced immediately when he told her, almost in passing, about his little bit of breaking and entering.

"Harry! What is it with you?" He dismissed her concerns, saying that nobody had spotted him, no harm had been done and that anyway, the place had been completely empty. As soon as he mentioned the nuclear waste report he knew he'd succeeded in diverting her attention. It was the author's name, Dr Poortmans, which really caught her attention.

"That's really strange. I know him, not personally, but he's at the university. He's got something of a reputation as a trouble-maker, always on demos, frequently gets himself arrested, only just escaped imprisonment after his most recent arrest and rumour has it he's on a final warning at the uni. Likes to push things to the limit so I'm told. You might get on well with him!"

Vos couldn't tell whether her comment was meant to be serious, but before he could ask her about it, she suddenly started talking about Kim, telling him that she'd been on the phone again.

"Did you speak to Anders?" she asked.

Vos had been looking forward to putting his feet up, eating a leisurely dinner and having an early night with Katerine. He didn't really want to start a long conversation about his daughter. Maybe they could keep it short. He told her Anders was keen about the baby.

"Well that's good. He'll have to try harder to convince her of that though, especially since Patrick's been bending her ear." Vos felt his heart sink. He'd assumed that his daughter's former boyfriend was completely off the scene. What was he doing sticking his oar in? The risk was that it would drive Anders away and he was one of the good guys. Suddenly he went into panic mode. Christ – what if the baby was Patrick's and not Anders', what if Kim had been keeping the pair of them on the go?

+ + +

In the early hours of the morning, unable to sleep, Vos went to the kitchen, poured himself a smoothie and started reading Poortmans' report. Each page was stamped 'draft' and 'confidential'. Most of the technical stuff was beyond him, but there was a clear message. More land was needed for storage of low level and medium level nuclear waste in the area between Dessel and Mol. The report stated that since it was no longer possible to reprocess spent fuel in the UK or France, additional storage capacity locally was urgently required. Some existing reactors were likely to be given extended lives and there'd also be the waste demands of decommissioned sites to take into account. The obvious place to create additional storage facilities was in the vicinity of existing waste sites. The authorities would work on the assumption that there'd be less likelihood of local opposition to such proposals, because of the benefits of extra jobs. There'd be opposition from national and international environmental organisations – but that would be sparked wherever proposed storage sites were proposed. This fitted in with what Franke had told him.

Vos was starting to nod off when his eye was caught by a detail in one of the appendices, reservations that had been expressed about the geological conditions beneath a large potential storage site owned by a company called GreenEarth. That was the kind of sensitive information that any landowner wanting to sell, would like to see buried.

One odd point was that a note – *RWL?* – had been written in pencil on the top of a couple of pages in the main body of the report. He wondered what significance this had – if any.

Vos doubted that the report would ever be made public. Maybe Vervloet had got out of his depth and paid the price.

Seven

Lights were on in the house when Vos pulled up on his driveway. He wasn't worried about this as, at the last count, three people had keys to his home. But he was puzzled by the presence of the Citroen Berlingo that was parked ahead of him on the drive. Ryck bounded enthusiastically out of the house.

"Hope you don't mind, Uncle – we're all here. Would it be OK if we stayed the night, only I've been doing the garden and it's a bit late to go back tonight." Given that his nephew had been making up for his own lack of effort, Vos felt that despite his own tiredness, he could hardly say no. "And we've got some news! We'll tell you when we're inside."

The smell of food cooking hit Vos as soon as he entered the house, a very different aroma from his uncle's cassoulet. Magda kissed him on the cheek and told him to sit down at the table. A cold Polish beer was set in front of him and the other two sat down opposite, exchanging grins and holding hands. Sun was asleep in the pushchair.

"Are you two getting married?" Vos asked, thinking it was all a little quick.

"No, no, better than that, we're expecting a baby!"

With Ryck being a student, Vos had no idea how they could afford to bring up even one child let alone two? How could this possibly work?

"Well," said Vos, trying to keep the hesitancy out of his voice, "this calls for a celebration." The words were hardly out of his mouth when three of his rarely used champagne glasses appeared on the table and a bottle was removed from the fridge. Ryck did the honours and filled three glasses – very professionally, Vos observed. A toast was made and they sipped their drinks. Vos slowly steered the conversation around to the practicalities.

"So, what will you do about work, Magda – I mean with Ryck being at college?"

"Oh, I plan to have a month off and then go back. Mum will do the childcare, like she did last time. She's very good like that. Dad's still driving his trains so he won't have much time to help out, but he'll do his bit as well." All planned out then, thought Vos.

"And now Josina has moved to Antwerp, she's offered regular babysitting as well," Ryck added. Vos was pleased to hear that the daughter he'd only found out about a few months previously had developed good links with his nephew and now Magda. He saw her when he could, but he never felt it was often enough.

"I've not asked you before, but how did you two meet in the first place?" Vos said. Again that exchange of grins.

"We met in a massage parlour," Magda said, deadpan. Vos didn't know how to respond. Was this a wind-up? What on earth was Magda doing working in one of those places and, just as bad, or was it worse, what was Ryck doing in such an establishment?

"How…er…did that happen?" Vos wasn't sure he wanted to hear the answer.

"Oh – you know," Magda said, still smiling.

"I'll put you out of your misery, Uncle. Magda provides massage as part of her holistic therapies package. I'd been a bit stressed about things at the time and I thought a massage session might help. All strictly above board, but we love to see people's reactions when we tell them. Now, before we start on Magda's kasha, how about a quick tour of the garden to inspect progress?"

"That sounds like an excellent plan," Vos said. "Oh, by the way – that Berlingo? Isn't it the same one I borrowed from the garage in Berchem when the Vectra's old engine packed in?"

"Well spotted,Uncle. Yes, they've given me free use of it for as long as I'm working there. It makes things a lot easier."

The two men poked about in the vegetable patch whilst Magda put the finishing touches to the dish, sprinkling grated cheese on top of the barley, mushrooms and kabanos.

+ + +

The following morning, with breakfast out of the way and his visitors on the road back to Antwerp, Vos turned on his computer. It was in one of its frequent slow moods and he waited impatiently for the site to load, muttering to himself. A bit of light internet browsing was the order of the day, using a couple of the sites that Albert had told him about. His uncle had made the process of unearthing details about old soldiers sound almost easy. But Vos' own Demotte-related searches produced only patchy and confusing information. It didn't help that he also got distracted into reading about other soldiers who had clearly been real heroes. In his view, it would have been an heroic step even to have joined the resistance and he wondered, not for the first time, how he'd have reacted in a similar position. It was all very well thinking that of course you'd have got involved, but there were plenty who hadn't, often with very good reason.

In the end he gave up his rather fruitless efforts and switched his attention to Mrs Waarschoot. His searches threw up a Mrs De Vocht, an enthusiastic user of Twitter, who kept up a running commentary on her daily life. This included a very recent reference to a visit with Mrs W to a local restaurant. Having found a phone number on her business website, it took him three attempts to get through to De Vocht. Her voice sounded distant and superior.

Vos had to work hard to get anywhere. He used a cover story of being a customer of Mrs Waarschoot's photography business with an urgent deadline to meet. If he'd been open about his PI role, it might have set all sorts of hares running.

"What I can't understand, Mr Vos, is why you're contacting me about this matter." Mrs De Vocht's condescending tone echoed down the line. "Presumably you've tried ringing or emailing her yourself?" Vos confirmed he had. "I see. I have to tell you that whilst the lady is a good friend, I haven't seen her recently." He decided against referring to the details he'd read on her Twitter account. He was, after all, supposed to be just a potential customer, not an expert on Mrs W's movements.

"I'm sorry to be bothering you, but from what her husband told me, I thought you two had been due to meet up yesterday. I probably got hold of the wrong end of the stick." Vos hoped he'd struck the right balance.

"Well if he's already told you that, I can see why you're making the call, but I'm unable to help, as she's already moved on. I may be able to get a message to her, but naturally it will be up to her whether she responds."

Another dead end, Vos thought – first the failure of his internet searching and then being given the brush off by Mrs Haughty.

The information in the incoming email from Uncle Albert demonstrated how a professional searched and found the detail he was after. Vos decided that in future he wouldn't waste time on his own amateurish attempts. Albert's conclusion was that Demotte senior had probably been a member of a group that had split off from the Legion Wallonie. The splinter group had claimed to be the only true leaders of the 'spirit of Wallonia', uncorrupted by power. However, it was clear that because of their uncompromising approach they were temperamentally unsuited to resistance infiltration and made an equal mess of developing links with the local divisions of the Waffen SS, who viewed them as ill-disciplined adventurers. So they'd ended up getting embroiled in brutal skirmishes with resistance units and there were accusations that they'd executed civilians who had crossed them in one way or another.

Albert thought that on the basis of the evidence he'd unearthed so far, there was a strong likelihood Demotte's unit had been involved in war crimes.

Vos wondered whether he should go any further. Demotte was in a home and maybe wouldn't last much longer. Was it really worth stirring up the past with such accusations? Perhaps he should he let sleeping dogs lie. But his instinct told him that he couldn't take this line. This kind of activity had to be exposed, surely!

+ + +

He was woken from his after-lunch nap by a knock at the door. It was a youngish woman, not attractive but he felt there was something sparky about her, even though she was doing nothing, other than standing on his doorstep. The way her dark hair was pulled back tightly into a ponytail, gave her face a rather severe look. She had a cluster of bracelets on her right wrist and half a dozen rings in her left ear. He thought the small scar on her forehead gave her a certain look of vulnerability.

"Harry Vos?" He nodded. "I'd like to talk to you about Charlie. I'm Edith Brulet."

He couldn't believe his ears. Ushering her into the kitchen, he put the kettle on and fetched mugs and plates. She gazed round the room, eyes flitting from object to object, wrapping the loose end of her ponytail round and round a finger.

He offered his condolences. She was Charlie's former girlfriend, but nevertheless it seemed the right thing to do. She seemed to appreciate his comment. There were so many questions he wanted to ask, but he started with the simplest. How had she found him?

"I don't trust the police so I've been making my own enquiries, checking out places where Charlie had some kind of connection. There was a business card in his apartment for a tattoo parlour in Mons. I told him he should never have had that tattoo done but he didn't listen. But it's not surprising he decided to get it removed after we split up. When I dropped into the parlour, the guy there said he'd done a couple of removal sessions, said that you'd been asking about it and gave me your details."

"Well I'm really glad you've been able to catch up with me. But I'm puzzled. You're calling him Charlie. What was his real name?" She was immediately on the defensive, saying she couldn't reveal that information yet. Vos was puzzled, but decided not to push the issue for the time being. "How did you know that it was your Charlie they found?" he continued. "Was it the e-fit?"

"When I saw it, I thought it was him, even though it wasn't that much of a likeness. But what convinced me…I'm sorry it's a bit embarrassing for me…it was the birthmark." Ah – the one on his inner thigh, Vos remembered. She reddened and looked away. It took a few moments before she turned back to face him.

"And when did you last see Charlie?" He tried to respect her feelings by keeping the excitement out of his voice. But he felt elated. He was the one who'd made the link from the boots, to the boot shop, to the tattoo parlour in London and eventually, thanks to Antoine, to the tattoo shop in Mons.

"It was about a year ago. I'll never forget it, we had a blazing row, I walked out and that was it. Not even a phone call from him." Vos thought that apart from her initial reaction to the mention of the birthmark, she seemed remarkably composed, not detached exactly, but none of the body language he'd have expected – nervousness, hand-clasping, hesitancy, watering eyes.

"I know very little about what he was up to over the past year. He always led a very solitary life. I was a real exception for him. I think he decided I'd got too close and the row was his way of getting rid of me. But to be honest I couldn't really handle him. I don't think he died of natural causes though." Taken aback, Vos asked why she thought that. "I have my reasons and I'll decide when to tell you," was her cryptic reply.

If things continued in this way, he wondered if he'd be able to get anything helpful from her. He poured coffee and cut slices of his mother's fruitcake. Edith ate slowly and deliberately, chewing her food over and over before swallowing and watching him intently as he described what he'd found out so far. It made him realise just how little he really knew about Charlie and his earlier feeling of elation began to dissipate. Maybe she knew little more than he did. But she had known *him* – that was the difference.

"It's bound to be something environmental," she said. "He lived and breathed it. I told him he took too many risks but he never listened. That was his big problem – he never listened. We need to find out what he was doing there, by the river – unless he was taken there after he was killed." Vos focused immediately on the word 'killed' and almost missed the word 'we'. Although he'd sort of assumed that the death wasn't down to natural causes, there hadn't been any sign of *foul play*, as the coppers loved calling it. And what did she have in mind in relation to the 'we'? Was it just a slip of the tongue? He was hesitant about asking his next question.

"Look, I know this won't be easy for you to think about, but there's one detail about Charlie I need to ask you about. There was a needle mark on his body, consistent with use of a hypodermic. Did he have any history of drug use – with a needle I mean?" She told him in a matter-of-fact way that, apart from cannabis, Charlie had never touched drugs.

"Here, I've brought you this," she continued quickly, pulling a file out of her bag. "Do you think I could have another coffee, Mr Vos?"

"Please – call me Harry. Pass your cup."

Vos leafed through the typed pages in the file. They contained details of a geological survey in the Sambre valley, south west of Charleroi. Charlie's body had been found slap-bang in the middle of one of the survey areas.

"The report's all to do with fracking. You know about fracking?" That same look of intensity on her face. Vos told her that what he knew about it could be written on the back of a beer mat. "Well it's the way they get shale gas out from underground, basically by pumping in water and chemicals at high pressure."

"So what's the problem with that?" he asked.

"Where do I start? First of all it can contaminate water in the ground and on the surface, then there's the air and noise pollution, the release of greenhouse gasses such as methane and the risks of seismic activity. Do you want me to go on?" Vos said he'd heard enough. "Anyway, the company that commissioned the survey's called X-Tract," Edith continued. "They do this kind of thing all over Europe and, naturally, have a big lobbying operation which targets national governments and the EU. It's their job to get drilling access for the fracking companies. I've no doubt they'll be trying to get the Government to lift the ban on fracking here. There's an awful lot of money to be made, so anyone who gets in their way is likely to be a target. I don't have any evidence, yet, that they were involved in Charlie's death, but I have my suspicions."

Vos couldn't work out whether Edith was overly susceptible to conspiracy theories or whether there might be something in what she was saying. Either way, he wanted to find out more.

"Did you get this report from Charlie?"

"No – as I said, I've had no contact with him for ages. I got it from a friend of his but I'm not going to tell you his name."

"What do you think needs to be done next?" he asked her, wondering again about her refusal to release what she clearly viewed as sensitive information.

"Well, correct me if I'm wrong, but you're doing what you're doing at the moment out of curiosity. From what the man in the tattoo parlour said, there's no money in it for you and you've no other vested interest. So, in my book, you're the ideal person to work with me to make further enquiries. I'm afraid I couldn't pay you though."

He was already involved with the case and had the time and the interest. But did he really want to risk flirting with danger again quite so soon after the people-smuggling case. He did his usual trick and imagined himself a month down the road having declined the case. How was he feeling, was he regretting it, did he want to turn the clock back? He felt that before making such a decision, he should try and persuade Edith to talk to the police and mentioned his own links with Antoine.

Her response was firm.

"They can carry on doing what they're doing but please don't tell them about me. You and I are in a better position than the police to delve into a number of things and we'll be more committed. I'm the only person who cares about him – despite what happened at the end of our relationship. He got on well enough with his dad, but sadly he's dead. His mother's a cow – left years ago and lives somewhere in Spain with a car salesman." Vos thought that, despite this, surely the mother had a right to know about her son's death. But maybe Edith had good reason for the view she held. "The other thing is that if we reveal his identity now, it'll get splashed all over the papers. Wouldn't take long for some journalist to find out about Charlie's eco-links and then there'd be conspiracy theories galore about his death. It would be a huge distraction. Anyway I don't want *them* to know that we're on the case."

When Vos asked her who she meant by *them*, she wouldn't elaborate and he had the feeling that she didn't actually know. He was in two minds about whether to mention Vervloet's death and his hunch that there might be some sort of connection to Charlie's death. From what she'd told him about Charlie's fracking report, maybe there was an environmental link – after all, fracking and nuclear waste dumping might stir up similar kinds of conflicts. In the end he decided there was nothing to lose by mentioning Vervloet. As soon as he said the name, she went very pale and he was immediately worried. But after a minute or two she seemed to recover and said it was just tiredness. She asked him to tell her about the second death and why he thought there might be a connection. When he finished explaining, she sat very still, made no comment and seemed to disappear into a world of her own. Realising he wasn't going to get any further, he tried to get her back on track.

"What was Charlie like to live with – if you don't mind me asking?" Vos was keen to find out more about the everyday Charlie.

"I never really lived with him. He'd stay at mine for a few days and then I'd go round to his. We lived quite close to each other. That was about as much as either of us could take. He wasn't very good at tolerating company and I guess I'm a bit the same. He'd only had a couple of girlfriends before me and neither of them lasted long. Look – I've been thinking. You might want to take a look at his apartment. There's not much in it but you never know, you might see something that I've missed. I've still got a key – never gave it back to him after we split up."

Vos knew this was the moment when he had to make a decision – make the 'we' a reality or pull out there and then. His *month down the road test* told him he was in.

Edith pulled a bunch of keys from the zipped pocket of her rucksack and removed one from the ring, distinguished with a red plastic cover over the head. As she handed the key to Vos she stifled a cry and took a packet of tissues from her bag. Vos had been puzzled about her previous lack of emotion, but clearly she'd been bottling things up. He poured another coffee and waited for her to recover.

"How come nobody's reported him missing?" Vos asked. "Wouldn't the neighbours have noticed and what about things like bills being unpaid?"

"The neighbours there don't have much contact with each other," she said, her voice shaky. "And some of the apartments have been empty for a while. I remember when I was there, I seldom saw anybody else about. With the bills – they're all paid by direct debit. Charlie was left some money by his dad. I don't think it was a huge amount but enough to cover regular payments for things like fuel and rent. They'll still be going through."

"But surely somebody would have noticed his absence?" Vos wondered if this was what it was like these days, everybody in their own small bubble, unaware of what was going on around them.

"Obviously not or they'd have been in contact with the police. He didn't have a job, so no one would miss him there. He was pretty much a full-time environmentalist, often away for days or weeks at a time – on manoeuvres as he used to call it – one campaign after another. It's what he lived for really. You mentioned before about him being in London – the new boots and the tattoo removal and all that. Well he probably went there for a demo, used to go all over the place – hitchhiked a lot to keep his costs down." Her comment rang a bell with Vos.

"Interesting you should mention that. You'll know he had a train ticket as far as Charleroi but I've been wondering how he got from there to the Sambre valley. From what you say, he might have hitched."

"Quite possibly but he was a great walker too so he'd be just as likely to have gone on foot."

"And talking of the boots, why do you think the labels had been cut off?" It was something that had puzzled Vos from the start.

"Oh he'd have done that himself – couldn't stand logos and labels, said he didn't want to help the capitalists make even more money by advertising their products for free. That was him all over."

Vos was beginning to build up a better picture of Charlie, clearly a man with very firm views.

"Just a thought – if he was short of money how come he'd buy an expensive pair of boots?"

"I was wondering about that as well," Edith said.

Vos thanked her for the key and asked if he could have Charlie's address as well.

"Oh yes," she replied. "I suppose that would be useful." A thin smile, as she wrote down the details.

"So do you live in Marolles as well?"

"Yes. That's how we met, in our local café, the one where I work. He was talking to a man about *Daft Punk* and as they're one of my favourite bands I took an immediate interest. Music was his other passion – after the environment I mean."

Vos reflected sadly that Edith probably hadn't been one of Charlie's few real passions.

+ + +

His mother had said it would be fine for her and Mr Wouters to continue to have Barto while he went off to Brussels. Vos didn't want to have to take a dog around the city with him. But he knew that the downside to not having the dog – perhaps the only downside – was that he missed the twice daily walk. He

got little enough exercise anyway and he was putting on weight
again.

Once on the train, he took the opportunity to phone Katerine
and tell her about Edith. By the time she'd finished all her
questions, the train was creeping through the middle of Brussels.
He checked the address in his notebook. Emerging from Zuid
station, shading his eyes from the bright midday sun, it took him
about fifteen minutes to reach Charlie's apartment near the Place
du Jeu-de-Balle. He stood in the small hallway to catch his breath
after climbing the stairs and wondered if the visit would turn out
to be a waste of time. If Edith hadn't found anything useful in the
place, then it was unlikely he would suddenly unearth a missing
piece of the jigsaw.

She was right – there wasn't much in the apartment;
minimalist, but perhaps not in a planned way. A small fridge,
hotplates but no oven, a fold-up table with two fold-up chairs,
an armchair of 1950's vintage, a sofa bed that looked particularly
uncomfortable and a radio. That was it. Not even a TV. Charlie
had clearly not spent money on anything other than the bare
necessities. Maybe, as Edith had speculated, his father's legacy
had been only enough to cover basic running costs. Or perhaps
Charlie just liked it that way and saw not consuming as part of his
environmentally aware, anti-capitalist, way of life.

The few books on the windowsill all had an environmental
link. Where were his bills, his personal papers? Vos' search
for anything which revealed more information about Charlie,
perhaps even his real name, proved fruitless. Had somebody been
in the place and spirited away all his personal papers – just like
in Vervloet's apartment? Was there anything left in some secret
hidey-hole? As he sat in the armchair, which turned out to be
surprisingly comfortable, he tried to work out where he would
hide things in this shoebox of an apartment. There was a steady
swish of car tyres on the road outside and the intermittent rise

and fall of emergency sirens, but there was no noise from the adjacent apartments. Maybe their occupants were out or some of them were empty as Edith had mentioned.

It was a good chair for a snooze and Vos struggled to fight off the temptation. He found himself staring at the light-fitting which was of a similar vintage to the chair, an opaque glass bowl decorated in leafy patterns. A scene from an old black and white film popped into his head. He grabbed one of the fold-up chairs, hesitated, wondering if it would take his weight, before deciding to take the risk. The chair gave him just enough height to be able to fish around in the bowl hoping his fingers would close around a hidden object – just like he'd seen in the film. There was nothing there of course and in that moment of disappointment, he lost his concentration, then his balance and fell heavily to the ground.

Lying on the worn carpet, reluctant to test out his bruised limbs, he gazed upwards at the small table and spotted a small envelope taped to the stained wood of the underside. Gritting his teeth against the pain, he crawled under the table and retrieved the envelope. Inside was a small key. Just what he was after!

The sudden knock on the door surprised him. Perhaps the noise of his fall had disturbed one of the residents. It took him a while to get to his feet. His bad knee was playing up, which after the fall wasn't at all surprising. The knocking was repeated, louder this time. He hobbled across to the door and opened it. An old woman stared at him through spectacles that were too big for her. Grey cardigan, fully-buttoned despite the warmth of the day, a tweed skirt which looked to be of good quality, dark woollen stockings and grey slippers which had seen better days.

"You're not Rudy!" She peered around Vos as if he might have hidden this Rudy somewhere in the apartment. "How did you get in here?" So that was his name! Vos had got so used to thinking of him as Charlie that it was difficult to take his real name on board. The old woman spoke French in a very cultured way and he couldn't help wondering how she'd ended up living in this run-down block.

"You're quite right. I'm not Rudy. I'm Edith's father. You remember Edith who used to live here sometimes? She lent me her key – that's how I got in. She asked me to pick up something she'd left here last year."

The woman stood completely still for a moment assessing the information she'd just been given.

"I think you could be telling the truth, Mr…?"

"I'm Harry. I'm afraid I fell off a chair and made a bit of a noise. Did it disturb you?" She nodded. Perhaps she lived in the apartment directly below.

"You see Rudy hasn't been around for a while and I wondered whether he was back or whether somebody had broken in – not that they'd find anything much to steal in here – would they?" She walked past Vos, wandered around the room and bent down suddenly to retrieve the key from the floor where he'd left it. "You must have dropped this when you fell. Here – you take it. Now, when will Rudy be back?"

Because of the deceptive stance he'd taken, he felt on the defensive. But she didn't know he was playing a part. He could carry on making things up as long as they sounded convincing enough and told her that as far as he was aware Rudy would be away for a while longer.

"As you may know, my daughter is no longer with Rudy, so she only picks up secondhand what he's doing. I understand he's off on one of his environmental jaunts." He'd guessed the woman would know about this part of Rudy's life and she didn't seem surprised by his comment.

+ + +

After she'd departed, he examined the key which looked like it was for a left-luggage locker and was stamped with the number 29. With expert help from someone who worked on the railways or one of the locker manufacturers perhaps, he might be able to track down the location of the locker. He had a feeling he'd been told recently about somebody who drove trains, but couldn't remember who it was.

Not wanting to return home, he booked into a budget hotel on the edge of Marolles, where the bed was hard and the noise from an adjacent disco went on until the small hours. In his sleepless state, his mind rambling aimlessly, he suddenly remembered the railway connection. Magda had mentioned that Zyg, her father, was a train driver.

+ + +

A few phone calls the next morning established that Vos was in luck. Zyg was not in his driver's cab, but was attending a union conference in Brussels. After a series of texts, a brief meet-up was arranged in a café close to the conference venue, near the Park Van Brussel.

He took an instant liking to the Pole, a large jovial man who wanted to know all about the case. He took the locker key and promised that he'd return it the following day – same time, same place. In the meantime he'd speak to a man who knew a man. They parted with plans for a get-together once they were both back in Antwerp.

Vos had time on his hands. Still not feeling like returning home, he decided to switch hotels, pray for a more comfortable bed and stay another night in Brussels. There was no reply when he phoned Edith to tell her about the key and he left a message. Sitting in the park, the sounds of a brass band rising and falling in the distance, he tried his mother's number, well aware that since she'd moved in with Jan Wouters, he'd been less than dutiful in contacting her. Katerine had told him that if he was going to broach the topic of Albert with his mother, he should do it face to face. But his view was that a phone call had the advantage that it could be terminated if things got difficult. At least she was in.

They talked about other members of the family for a while until Vos gradually steered things around to the wedding which she hadn't wanted to attend and *oh, by the way, whilst I was in Mons I decided to go and see…*Much to his relief, she didn't end the call there and then. He proceeded cautiously, suggesting, very tentatively, that she might want to meet up with her brother. Sweating all over, gripping the phone far too tightly, he was fearful of how she'd respond.

"I think I would like that, Harry. Could you arrange it?"

+ + +

At last he was on his way back to Heist. He'd drunk a little too much Vedett the night before, but the jazz had been excellent: two drummers, a saxophonist and, instead of a bass guitar, a tuba. One of their pieces was still running through his head, conjuring up images of a deserted nocturnal highway, streetlights flickering by.

The locker key was back in his pocket. Zyg had been impressive and, through his network, had managed to find out that the locker was at Aalst station. Vos' plan was for him and Edith to open the locker together, but he was still awaiting a response from her.

On the walk home from Heist station, Katerine phoned him, wanting to know more about progress on the case and he tried to stop himself getting too carried away. Walking was painful. The fall from the chair in Charlie's apartment must have aggravated something and he hoped it was just a temporary affliction. Ever since his mountaineering accident in the Dolomites years ago, his leg had been his vulnerability. But it could have been even worse and he could still recall the dread of thinking, in the immediate aftermath of the fall, that he might never walk again.

A text pinged on his phone: *Forgot to say. Still haven't managed to speak to Poortmans. Will try again. Love K.* For a moment Vos was at a loss to remember who she was referring to. Then it came back to him – the specialist in nuclear waste, the man who sailed close to the wind. Ah well, there was no particular hurry to hear from him.

Back home, slumped in front of the TV, watching a remake of a gameshow he'd first seen in his teens, he fell asleep.

Maes

I'm still finding it difficult to accept the official version of Vervloet's death. It's yesterday's news as far as the boss is concerned – hit and run, police couldn't find the driver, end of. I've always toed the line in the past. When a job pays well, you tend not to bite the hand that feeds you. Maybe I should have been a bit more inquisitive.

I won't be able to find out any more through the Company, but I reckon I've got an alternative route. After V and I had our evening out in Antwerp, we went back to his apartment and bumped into one of his neighbours, just as she was leaving her place across the foyer. The three of us had a quick chat and she struck me as someone I wouldn't mind seeing again. Up until now, I've not managed to get round to it.

She's in, which is my first stroke of luck. The second is that I'm pretty certain from her welcome that she fancies me! We do the introductions. Hanne she's called. Then, before I have a chance to say anything, she starts talking about Vervloet and gets quite upset. Tells me the last time she saw him, he was very on edge, but wouldn't say what the problem was. Very interesting though – like me she's not convinced that his death was a simple hit and run and tells me a little story about a man breaking in to Vervloet's apartment!

He's oldish and she watches him get in through the back door, a few minutes later hears him come out the front door, then through her spy hole sees him break into Vervloet's mailbox, sift through the post, remove an envelope and pocket it. Thinks about calling the police, but decides not to get involved – witness statements and all that.

From what she says I reckon this must have happened the day after I cleared out the apartment. But the question is, does it have anything to do with Vervloet's death? I'm already suspicious because of that report he had. Was there something just as incriminating in the envelope the burglar took?

Eventually we stop talking about Vervloet and get onto more enjoyable subjects. The two of us spend a very pleasant night together and as I leave, it's clear she's definitely up for meeting again.

I decide not to tell Mertens anything about the old man and the burglary. I've already been given the details for my next job which is in Chooz, in France, but only just. More land required for nuclear waste. I've got options to follow up either side of the border.

Eight

Edith had lived for most of her life in the Marolles district of Brussels. The only time she'd spent away was in her mid-teens. After her mother's death, her father decided to take a job in Paris. She spent a couple of years there but couldn't settle. The girls at school were awful – called her the 'weird Belgian'. So she moved back to Marolles to live with her grandmother. They got on very well, the old lady quirky and non-conventional – still using the Marollien dialect, even though there were very few people left who could understand her – the teenager mad on music and acting, out all hours of the day and night.

Now Edith had her own apartment in the district.

She pulled some press cuttings about the two investigations from a clear plastic wallet and spread them out on the table, Charlie's on the left and those about Andries Vervloet on the right. She shuffled the cuttings around, trying to get some inspiration about what had really happened. The strange thing was, she'd known both of them. The two men had been school friends, drifted apart and met up again almost by accident. It was Charlie who'd introduced her to Andries. She'd thought he'd seemed wide-eyed and innocent. Something had suddenly sparked his concerns about nuclear energy and he'd been very keen to find out more.

They'd spent some time together following her break-up with Charlie. She recalled the tense atmosphere at the Green Guards meeting they'd attended, where plans were being drawn up for a big demo near Dessel. Some of the guys there had been quite scary – some of the women too – but their talk of direct action had really grabbed her. After a very brief encounter, Charlie had always steered clear of the Guards, saying they weren't to be trusted, but she felt that at least they got on with things.

Because she'd had no direct contact with Charlie, it had taken her a while to realise that he'd disappeared for longer than one of his usual absences. His few friends had no idea where he was. She'd used her key to get into his apartment, searched the place and convinced herself that something wasn't right. Desperate to contact Andries, to find out what he knew about Charlie's whereabouts, she'd been unable to contact him by phone and at the time had no idea where he lived, though she'd found out since.

When news of the body found in the Sambre valley had been splashed across the media, she'd studied the details, examined the e-fit and come to the dreadful conclusion that it was her ex-boyfriend. And still, in her desperation, she'd been unable to contact Andries.

Given the way Charlie had ended their relationship, she wasn't quite sure where her continuing sense of loyalty to him came from. But she was convinced the police wouldn't get far in their investigations and that she'd need to be the one to find out how Charlie had died. It had proved difficult doing it all on her own and she'd been almost at the point of giving up when she'd stumbled across the tattooist in Mons. And that had led her to Harry Vos.

She wasn't sure what to make of him. Why was he so interested in investigating both deaths when he wasn't being paid by anyone? Maybe it didn't matter. He was making progress, finding the locker key, their first real breakthrough, and making enquiries about the location of the locker. When he'd mentioned the name Rudy, she'd told him that it had been a nickname of Charlie's, not his real name.

Checking her phone, she found she'd missed an incoming text.

I've found out where the locker is. Ring me. Harry V.

+ + +

Aalst? Edith couldn't remember any connection Charlie had with the place – but that was the location of the locker according to Harry.

There was something about the man sitting a few seats away from her. She was sure she'd seen him somewhere before, but couldn't remember where – just a fleeting contact, she seemed to think. When he disappeared off down the carriage, she stopped trying to place him.

Harry was there on the platform to meet her off the train.

"Have you been to the locker – have you opened it?" she asked, trying not to sound too excited.

"No – not yet, I was waiting for you!" She was pleased. Had their roles been reversed, she'd have already put the key to good use.

Walking towards the lockers, it all happened so fast. As Vos showed Edith the key, a man appeared from nowhere, snatched the key from his grasp and hit him over the head. She watched in horror as Vos slumped to the ground. Her attempts to block the man's escape were futile and he ran away in the direction of the lockers.

It took a few moments for Vos to pull himself together. He said he was OK. She helped him to his feet and retrieved his stick.

"That's that then!" he said, staring ahead of him. "Whatever was in the locker, it will have gone by now."

"That man … he was on the train …must have followed me from Brussels … how did he know about the locker key? Who the hell is he?" Edith collapsed onto a bench breathing heavily. Vos sat down next to her and listened to her story, trying to comfort her as she spoke.

"Let's go and check out the locker – just in case." He rubbed his head. "It's painful but at least there's no blood." Edith asked whether she should call an ambulance, but he said he was fine. They shuffled arm-in-arm towards the lockers.

As expected, the door to number 29 was open and the locker empty. Vos was just about to turn away to find a seat and a coffee in the station bar when he noticed a small sheet of paper at the very back of the locker. The thief must have missed it in his hurry to get away. Stretching to reach the paper, Vos felt his back muscles complaining. Once it was in his grasp, he pulled it out and stared at the handwritten message. He was unable to understand a word of it.

"This can't be anything to do with Charlie surely." He handed the note to Edith who screwed her eyes up in an attempt to read it.

"Wait a minute – I'll have to put my glasses on. It's a damn nuisance, my eyesight used to be fine." She rummaged in her bag until she found her glasses case, then perched the glasses on the end of her nose. "No – I can't make head nor tail of it either, but I know someone who will be able to – my gran. It's written in Marollien. Have you heard of it?" Vos said he had. "This is Charlie's handwriting. He taught himself the dialect – goodness knows why. I need to speak to Gran."

+ + +

Edith scanned the train carriage which was taking them back to Brussels, half-expecting the assailant to reappear. Vos tried to reassure her that this would be unlikely.

"Are you sure you don't need to get your head examined?" she asked.

"No, it's just a bump. I've had far worse. Anyway, I've got a plan. Tell me what you think of it. I think that guy must somehow have found out where you live and followed you from there today. He must have already known about the key – although God knows how. What's clear though is that he's a big worry. So rather than going back to your place now, why not come back with me to Heist? I appreciate you probably don't like the idea of being propositioned in this way by an old man, but if it's a problem, there's an alternative. You could stay at my mother's house – well it's not hers, but it's where she lives. Then we can plan our next move."

She told him she certainly wasn't keen on returning to her apartment – at least for a while – and that staying at his place would be no problem at all. To satisfy her concerns, they walked the full length of the train to double-check that the man wasn't onboard, opening toilet doors as they went. Only one was occupied. They waited there for a while and were relieved to find that it was a large middle-aged woman who eventually emerged. Their inspection of the train complete, they disembarked at Zuid station and took a circuitous route to their departure platform. Once Vos had convinced her that they weren't being tailed, they boarded the Leuven train. As soon as they'd settled into their seats Edith turned to him and said she had something she needed to tell him

"I've decided I can trust you Harry. The weird thing is, about Charlie, that's his real name!"

"What? You're having me on surely!"

"No. Most people knew him as Rudy, but, as I told you, that was just a nickname. It came from some British pop song. His actual name really was Charlie. So you can carry on using it, although I still don't want to reveal this information to the wider world."

Vos, still surprised by her revelation, decided to respect her decision.

"By the way – I meant to ask you. Will you able to get some kind of temporary leave from your job, so you can spend more time trying to find out what happened to Charlie? Of course – I don't actually know what you do." Vos hoped he hadn't put her on the spot. Maybe she didn't have a job.

"Well, I'm an actor, but you know what acting's like – sometimes you are and more often you're not. It's a community theatre so it's pretty up and down. When I'm 'resting' I usually work in a café near home – the one where I first met Charlie – but they're having some repair work done just now so, as it happens, I'm a free agent for a while."

Vos couldn't stop himself nodding off on the final leg of the journey from Leuven, but Edith woke him just before they reached Heist and the walk home from the station revived him.

As soon as they reached Vos' house Edith phoned her grandma.

"Gran – how are you?" For Vos' benefit she put the call on speakerphone. The two women exchanged small talk, before Edith got round to reading out Charlie's message, spelling each word as she went.

"You'll need to go a bit slower Edith so I can keep up with you as I write this down." The old woman's voice was clear and strong.

"OK I've got it all now. Give me a mo while I translate it." Vos could hear her singing to herself as she worked away.

"It looks like a list of things to do. The first one says: *How does the Company link to T.I.?* That's Company with a capital C. Got that?" Edith said she needed a moment as her pen wasn't working properly. "OK now? Good. Second one: *Find out how X-Tract operates.*" Edith's gran waited for the go-ahead before moving on to the next item on the list. "*Ask V if he can get hold of Mol report.* And the final item just says: *Get on the inside!* Do you know what any of this means, Edith?"

"Just a sec, Gran, while I finish jotting this down. Right – that's it. Some of this rings a bell but not all of it."

"What are you getting involved in, Edith and where are you now?" Edith paused before replying.

"I'm at a friend's house, Gran. She's a linguist and has this assignment to complete. I'm just helping her out." Edith looked at Vos and smiled.

"You've almost convinced me. Well be careful whatever it is you're really doing."

"OK Gran. I will. Thank you so much. Bye now."

"Not much gets past her!" Vos said. He switched the kettle on and found some music on the radio. The string quartet sounded familiar, but he had to check the read-out to find out it was one of Bartok's.

"I didn't want to worry her by saying anything about that dreadful man," Edith said. "She'd worry like mad if she knew."

"Yes, I think you were quite right not to mention it," Vos said. "So that list does make some sense to you?"

"Look Harry. I'm afraid I haven't been straight with you up to now." She bowed her head and looked away from him briefly. "I was waiting to see how far I could trust you and I'm definitely OK with that now. So, that's my confession and now I'd better fill you in with the detail. You see the thing is, I knew Vervloet, not well, but I met him a few times." Vos wondered if he'd misheard and had to ask her to repeat herself. He'd never guessed. "In fact, I was the one who phoned up the cops in Turnhout," she continued, "to tell them it was Vervloet they'd found. I recognised their e-fit." Vos was completely thrown by this and disappointed that she hadn't felt able to confide in him when they'd first met. But he didn't want to make anything of it. "Not only that, but Charlie and Vervloet knew each other as well."

"Well I'm glad you told me and it certainly throws a different light on things. Presumably the 'V' Charlie refers to is Vervloet." Vos was finding it hard to digest all this new information.

"Oh yes, definitely."

"Between us we might get somewhere, you know. I've actually got a copy of the Mol report." It was Edith's turn to look surprised.

"How on earth did you get hold of that?"

"Oh it's a long story. You can read it if you like." Vos decided he didn't want to go into the details of his break-in at Vervloet's just yet.

"Yes I would like to see it. The next item on the list is X-Tract and we already know about them," Edith continued. "They're the specialists who do the site testing for fracking. But I've never heard of T.I. Have you?" He shook his head. "And I wonder what he meant about 'getting on the inside'? I think we've got some work to do."

"Yes, it's good to know our trip to Aalst wasn't a waste of time after all," Vos said, trying to ignore the pain in his head.

He knew he had to phone Katerine to let her know about the attack. In the end he played it all down. Edith watched him as he spoke – eyebrows raised.

Nine

"No, no, I do like the dog. It's just that I've only just put this suit on and I'm not sure how…how clean he is. But he's very nice." Kim moved her legs further to the left to avoid any more contact with Barto. "But what about you, Grandma, how are you and when will I meet your Mr Wouters – Jan isn't it?"

Mrs Vos nodded and said that unfortunately Kim wouldn't be able to meet him just yet as he was out at the bowling club. She poured fresh cups of peppermint tea and cut two small slices of jam sponge. She couldn't remember the last time Kim had visited her at home – even though it was only sort of her home. So far, the real reason for the surprise visit hadn't emerged, but she was patient. She'd heard all about Anders and their apartment, about Kim's job – which she didn't understand the first thing about – and about London life, which seemed to revolve around meeting large groups of friends and drinking expensive fizzy wine.

She was pleased that the visit had taken her mind off her own big problem – what to do about her brother Albert. She'd got so used over the years to not thinking about him that she wasn't sure how she should react to the possibility of a reunion. Her son seemed to have managed it well enough but it was easier for him. If they did meet up – where would this be, how long would it last and would she be able to escape quickly enough if it became obvious that it was a mistake? When she'd raised it with Jan he'd been his usual placid self and told her not to worry – just to give it a go – and that he would come along if she wanted him to. He also suggested taking the dog as a sort of ice breaker. She couldn't remember whether her brother liked dogs or not.

The pause in the conversation wasn't a comfortable one and Mrs Vos realised that Kim must have asked her a question – an important one judging by the look on her face.

"I'm sorry, my dear. My hearing isn't what it used to be. Could you repeat your question?" But when it came, it really wasn't the kind of question she wanted to hear and she had no idea how to answer it tactfully. She'd always considered abortion to be a sin. There'd been one or two friends whose daughters had faced the problem, even one of her nieces, and she'd always pointedly refused to comment when the subject had been raised. But this was different – apart from anything else, she couldn't escape. With this kind of conversation taking place, she was very glad that Jan was out and hoped fervently that he wouldn't return early from his bowls match. But through the kitchen window, the sky looked threatening and there was always the danger of rain stopping play.

"It's very difficult for me, Kim. I'm so out of touch, you see. In the old days it was very black and white, not to mention illegal and dangerous. And with the church – well it was …" She found she couldn't say 'a sin' – not to her own granddaughter. She settled on the phrase 'frowned upon' which didn't express what she felt at all. "Have you spoken to your father about it? And what does Anders think?"

"Well they both said that it was my decision – that's the scary part, although to be fair to Anders, he told me he wants to become a father – and he is the father."

"So it is all over with your old boyfriend then?" Kim nodded but didn't speak. Mrs Vos gritted her teeth and decided she couldn't sit on the fence on a matter as important as this. "It seems to me, my dear, that thanks to your own hard work you have a lot that's good in your life and a baby could be something very good. You are just the right kind of age to become a mother and perhaps you would be able to pay for a nanny to help you bring up your baby, so that you could carry on working. And if Anders is supportive – well that's wonderful. Of course it is your decision…" Mrs Vos felt she'd managed both to stay true to her principles and emphasise how positively she felt about the baby.

Kim sat silently for a while, before asking for another cup of tea. Barto, asleep at her feet, shook his legs as if dreaming of a walk. The silence continued and Mrs Vos began to worry that she'd been too definite in her views. Just as she heard the rain starting to spit against the kitchen window, the front door slammed. The bowler was back.

+ + +

Although Kim and Anders had dropped in to see her father, she'd purposely avoided staying at his place – keen to avoid the risk of a row. To be fair, his last London visit had gone much better than she'd expected, but that might have been a one-off. The hotel in Antwerp was the kind of place she liked staying, comfortable, pleasantly expensive and located in the heart of the fashion quarter where all the luxuries she might want were available on tap.

Anders was a marvel, putting up with her moods, soothing her fevered brow – and taking her out for meals. They'd visited her brother and his family, briefly, just long enough to introduce Anders, so Eddie could see that, this time, she'd got it right. Her two nephews had been as wild as ever and she'd been thankful to escape to the sanctuary of the hotel.

She told Anders about how her grandmother had managed to stop short of using the word 'sin' and of how she'd been upbeat about the prospect of another grandchild.

"Well, as I've said before, it's your decision of course. But I'm as upbeat as your grandma sounds. Maybe I could meet her sometime. And what about her fancy man?"

"Anders, you can't call him that. I'm shocked," she said, laughing. "Actually he's a sweetie. They're just right for each other. Grandma was really on edge when he arrived home earlier than planned but she needn't have worried. He took me and my predicament in his stride."

"That's good to hear," Anders said. "Are you going to phone your dad – just to reassure him about your grandma?"

Kim wanted to put the call off. She'd had a very reassuring supportive discussion with Katerine and was worried that her feeling of calm would dissipate if she spoke to her father. When Anders handed her the phone, she grimaced but dialled the number. A woman's voice, one she was certain she'd never heard before, answered and told her that Mr Vos was out but would be back shortly. What was he up to this time?

+ + +

When Edith told Vos about his daughter's message, he said he'd call her back later, keen to avoid immediate distractions.

There were two columns in his notebook, on the left the things they knew and on the right what they had to find out. The left hand list was by far the shorter, but then, not long since, it had been almost blank.

"That name in the right hand column," Edith said. "Who is Poortmans and how does he fit in to the picture?"

"Oh him! He's an expert on nuclear waste, wrote the report on Mol, the one I mentioned. The worrying thing is that Vervloet's body was found within the area covered by the report. Somebody – maybe Poortmans himself – sent a copy of this report to Vervloet, but unfortunately he was already dead by the time it arrived. I got hold of it when I broke into his mailbox."

"You did what?" Edith asked.

"Oh yes," Vos said, feeling somewhat sheepish. "I put off telling you before, but I'm afraid I forced my way in to Vervloet's apartment – this was after his death, I hasten to add. I wanted to find out more about him. The place was completely empty, but I found Poortmans' report in the mailbox."

"I see," Edith said. "You said before, I could have a look at it."

"Yes – sorry, I'll dig it out," he said. "Katerine's been trying to speak to Poortmans, but he seems to have disappeared temporarily, not for the first time. As soon as he's back in circulation, she'll get hold of him. They're both at the university. I'm hoping he'll be able to help us to find out more about Vervloet. By the way, do you know who he worked for?"

"No. I think he wanted to tell me but he was very nervous about it, said I wouldn't approve of the kind of work they did. But he wouldn't elaborate. Why don't I do some snooping around – talk to his neighbours?" Vos could see this made sense.

"OK. I'll do the same with Charlie's neighbours, as long as you don't mind me posing as your father, like I did before." Vos watched her whole face transform when she grinned.

"Not at all! He'd see the funny side of it. He lives in Paris so there's little danger of two men turning up at that apartment block, both claiming to be my father. I think you'd get on. He's a maverick as well. The thing I'm worried about is the man who hit you – no doubt you are as well. How can we find out who he is?"

Vos had been wondering about this. As he'd only caught a very brief glimpse of the man, there probably wouldn't be much point in him trawling through police mugshots. When he asked Edith if she'd consider doing this – after all she'd seen him twice, once on the train and then again at Aalst station – she said she'd rather not. The alternative was checking whether the assault had been picked up on CCTV footage. Perhaps he should ring Antoine. But he realised that could be difficult for his cousin to follow up, given his own unofficial involvement in the Charlie case and the fact that he hadn't actually reported the assault.

Then he remembered Zyg, Magda's father. Would he be able to help again?

+ + +

As it turned out, Zyg seemed to know everyone associated with the railways. He'd managed to get back to Vos surprisingly quickly saying he'd made a few calls and that the man he needed to speak to at Aalst station was called Koenraad, he liked craft gin and would be happy to see Vos and Edith, despite their lack of official credentials.

It was more of a cubicle than a room. Koenraad told them the main bank of screens was housed in a larger space further down the corridor. They huddled around the single monitor as he tapped in a reference number to select the footage for the relevant date and time.

"It varies a lot," he said. "Sometimes the quality's good and other times it's like the fog's descended." They watched as Koenraad fast-forwarded.

"Wait, wait!" Edith called out, her voice excited. "There's the two of us. It's not too fuzzy. We're in luck."

Vos stared at the screen as the man from the train suddenly moved into shot and struck him. Edith put her hand on Vos' arm and Koenraad whistled through his teeth.

"Crikey, that must have hurt," he said, rewinding the images and then pausing the footage so they could have a better look at the man's face. "There! That's not a bad shot of him. I'll print it off for you. Just don't tell anyone you got it from me."

Vos was pleased. He'd assumed they'd be unlikely to get anything useable from the system. It was nice to be wrong.

"Fuck!" Both men looked startled by Edith's unexpected outburst. "I've just realised that I've seen that man before – I mean before the Aalst trip. He was in a bar talking to Vervloet and he made himself scarce as soon as I arrived." She was speaking rapidly, almost gabbling. "I don't know why I didn't think of it before. He could be something to do with the Green Guards. I remember Vervloet saying he'd just come from one of their meetings." She pulled out a handkerchief and blew her nose. "A couple of people I know have got connections with the Guards. They might be able to help."

"That would be good," Vos said. Removing a bottle of gin from his bag he thanked Koenraad. "You've been really helpful and I understand you like a drop of this. Oh and don't worry, I won't mention your name when I get this photo checked out. I just wish I'd been better prepared. It would have been nice to have caught him one."

On the train back to Brussels, Edith asked Vos about his comment.

"Would you really have hit back at that guy if you'd had the chance?" Vos claimed it was just bravado and that he'd made the comment without really thinking.

"Anyway there's something I haven't mentioned to you yet. I've spoken to my cousin Antoine again to update him."

"What! How much have you told him about me?"

"Don't worry. I'm sticking to our agreement. I haven't mentioned you and I haven't told him that Charlie really is Charlie. Any information you come up with – well, I won't say where it's really come from. But it's very helpful having a direct link to Antoine and I'll use it to get the photo of my attacker circulated. Are you OK with that?"

"Yes that sounds fine to me and thanks for respecting my wishes. I appreciate that."

Vos asked whether she'd managed to get anything useful out of Vervloet's neighbours.

"I didn't expect to, but I struck lucky when one of them – a young woman – said she'd been out with him a couple of times. According to her, he'd been getting increasingly agitated about his work, felt he was being watched, but wouldn't elaborate. And she let slip that I wasn't the only person who'd been asking questions. A man she described as a right smoothie had also paid her a call, a colleague of Andries apparently, pretty cut up about his death and very suspicious about the official hit and run story. "

Another potentially useful line of enquiry, Vos thought. His own attempts to speak to Charlie's neighbours hadn't produced much, but there had been one little nugget – a comment from an older man who'd called Charlie *an aggressive bastard*. This didn't seem to fit with the impression he'd built up from Edith's description of the dead man.

+ + +

It felt like he was doing too much, travelling hither and thither, not eating proper meals and the assault hadn't helped. But Vos found it hard to make himself slow down. There was always one more person to see or one more piece of information to locate.

At least it wasn't far to Antwerp and he'd left the car at home. Chief Inspector Franke, the big man from Turnhout, had given him a name to follow up within the specialist police unit. Vos doubted he'd get very far with Dirken, but felt he had to try.

The officer on duty was dismissive, told him that his private investigator status meant nothing and there was no way he was getting to see the Chief Inspector.

"I think you may want to tell him I'm here," Vos said, smiling at the officer. "I'm here about a man called Vervloet. There's speculation that his death had something to do with the nuclear waste site out at Mol." The officer coughed and picked up a phone.

Grim-faced, Dirken looked like the kind of man you wouldn't want to cross. He led Vos along a series of corridors to a small featureless interview room.

"I'll give you five minutes and no more," Dirken said. "How did you get hold of my name?"

"I'll come to that in a moment." Even though his time was short, Vos was in no mood to be rushed. "First of all, Vervloet was a client of mine." He was pleased that Dirken looked surprised. "He was worried about being followed and bugged. The day before he died, he sent me a copy of a confidential report on nuclear waste in the Mol area, which contains some very sensitive information. It's my view that there might be a connection between Vervloet's activities in relation to the nuclear business and his death. The fact that your unit is involved here in Antwerp strengthens my view. If it had just been an ordinary hit and run, as the official story goes, it would have been handled by the local police in Turnhout."

"And what makes you think I have any involvement in nuclear matters?" Dirken was beginning to get irritated.

"Because your name crops up in the report." Although this was a complete fabrication, Vos was gambling that, firstly, Dirken wouldn't have seen the report which, after all, was still in a draft format and secondly, that it was not unlikely his name might be referenced in such a report. Because he was honour-bound not to say a word about his very helpful conversation with Franke, he'd decided to invent this alternative way of linking Dirken's name to the case.

The man flushed and scowled.

"Your information is wrong. However, given that you have admitted to being in possession of confidential information, I require you to hand over your copy of this report." Dirken seemed to be struggling to stay on top of things. He pulled at his shirt collar which was clearly too tight, then loosened his tie.

"I'm afraid I shredded it – even to a layperson like me, it looked a bit too hot," Vos replied. "But I felt it was my duty to inform you of both its existence and the implications it might have for the case. Now, there's something else I want to raise during my allotted five minutes. Media reports of the hit and run fail to mention two important facts. There's no reference to the body having been moved or to the theft of possessions from the victim. Yet the witness gave details of both these matters when she was interviewed. Don't you think that's odd?"

"How do you know about this if it wasn't reported in the media?" Dirken glanced at his watch. Time was almost up.

"I spoke to the witness in my capacity as Vervloet's private investigator." Dirken's face reddened further.

"Look here, Vos! This case is a police matter. Your client is dead and you are in no position to continue acting for him. Your comments will be passed on to the Turnhout force. They are the ones handling this case. But there are two points I need to make crystal-clear to you in the remaining minute you have available. Firstly, should I discover you are continuing to sniff around, you will be charged with willful obstruction of the police and with being in possession of confidential information relating to a matter of national security. And the second point? Well it's even more serious than the first and is in regard to your claim of a nuclear connection to this death. This is of course nonsense. But if it were to be the case, then the kind of interference and meddling you are involved in would put you at great risk. Next time your computer is on – I take it you have one, despite your age – just scroll through the legislation on the nuclear industry, specifically as it relates to penalties for breaches of security. Then ask yourself if you should continue behaving in such a reckless manner." He glanced at his watch again. "Your five minutes are up."

As he stared out of the train window on the return journey to Heist, passing field after field of grazing cows, Vos felt his discussion with Dirken had been worthwhile. He was now certain that there was more to Vervloet's death than a simple hit and run. However, he was equally certain that he'd be unable to penetrate the security wall that had been erected around the police investigation into the death.

Maes

I'm just back from a successful trip to Chooz. It's a strange area, a small French inlet surrounded on three sides by Belgian territory. They're facing the same problem there as elsewhere. Nuclear is back in favour because it doesn't churn out carbon but at the same time there's a problem about what to do with the waste generated. With recycling plants closing down and some of the old storage sites full, new sites are at a premium. And that's where we come in. It's simple. More waste, more storage needed, big money to be made – and we're benefiting. So I'm glad I've just managed to tie up some site purchases.

But Mertens isn't in a good mood. What a surprise! He acknowledges the progress I've made but in the next breath he's onto me about Vervloet, claims his boss has grilled him about it. Now of course he's taking it out on me.

I cleared the apartment. There was absolutely nothing left that might have caused us a problem. Mertens asks me if I checked the mailbox out in the entrance. Full of junk mail I tell him but nothing else. That's when he tells me about the camera. Shit. They're filming Vervloet's place and I've been making visits to the apartment across the landing! Am I also on film?

But when Mertens starts telling me about an old man they've picked up on the camera, my worries change track. He must be the ageing burglar that girlfriend Hanne spied going through Vervloet's mailbox – and I didn't report it. Mertens wants me to find out who this guy is and what he's up to, as if I'm some bloody detective. But, it will put me back in his good books if I can do this.

He gives me a copy of a still of the old man taken from the camera footage. It's not great but it should be enough to go on. The fact I'm being sent on this errand signals to me that there's more to V's death than they're letting on.

I'm totally unprepared for what follows. They must have had that camera in place for a while, because Mertens knows I'd visited Vervloet. He asks me point blank if I had a relationship with him. Me!! I try and keep calm, but I'm seething inside. The thing is, do I mention Hanne? Will it make things worse or better? I decide to tell him on the grounds that they might already have me and her together on their fucking camera.

He grills me for a while. I admit I broke the rules about socialising with another member of staff, but at least he drops the gay angle. It's a relief that he says nothing about staying away from the girlfriend.

I wonder where the camera is. Or maybe there's more than one. What else have they picked up?

Ten

For the first time, Vos was beginning to wonder about Mrs Waarschoot. Initially he'd felt her husband was fussing too much and that the simple explanation for her absence was that she needed some space. But maybe she had actually linked up with the 'old flame' that one of her friends had mentioned.

Her husband had been on the phone again, voicing his concerns about her lack of contact, not just with him but with a number of her friends. Vos had agreed to meet him later in the day.

Sitting in his own kitchen, halfway through his second coffee of the morning, Vos watched Ryck watering row after row in the vegetable garden. Edith was due back, having spent a couple of days with her grandma.

There'd been no recent developments in any of his enquiries. Sometimes he felt the distractions of his investigations meant he never had enough time for everyday life. But if he was honest, he got bored quite quickly with the ordinary things. It was all about getting a balance, but often that eluded him.

His mother seemed to manage it these days, helped, no doubt, by Jan Wouters' relaxed approach to life. He'd played the role of amiable host to a tee the previous Sunday, when Harry and his brother Pieter had been invited for lunch and the four of them had then accompanied Barto on his afternoon walk. There'd not been an argument in sight and his mother had even agreed to the suggested date for a meet-up with her brother Albert.

Inevitably it was the phone that stirred him from this reflective peace.

"Dad!" Of all the possible callers – it had to be Kim.

"Yes dear. How are you?"

She spent a while telling him and he was pleasantly surprised that most of it sounded positive. She and Anders had come to an agreement about the baby. He would switch to a four day week and they'd employ a nanny. Apparently Kim's employer couldn't do without her, so reducing her own hours was out of the question. And Patrick had been very supportive. Vos swallowed before asking the inevitable question.

"So is that OK with Anders – you talking this kind of thing over with your ex?"

"He might be my ex, Dad, but he's also a good friend. That's what takes priority and Anders is cool with it." Vos didn't believe this for a second, but said nothing. "And how are you, Dad? What have you been up to?"

Vos almost dropped the phone. When was the last time Kim had asked such a question? He couldn't remember.

"Well I've been quite busy. You see, there's this case involving a man called Charlie." He wondered whether she'd have the slightest interest in the story but she didn't interrupt him. Every now and then she even asked for clarification on a detail.

"So you want to find out more about a company called T.I. but they may be offshore? Is that it?" She'd taken it all in! "Maybe I can help out." This was becoming stranger and stranger. Listening, helpful, what next? But with her more than full-time job and a baby on the way, how would she have time to help? "We deal with offshores all the time. Like everything else, it's about who you know and about asking the right questions. What do you have so far?"

Vos told her – not that there was much to tell. It might take a few days, but she'd call him back. This was definitely a new Kim.

Before she hung up she asked him about the woman who'd answered his phone the last time she'd called. Not that it had bothered her at all – she just wanted to know. He told her about Edith's involvement in the Charlie case and said she had a personal link without explaining further.

He was hungry again even though he'd had a large breakfast and it was not yet noon. He used hand signals to communicate with Ryck through the kitchen window, getting confirmation that he could also do with a bite to eat. Four slices each from the loaf of olive bread, butter, a particularly runny brie, half a dozen tomatoes picked out from the group ripening on the windowsill and a pot of his mother's homemade chutney. He banged on the window to let his nephew know that it was time to eat and poured two glasses of fruit juice.

Ryck took his time describing the latest details about Magda's pregnancy. Vos didn't need these continual updates, but didn't interrupt until there was a pause in his nephew's monologue.

"Well that's interesting, Ryck. Thanks for working in the garden this morning. I seem to have been away quite a bit recently and haven't had time to do anything much out there. I have to say, this brie is…" Ryck waited for his uncle to finish the sentence, but there was just silence. He seemed to be trying to say something but nothing was coming out.

"Are you OK, something gone down the wrong way?" Vos still didn't speak but motioned to his nephew to fetch something to write with. He scribbled a few words down and showed the pad to Ryck. *I can't seem to speak.*

They carried on eating through the lengthening silence. Vos scribbled again on the pad and pointed to the words. *What do you think it is?*

Ryck wasn't sure. He was wary of using the little medical knowledge he'd picked up as part of his preparations for the course. But he remembered reading about mini-strokes and knew that speech was one of the faculties that could disappear temporarily. The question was, should he say anything? His own knowledge was very limited and he didn't want to dive in with a comment which might unnecessarily worry his uncle. Perhaps he should hold on and hope the episode would soon be over. But after fifteen minutes of silence he was getting really worried.

"That was so weird," Vos said suddenly.

"Well that's a relief," Ryck responded. "I thought you'd really lost it there. Um… the thing is … it might be something you should get checked out, Uncle."

"You could be right. Maybe I should make an appointment to see the doctor."

"No, no, I mean you should get it checked out now, today, at the hospital. I think you might have had something called a mini-stroke. The advice is to call an ambulance and to have things checked out immediately in hospital. There's a risk of having another, for one thing."

"Come on, Ryck! You haven't even started that course of yours yet. This is just something you've got from the internet isn't it?" Ryck was unsure how to proceed. It was true – he had just got it from the internet, but that didn't mean to say it wasn't accurate. Besides a friend of his had also talked about it – somebody he knew whose facial muscles had packed in temporarily.

"Well, I'm going to follow that advice. I'm phoning for an ambulance," he said, decisively.

+ + +

When Edith arrived back at Vos' house she was surprised to find he wasn't there. He'd told her he'd be in. It took a minute or two

before she noticed the note on the kitchen table, propped up
against the sugar bowl. His nephew had taken Vos to hospital.
She hoped it wasn't anything serious.

Before she'd had time to put her overnight bag in the spare
room, there was a knock at the door. The man said his name
was Waarschoot and he had an appointment with Mr Vos. Edith
explained what had happened, asked for his phone number and
said she'd pass the message on. There was something about him
she didn't like, but couldn't put her finger on it.

No sooner had she closed the door than the phone rang. She
was in two minds about whether to answer it, but curiosity got
the better of her. Besides, she'd given the number to a couple of
good friends. The call might even be for her. But it wasn't. It was
Harry's prickly-sounding daughter.

"I've tried to speak to my dad on his mobile but it's been
switched off for ages. That's why I tried the landline. Do you know
where he is?"

Edith told her about Ryck's note. Unfortunately, she didn't
know what the problem was or which hospital her father had
been taken to.

"OK – I'll try and speak to Ryck," Kim said, sounding suddenly
very concerned. "But I need to tell Dad something – something
important. It's about an organisation called T.I. ..."

"I know about that," Edith cut in, trying to keep calm. "You
could give me the information. They've got something to do with
the case we're working on."

"I don't think I can tell you. I need to be careful about who
I share this stuff with." Edith wasn't aware that Vos had said
anything to his daughter about the case. Why would he have
involved her?

"Look, this is personal for me," Edith said, making an effort to
keep calm. "Did your dad tell you about Charlie? Yes? Well he was
my boyfriend. His death hit me really hard as you can imagine.

I absolutely must find out how and why he died and we think there's a link to T.I. somehow, so anything you've got on them – well I would be really grateful if you could share it with me." She tried not to sound too pleading.

"Oh, you poor thing! I had no idea," Kim said. "Of course I'll share it with you. It's preliminary stuff – there'll be more to come. They're very well-hidden, so you can bet your life that there's an awful lot of money involved. If you give me your email I can send you the details." Edith gave her the address. "Please tell Dad about this as soon as you can. My source made it clear to me that anyone dealing with T.I. should be careful. Maybe you shouldn't try and go any further with this, but hand things over to the police." Edith explained that there really wasn't much to hand over, but reassured Kim that they'd be cautious.

Lying in bed in the small spare room, Edith found that although she was exhausted she couldn't sleep. She wondered why she'd got herself into this position. She'd loved Charlie, but doubted that he'd ever felt the same way about her and their break-up had been awful. If he'd still been alive, they wouldn't have been together – she was certain of that. Whilst in some ways he'd been quite worldly-wise and knew how to handle himself, at times he'd been almost shockingly naïve. So why was she pursuing this and putting herself in danger? She had the feeling that if it hadn't been for Harry Vos, she would probably have called it a day by now. But his interest had rekindled hers. Would he be able to continue his investigations or would the hospital keep him in and she'd be on her own again? She had no way of knowing, but there was no point in assuming the worst.

Lying back on the pillow, she drifted off. She was a little girl, out shopping with her grandma, Christmas lights bright in the December darkness. Inside the department store there was everything you could imagine. They rode up the escalator to one of the higher floors where they walked between sparkling displays, each one trying to outdo the other. She lingered next to the skates, the white boots brilliant under the fluorescent lights and gave her grandma that special look. Not a word was exchanged but she knew the skates would be hers.

Maes

Hanne's come up trumps! No, she's not found out who the old burglar is yet, but she's befriended a girl who's been sniffing around Vervloet's neighbours asking questions.

The girl's called Brulet, on a bit of a mission, quite intense. I'm wondering if I should try and speak to her. She's probably been picked up on that damned camera so I'd need to be careful. Maybe I should just get Hanne to ask some questions. I could give her a list. It's hardly the best chat-up line – 'can you do me a favour and give this woman a grilling' – but it's worth a try.

+ + +

It doesn't take long.

Brulet's been round to Hanne's place again. Apparently she really opened up which surprises me. Vervloet was a troubled man, unsure of himself, uncertain about his future, Brulet thinks his death might be linked to that of a man known as Charlie. I remember seeing something on the TV about him – found dead by a riverbank, somewhere near Charleroi, no ID. Speculation maybe, but who knows.

Then Hanne surprises me. Brulet has an accomplice. He's an old man!

I make sure Hanne knows just how grateful I am.

Eleven

Vos should have felt miserable. Banned from working, barred from driving, forced to adopt a pill-popping routine at breakfast time, a new diet which seemed to exclude everything he really liked and, perhaps worst of all, a reduction in his drinking.

But the upside was Katerine's decision. In order to keep a watchful eye on him, she'd insisted on moving in with him full-time for the time being.

Initially he'd refused point blank to get into the ambulance that Ryck had called, insisting that he was fine and had things that needed doing. But the paramedics had been very persuasive, their approach honed over many years of dealing with recalcitrant patients like him. After a blood test, blood pressure test, an ECG and an ultrasound scan he'd been questioned by a consultant. She'd eventually confirmed Ryck's internet-informed diagnosis and explained that he'd had what they called a transient ischaemic attack. This meant basically that there'd been a temporary disruption in the blood supply to part of his brain. In his case this had led to a temporary loss of speech. She told him that although the effects often only lasted a few minutes and were usually fully resolved within 24 hours, he would need to take statins and a blood thinner and have frequent rests.

Vos had left the hospital armed with two boxes of pills, a heart monitor which he was instructed to use for 48 hours and a list of dos and don'ts. The first of the don'ts told him that he shouldn't be on his own – for a week or two at least. Ryck wasn't in a position to uncle-sit. Until Katerine came to the rescue, Vos had faced the prospect of having to occupy the small box room in Mr Wouter's house under the watchful eye of his mother.

But Katerine set some firm ground rules and told him there was no way he'd be working on any cases for the foreseeable future. She'd seen the message from Edith about Mr Waarschoot's visit and phoned him to let him know that there'd be no further enquiries about his wife for a while. His few terse words in response barely hid his annoyance.

Katerine had been knocked sideways by the mini-stroke. After reading up about them in some detail, at least she understood more about future risks. Coming so soon after the attack on Vos at Aalst Station, she worried whether there was a connection. Her own doctor had told her it was possible but unlikely.

She was keen to make sure Harry would be sidelined for a while, although she was under no illusions that his inactivity would be anything other than temporary. But it wasn't as if he needed watching 24/7. As her students were on vacation and there were no immediate deadlines approaching for her research work, she would have some spare time available.

Standing in the garden shed to avoid the risk of Vos eavesdropping, watching the rain watering rows of potatoes outside, she phoned Edith. They agreed to meet in Antwerp.

+ + +

Having walked the length of the Sint-Anna Tunnel, they emerged onto the Scheldt embankment, found an empty bench and joined others gazing back across the river to the city skyline. Edith was very concerned about Vos and Katerine tried to reassure her as best as she could that he was tired but OK.

"Of course he's not allowed to continue his investigations for a while so I thought maybe you and I could work together to try and find out a little more." The two women were a contrasting pair: Edith in tight black jeans and heavy boots, a light tartan scarf tied loosely around her neck, Katerine in her work clothes, a dark trouser suit over a pale lilac blouse, briefcase at her side. Dog walkers passed by, squinting into the sun as they watched the heavy barges chugging upstream.

"Harry has a dog like that one," Katerine said, pointing towards an Irish wolfhound "but he's temporarily loaned out to his mother, so you won't have met him yet." Edith shook her head.

"I'll tell you what's bothering me." The younger woman let her gaze follow the dog as it sniffed at a discarded bag of rubbish. "I think Charlie and the other man, Andries Vervloet, were both killed, not by the same person necessarily but by the same organisation. I think they both uncovered stuff that should have remained buried. That could make it dangerous to carry on digging. I need some convincing before I can be sure about going ahead." Her hands shook as she lit a cigarette. She blew the smoke out rapidly as if she didn't really want it inside her in the first place.

Katerine was also in two minds. Based on what she'd heard from Vos, she'd come to a similar conclusion, but had been reluctant to put it into words. With the people-smuggling case it had been different. Although she'd known it would be dangerous from the start, she was familiar with the goings-on in that particular world so it hadn't scared her too much. But she didn't know much about the worlds of nuclear waste or fracking. She'd no doubt that at the root of it all would be money – big money. And that made it risky.

Although Vos' head injury hadn't been serious, it had been a warning. Edith was right to be cautious. But somebody needed to find out what had happened to the two men – didn't they? And the police didn't seem to be getting very far. One death was officially down as a hit and run, with a driver who'd not been traced and probably never would be. The other seemed to be regarded by the police – and the press – as more of a puzzle to be solved than an investigation of a suspicious death. If she, Edith and Vos didn't pursue things, maybe nobody else would. And as her man was off the case for the time being, it was really down to her and Edith to make progress. Katerine felt she had to try and keep the young woman on board.

"I do understand your concerns, Edith. But I know Harry. As soon as he's able, he'll be back on this and I won't be able to stop him. If we can make some progress in the meantime, there'll be less for him to have to do further down the line. I'm not sure how far I'd get on my own. You know much more about all this than I do."

An older man sat down on their bench and immediately started telling them his life story. Everything about him drooped, his hair, his moustache, his eyes and his voice. As one, the women nodded politely, rose from the bench and walked off along the embankment.

"I think we've got enough of our own troubles just now without listening to his," Katerine said. "Look I'm off to meet the man I mentioned to you on the phone – Dr Poortmans? He's the one who wrote that report that Harry got hold of, an expert on nuclear waste issues and things that go on behind the scenes. We're in need of that kind of expertise. If you feel up to it, I'd be really grateful if you could come along with me."

Edith asked her to wait for a minute. She stared out over the river and then turned to tell Katerine that she'd made her mind up. She wanted to meet this man.

+ + +

Dr Poortmans had a reputation. He'd flirted with dismissal from his research post for years but had somehow managed to avoid the final chop. It helped that he was very good at what he did. It didn't help that he upset almost everyone in the way he did it.

His desk was a mess and they sat around an oval table that was mercifully free of debris. He carried three flexible plastic cups of coffee between his hands and Katerine was convinced that the whole lot would end up on the vinyl-tiled floor. Miraculously he succeeded in getting to the table without spilling a drop.

"I'm afraid the only milk I've got resembles a biological culture, so we'll have to drink this awful stuff black. Do feel free to smoke, by the way. I don't follow that particular university rule."

Or any others, Katerine muttered under her breath.

"Now! Let's see what I've got for you." Poortmans walked to his desk and pulled out a green file from underneath a lopsided pile of magazines. "Ah yes, I'm sure you'll find this very interesting." He ignored the sound of the magazines slithering onto the floor, pulled out a map centred on the town of Mol and pointed to a thin red line that had been drawn around an area some distance to the north and west of the town.

"This is what the Company does," Poortmans said, lighting a small cheroot.

"Which company?" Katerine asked.

"The insiders just call it the Company with a capital C. Its registered name is Redline." The two women glanced at each other but didn't speak. "They're part of an interlocking network of companies. I've only been able to trace part of it." He pushed his glasses back up the bridge of his nose, a pointless action as they immediately slid back to their original position. "Anyway what Redline practices is really a form of gambling. Step one is about research, finding out about plans for development at a very early stage. An obvious example, and the one I'm personally most interested in, is the need for more nuclear waste sites. But the same approach is used for fracking sites and other developments. It's important for the Company to get in very early before there are any publicly declared plans. That way they can steal a march on any likely competitors. So they make contact with people in the know in the right organisations and offer cash – a bribe – to encourage them to divulge confidential information about future plans. Even people in relatively senior positions can be bought. Some just want the extra money, while others have debts to clear, over-lavish lifestyles, gambling problems or maybe a skeleton in the cupboard. Are you with me so far?"

They both nodded. Katerine wished he would stop smoking the vile-smelling cheroot, but was too interested in what the man had to say to risk annoying him.

"Step two involves identifying potential sites suitable for the anticipated development. This again depends on good research. Step three involves approaching the unsuspecting current owners of said land. Wave money under their noses and they'll often sign up happily. The strategy is dependent on secrecy at all stages. So the Company exerts a strong degree of control over its operatives but pays them well for what they do which, in turn, buys their loyalty. From what I've heard, leaks of information from their operatives are rare."

Poortmans paused, blew out a perfect smoke-ring and took a sip of his weak black coffee. He smiled smugly and looked as if he was enjoying the attention of the two women.

"What happens on the ground – literally – is that the Company man, posing as an ordinary Joe with a dream of buying his own bit of land, comes along and asks an unsuspecting landowner if they'd consider selling their plot of land. A deal is agreed, which includes a secret cash bonus on top and the purchase is completed with a minimum of delay. Then a back-to-back sale to one of the companies within the network takes place. Once all the required plots have been purchased, an approach is made to the organisation which wants to develop the complete site – whether it's for nuclear waste, fracking, redevelopment or whatever – and the land is sold on. The profits can be very significant. That's how it works."

Katerine was impressed by his assessment but wanted to know more about the Company. How extensive was the network?

"I can't answer that yet. The enquiries I've made so far all come up against the problem of secrecy. If you want to avoid tax or keep your ownership details away from prying eyes – or both – there's never been a better time to do it. You can follow the links back so far and then there'll be a trust with a lawyer as the only contact and you can't get any further. I've just compiled another report on Redline – with the help of a colleague. We share the same approach. I'll let you have a copy of it. But let's get back to the Company's *ordinary Joes*. I'm certain Vervloet was one of them and I'd put money on it that your Charlie was another."

Edith gasped.

"How can you possibly think that? You obviously know nothing about him. He was on the opposite side of the fence completely. It's far more likely that he ended up dead because of his activism and that somebody from the Company, as you call it, might have been behind his death." She was struggling to keep control of her voice.

"It's understandable you have that view," Poortmans continued, "but I'd ask you to consider a few facts." It was clear to Katerine that the man had no appreciation of Edith's vulnerability. He was enjoying himself too much. "The map he was found with just happened to include a potential fracking site, although this potential wasn't publicly known. Given what you say about Charlie's background, you'd assume that he was checking the site out because he was an anti-fracker. But it's also possible that he was badly in need of money and had decided to join the other side. After all, you mentioned he had that cash on him, three thousand euros. Not an insignificant amount," he said, looking at Katerine. "I know he'd been in contact with our friend Vervloet and the two of them had been planning something together."

"How on earth do you know that?" Edith cut in, her voice no longer shaking.

"Simple. Vervloet told me. Called him Rudy, but I'm pretty certain it was your Charlie. Bear with me. This is how things could have developed. Let's assume Vervloet worked for Redline, but harboured doubts about their methods. He'd been trying to find out more about what was really going on and in his travels came across Charlie who was coming from the opposite direction, part of the opposition. Something pulled them together. My hunch would be that Charlie wanted to get inside the Company – for whatever reason – and Vervloet helped him to do this. Look, he sent me this text."

Poortmans flicked through several screens on his phone before handing it over to Edith. She went pale as she read the message.

R's disappeared. Maybe it was a bad idea getting him on board.

Just as Katerine was about to ask her about the message, the office door opened. A young woman dressed in a short skirt and high heels appeared, looking flustered.

"I'm sorry to interrupt, Dr Poortmans, but there's a policeman in reception saying he needs to see you right now. He's very insistent."

Poortman looked only mildly concerned. Without a word, he stubbed his cheroot out in a saucer, picked up a battered briefcase, headed for the door and turned left down the corridor.

"Reception is the other way, Doctor!" But the young woman's words were wasted. Katerine guessed that Poortmans would have previous experience of police avoidance. "Oh dear, he'll be in trouble again for this. Unfortunately the Doctor can be unpredictable. I doubt he'll be back for a while."

As they walked to Katerine's office, Edith couldn't hold back.

"What I've just heard has really thrown me. Maybe Charlie wasn't all he seemed. He lived and breathed all the environmental stuff, but I have to admit, now and then he'd do things that just didn't add up."

Twelve

There were just the two of them in the clinic waiting room. Amongst the posters covering the walls were a couple promoting stroke awareness. There appeared to be a local support group in Heist but Vos thought it was the last thing he'd consider joining. Why would he want to mix with other people when he'd have only a single thing in common with them?

He pulled a book from his bag, a history of events in the Ardennes in 1944, removed the marker and started reading. At the back of his mind, thoughts about Demotte's wartime experiences drifted around.

A name flashed up in the orange lights of the display screen followed by instructions to go to room 4. Vos looked at the other man who stared back at him.

"Someone not turned up then!" the man said and Vos nodded. A few minutes later, when the name *Demotte* appeared on the screen, he thought he was imagining things. *Think about the man and his name comes up in lights.* What was going on? His fellow patient walked off to room 4. Was it his Demotte? Well, his care home was in Heist so it was a real possibility. Vos regretted that he'd missed an opportunity for a potentially very interesting conversation, but then reminded himself that there was absolutely no way he could have known about this serendipitous occasion in advance.

"Something's cropped up. There'll be a bit of a delay." Demotte was back in the waiting area talking to him and Vos realised that he must have dropped off. "We could go and get a coffee. It'll be half an hour or so, they told me." The pair of them trooped off to the hospital café which looked just like a real café with a proper coffee-making machine.

They sat at a table which gave a good view of ambulance arrivals. Vos wasn't going to waste this unexpected opportunity. He pulled the book from his bag again.

"I'm about halfway through this," he said. "It's all about what went on in the Ardennes in '44." He paused, hoping for a reaction. Demotte looked at him and for a moment, Vos thought he was going to get no further. But then the old man started talking and gradually his story began to come out. He was hesitant and repeated himself several times. Vos wondered if he was having difficulties with his memory.

From the details he mentioned, it soon became clear that Vos had the right Demotte in front of him. But the emphasis of his story was very different from the one Albert had outlined. He talked about his involvement in something called Groupe G, helping allied airmen to escape capture by the Germans and sabotaging military assets, as he called them. Vos wanted to probe deeper.

"This is really interesting. I've been talking to my uncle, who was also in the Ardennes at that time and he told me that some men made up stories about what they'd done during the war. They claimed to have been involved in the resistance. In reality they'd been on the opposite side and tried to cover their tracks. They fabricated a different kind of past for themselves. Did you come across people like that? I mean it was all very confused at the time and records went missing." Demotte sipped his coffee and tried to extract a biscuit from its cellophane wrapper, struggling to find its weak point. Vos helped him out.

"I don't suppose you can smoke in here," the old man asked. Vos shook his head and pointed to the shelter beyond the café

window. Three smokers were standing there, looking, from the
way they were throwing themselves around, as if they were telling
each other jokes. "I hope you're not implying I was one of these
fabricators – trying to re-invent myself. Your generation has no
idea, you know. It was fucking awful back then. Apart from your
close mates, you didn't know who to trust. It was dreadful and I've
no idea how I survived it all. I took a bullet here," he said pointing
to his chest. "I must have had a guardian angel, not that I believe
in that sort of thing. I found out later that the bullet went right
through me but missed all the important bits. It was the cold that
almost finished me off, not that bullet, spent a night in the snow,
before I was found. Some locals took me in and nursed me when
they could easily have turned me in, or worse. I'll never forget
them. So there's your answer."

Vos felt chastened. The man sounded completely genuine,
speaking from the heart. But how did all this square up with
Albert's research?

Back in the waiting area, Demotte's name came up again on
the display. He walked off to room 4 without another word. Vos
couldn't tell whether he was angry or just drained.

By the time it was his turn to see the consultant, Vos was
feeling uneasy about the conversation he'd just had. He should
have been upfront with Demotte about who he was. The doctor
seemed pleased with his progress and told him he should be OK
to drive again after a further check up in a fortnight.

Waiting for the taxi home, he wondered which of the Demotte
stories was the true one.

+ + +

It was a relief to get back and put his feet up. He made the mistake
of checking his phone which had been switched off. There was
a voicemail from Mr Waarschoot who explained that he knew

all about Vos' indisposition, but wondered whether it would be at all possible to have just five minutes of his time as there had been a serious development. Vos decided to forget, temporarily, about Katerine's ban on his investigations and he phoned back to confirm a brief meeting.

It didn't take long for Waarschoot to arrive from Lier. Vos wasn't sure if he really liked the man. Once the outwardly considerate veneer rubbed off, there was something rather self-righteous and superior about him.

"Look," Vos explained. "If my carer returns, just pretend you're here to talk to me about my stroke. I'm under strict instructions not to get involved in any work just yet."

"Oh, I'm sorry!" Waarschoot looked perturbed. "I didn't think things were serious enough for you to need a carer. If I'd known…" Vos smiled.

"Well she's my partner actually, but also my self-appointed carer. I don't want to be caught stepping out of line, so if she returns, whilst you're still here, I'd be grateful if you could pretend you're visiting to talk to me about the local stroke club. Is that OK?" Waarschoot looked as if this idea was far from OK, but nodded his assent. "Good, now let's sit at the table and you can explain the latest problem."

"It's her debit card," Waarschoot said, pulling two sheets of paper from an expensive-looking leather briefcase. "I know I shouldn't have opened her statement but I was worried." Vos felt uncomfortable about the man's actions, as there didn't seem to be sufficient justification for this kind of step. "Anyway, I'm glad I did. There are a number of transactions that mean nothing to me. We've never had any secrets between us before, so it's disturbing that these payments are being made." He handed the statement over to Vos, who thought it highly unlikely a couple would have no secrets. He took a while to run his finger down the column of figures on each sheet.

"Hmm! It's not immediately obvious where the problem lies," Vos said, wanting his client to identify where the questionable transactions might be. "You'll have to be more specific."

"Look, take this entry here for a start," Waarschoot said brusquely, pointing to a sum of one thousand euros paid to a firm called Lambrecht. "I checked online and they're property agents. Even though I knew I was wasting my time, I phoned them, but of course they refused to tell me anything about my wife's account – confidentiality rules! Now take this one here," he continued, pointing to the second sheet. "Seven hundred euros paid to this travel firm. It's clear I won't be able to make any progress finding out what these payments are for, so I want you to find a way of checking what's going on – when you're back on your feet again, of course. But I think it's pretty obvious what she's up to. The Lambrecht payment is for some kind of love nest and she and her fancy man have had at least one holiday together."

Vos was concerned at this sudden change in his client's approach. Although he'd had his suspicions that something might be going on and there'd been that reference to an old flame, he wasn't yet convinced that Mrs W was having an affair. But he didn't have enough energy to argue the toss with Waarschoot there and then. His lame statement that he would look into things when he was fit enough left a sour taste. When he heard a key in the front door, his heart sank. He'd almost got away with it. Now things would depend on how good an actor his client was.

On the R1

Standing on a bridge, overlooking the Antwerp Ring Road, the twelve year old recorded the make and type of each vehicle that passed beneath him. As usual, the road was busy, which meant he had to work quickly. But he was an expert. A quick glance was all that was required to be able to tick the correct column in his notebook.

He should have been at school, but escaping the bullying there was a higher priority for him than avoiding any punishment by the adults – at school and at home – that inevitably followed his frequent absences. Besides, his dad never seemed to be completely serious with his tellings off. Maybe he'd had similar experiences in his own childhood.

The big old Opel was already going too fast as it approached the next bridge. The boy wondered whether he'd imagined it or whether the Toyota Land Cruiser following immediately behind really had nudged the Opel ever so slightly. Part of him wanted to close his eyes, but he knew he wouldn't. The noise of the impact with the bridge support was appalling, a screech of tyres, an almighty bang at the moment of collision, a racing engine, a suddenly blaring horn.

The Toyota continued on around the bend. The boy made a note in his book.

He knew there was no way the Opel driver could have survived and that other people would call the police. He waited there a long while and watched the flickering blue lights arriving, the closure of the road, the removal of the body from the crumpled vehicle and the technicians checking their distances and angles.

The Toyota would be his secret. He wouldn't even tell his father.

+ + +

In his bedroom, six floors up, his laptop glowing, he watched the news. The police officer read from a clipboard – a case of excessive speed, previous convictions for speeding, no trace of alcohol or drugs in the body, condolences to the family.

The boy made up his own story about the man in the Opel, middle-aged, on the run, unable to escape his pursuers. Probably had no family and only a handful of people would attend his funeral.

< why the fuck did you do it?

< it wasn't me

< what do you mean?

< either an accident, like it said on TV – or somebody else
  wanted him silenced

< well, well!

Thirteen

Sometimes Kim felt she'd never really been a full member of the family. Even as a child, she'd felt out on a limb. Her brother Eddie had always been the favourite. She'd got on fine with her mother, but her father – well she didn't remember him being around that much, working long shifts at the factory, then out with his workmates or tied up with some boring union business.

She'd grabbed the opportunity to study away from home. London was her kind of place, somewhere she could lose herself, be anonymous and shake off her provincial upbringing. Getting her first job in the City happened almost by accident. She'd been about to take a job with an accountancy firm, safe but rather boring, when she'd met a man in a Canary Wharf bar. By the end of the evening he'd offered her a job in his brokerage firm, she'd become an investment advisor and never looked back.

At first, the idea of becoming a mother had terrified her, but now it felt a much more natural step to be taking. Anders was a big part of this, of course. Without him she felt she couldn't have kept level-headed. And Patrick, bless him, had been a dear.

The cursor on the screen awaited her instructions. She re-read the details in her notebook. The network she and Jan had traced was extensive and impressive. It had been hard work finding each link in the chain, but they'd finally tracked down the organisation at the apex – Terra Incognita, the unknown land, 'T.I.' as Charlie had referred to it.

She'd worked with Jan in the early days. Having made more than enough money, working for 'the Man', as he'd put it, he'd quit his job to sample Caribbean life in Aruba. Since then he'd split his time between offshore fishing and investigating the much murkier waters of offshore finance. It was Jan who'd helped her to navigate these waters, who'd identified the lawyer fronting the blind trust, behind which sat T.I. Although they knew it was there, they'd been unable to get much further.

But they'd uncovered plenty of detail about what sat beneath T.I. and Kim attached a summary of this information to the email she was sending to her father. She'd started to feel differently about him recently – wasn't sure why. Now she was doing something important for him and it gave her a warm glow. Not that she was under any illusions that their relationship would be instantly and magically transformed, but it was a good start and did wonders for her karma.

Typically, he'd underplayed his recent health scare. She'd been about to jump on a plane to visit him but he'd said he was fine, was resting and was well looked after. Being even busier than normal, she'd decided to defer her trip.

+ + +

The Director's summons took her completely by surprise. It had to be trouble. When things were running smoothly, he was never to be seen. She printed off a copy of her latest performance matrix, just in case it was needed, but had a nagging feeling that this invitation was not related to her success rate.

"Kim – please take a seat. This is rather difficult, my dear." Oh God, another man who couldn't resist being condescending to a female colleague. "You see, I've had a call from …well let's call him Lord X. He's a peer of the realm, but I'm sure you'll understand that I can't give you his actual name." So this accusation – that's what must be coming – will be anonymous. Fantastic! "Our IT people have picked up some rather out-of-the-ordinary enquiries on your machine, you know, not the kind of thing we actually pay you very well for." Kim was seriously concerned. She'd done all her research for her father on her laptop at home. It would have been far too dangerous to have used the company's network. Something else must be going on here. "Lord X doesn't take kindly to anyone who attempts to breach his confidential business records and as, of course, ours is a business built on trust, you can appreciate his and my concern." The Director stopped talking abruptly and looked at his employee, expecting a response.

"Well, sir." She tried to keep the sarcasm out of her voice when she used the word 'sir'. "If IT can clarify the nature of these enquiries maybe I'll be in a position to respond."

The Director reached for a clear plastic wallet and handed it to her. She removed the two pieces of A4 and looked at them, recognising the details immediately, the network of companies that had Terra Incognita at its apex. She would have to tread very carefully.

"I'm puzzled, sir. I've never had this kind of information on my computer. How did IT get hold of it?"

"Are you saying you've not seen it before?" Irritation was beginning to show. Perhaps he'd been led to think it would be a simple matter to resolve.

"I'm asking you where it came from." Although she wasn't used to dealing with her boss in this way, she found she could handle it.

"I'm not sure that's important, Ms Vos." No more *my dear*. At least that was a relief. "As you refuse to tell me whether or not you have seen this information before, I have to assume that you are hiding something. This puts you in a very difficult position."

"On the contrary, and with the greatest of respect, Director, it puts you in a difficult position. Your allegation is completely unsubstantiated. Perhaps IT could throw some light on this."

The Head of IT was in the Director's office within a minute, clearly hidden away nearby in reserve. Kim had never got on with the woman.

"Explain to Ms Vos here how you obtained the information we spoke about earlier this morning." The Director's speech had become clipped, his face rigid.

"It was in an attachment to an email you received. You deleted both immediately and you must have thought you'd done the necessary to remove traces of both from the system. You succeeded with the email, but failed with the attachment and as you can see it has your initials in the header. There are no other KVs in the company. As you will be aware from the IT policy that you sign annually, we are authorised to monitor all emails and other documents on the system and that is what we have done." The woman was still standing. She was tall and Kim felt dwarfed sitting in the low chair adjacent to the Director's desk – but not intimidated.

"Come on! This is laughable. At least credit me with the nous that if I'd done what you've just accused me of, I wouldn't have been dumb enough to leave my initials on the document. This is a complete fabrication. If you persist with these claims, I'll have no alternative but to involve my lawyer," Kim said, her voice steady. "Unless you tell me I'm suspended, l shall continue with my work here."

Back at her desk, she couldn't stop herself shaking. Either they'd hacked her home laptop or someone had hacked Jan's system.

Despite the current state of his health, she knew she needed to tell her father about how T.I. operated.

Fourteen

Katerine had guessed straight away that the man who'd been sitting in the armchair in Vos' sitting room had nothing to do with stroke care but she'd gone along with the deception. Vos finally confessed later in the evening and explained about the debit card statement and Waarschoot's revelation that he thought his wife was having an affair. Katerine said she thought he was out of order and added that she'd taken an instant dislike to him.

Katerine was unsure whether to tell Vos what she'd found out. The news had been all round the university. Although she was trying not to overload him with stressful information, she didn't feel it was right to hold back the details of Poortmans' death.

When she told him, he looked stunned, but immediately wanted all the details. She ran through what had happened the previous day on the R1, car speeding when it hit a bridge support, no other vehicle involved, driver died instantly, police treating it as a fatal accident. Then she mentioned the connection between Poortmans and Vervloet.

First Charlie, then Vervloet and now Poortmans – the environmental activist, the land buyer with a conscience and the law-breaking academic. Vos was sure there must be a link between the three deaths.

"When Edith and I met him," Katerine continued, "he told us he had another report in the pipeline about the Company. But I don't suppose we'll be able to get hold of it now."

Vos gave her a hug and went to put the kettle on, unable to raise sufficient energy to think any further about Poortmans. He went through the coffee-making process automatically.

Sipping his drink at the kitchen table, he remembered the email and the subsequent phone call he'd had from his daughter, late the previous evening. It was a real surprise that she'd been able to provide him with information about Terra Incognita. Unfortunately, not only had she succeeded in digging out this information, but she'd precipitated an almighty problem for herself in the process. What had amazed him was how calmly she'd spoken about the prospect of losing her job. He told Katerine about Kim's email and the threat to her job.

"Harry! Why didn't you tell me this before now?"

"Unfortunately this is the kind of thing that happens when I'm so short of energy."

"Sorry, love, I wasn't thinking. But this is really worrying. How's she taking it?"

"Surprisingly well, but I'm very worried for her."

"I have to say though, Harry, this makes me more determined than ever to try and get to the bottom of what's going on. She's a star, your Kim. Edith and I can do the legwork on this for the time being. You're not ready yet, are you?" He had to agree, but said he wasn't sure that anybody except the police should be investigating

"After hearing about Poortmans, I'm worried about what might happen next. Maybe we should steer well clear." Because of his tiredness he was hoping that Katerine would agree with his assessment. But from the look on her face, he thought this was unlikely.

"I know what you mean, Harry, but the police aren't going to do anything much because there's so little to go on. Look what we've got – a hit and run, a nasty traffic accident and a mystery man who, even months after his death, nobody apart from Edith seems to miss. There's no evidence that any of them were deliberately killed and nothing official that links the three of them together. Even we can't be certain. It's still just speculation. Kim's information could be crucial, but we need to find out more about the Company – Redline, Poortmans called it. I know Edith will be keen. She had a bit of a wobble, but she's OK now."

"Can we mull it over in the morning and then make a decision. I need to go to bed now."

As he kissed her goodnight, his phone rang. It was Antoine. Vos gave his cousin a run-down of his state of health and the quarantine that had been imposed on him. Katerine's hand signals indicated that he should terminate the call as quickly as possible.

"Well I'm really sorry to hear about your health problems," Antoine said. "I do have some Charlie news for you but I guess it can wait."

"News – what news?"

"Are you sure you're OK to do this?" Vos said he was. "Right! It's really more speculation than news. One of my officers spoke to his oppo in Turnhout about their dead man. What was his name again? Vervloet, that's it. You remember he had a large amount of cash and a map on him when he died but these items were taken by the hit and run drivers."

"Yes, I remember. It was part of the evidence given by that witness."

"Well that matches what was found in Charlie's rucksack. Anyway my man's theory is that Charlie might have been involved in the same business as Vervloet, buying up land to sell on and making a profit in the process, maybe even working for the same company."

"Hang on!" said Vos. "Charlie was on the opposite side completely. He was Mr Environmental and wouldn't have approved of that kind of thing at all." He tried to ignore Katerine's raised eyebrows.

"That's what we thought at first, but what about this possibility?

Charlie has money problems and it's enough to turn him. He's perfect for the job, knows the scene inside out and would be anything but a pushover when it comes to negotiating. If it had happened just prior to his death, there'd have been no time for word to get out about his switch of loyalties, except maybe to one or two in the know."

But surely Edith would have noticed such a big change, Vos thought, before remembering that she'd had no contact with Charlie for months prior to his death and would have been unaware of any change. "OK, for the sake of argument, let's pursue this a bit further. He's in the same game as Vervloet, but who would have gone so far as to have the both of them killed?"

"I don't know about Vervloet, but with Charlie it could have been a group like the Green Guards." Antoine had to remind Vos who they were. "Just a sec!" Vos could hear his cousin sipping something. He imagined a full glass of red wine which set off his own cravings. "One or two of them have been known to go over the top," Antoine continued. "They keep a careful eye on what's happening on the ground with all the big environmental issues – nuclear waste dumping and fracking in particular. If they picked up that Charlie had switched sides – and for money – well that wouldn't have gone down well. Maybe they didn't intend to go as far as killing him. Perhaps it was an argument that got out of hand. Who knows – but it's possible." More sipping at the other end of the line. "I accept this is all speculation, Harry. We don't have any hard evidence and I can imagine what my boss would say if I asked him for more resources to investigate this kind of thing."

Vos wanted to keep on talking, but he found he couldn't ignore Katerine's frowning expression or his own drowsiness any longer. It was only after he'd put the phone down that he realised he hadn't told his cousin about Poortmans' death or T.I. or any of the other recent developments. It would all have to wait.

Katerine's previous look of annoyance over his too-long phone call had changed to one of guilt.

"I gathered Bernard was telling you Charlie might have switched sides. Well Poortmans came up with something very similar when we met him. I didn't mention it because I'm trying to limit what you're doing on the case for the time being." She followed Vos into the bedroom. "Listen, I've been thinking again about Poortmans' death." She was deliberately moving the discussion on, wanting to avoid a prolonged late night discussion about what Charlie might or might not have done. "It could just have been just an awful traffic accident. He was a terrible driver, was always in scrapes. I travelled with him once and it was a nightmare. I was so relieved when the journey was over. So maybe it was just an accident pure and simple." She hoped she'd said enough to calm his concerns about the third death.

During the sleepless early hours of the morning, Vos found himself coming round to the idea that Charlie might have switched sides and wondered what Edith would make of it all.

Maes

Here in my bed, I feel like death warmed up. It must be something I've eaten. Any day I don't work is a day I don't earn. They may pay us well when we're out on site but otherwise – sick pay, holiday pay – forget it.

I need to stop trying to find out about what happened to Vervloet. It won't do me any good. At least I've discovered who the old man is, name of Vos. Claims to be a private investigator, but doesn't seem to have a client. Perhaps he's one of those weirdos who reads about a death in the papers, then ferrets around to test out their own private theories about what might have happened. I have to say though – sometimes these guys do uncover things.

With a bit of luck, identifying Vos will get me back in favour with Mertens. Sure I've broken a few rules, but nothing too serious yet. That's why I need to stop now. The good news is that the girlfriend is still on the go, so once I've got rid of this damn food poisoning, things should start to look up again.

Damn! There's knocking at the front door and however much I try to ignore the sound, it's not going away. I'll have to answer it.

It's a woman, not exactly a looker although there's something almost animal-like about her which I find strangely attractive.

Very polite, asks if I'm Mr Maes, definitely not god-squad, maybe some kind of do-gooder. I'm really taken aback by her next question. She wants to talk to me about Vervloet! She must be Brulet. What to do? Shut the door in her face or whisk her inside before anyone sees us talking.

She sits at the table, a mug of tea in her hand, a cigarette in my own shaky grasp. I tell her that I'm not well but I don't think it's catching. It doesn't seem to bother her either way – doesn't look worried or sympathetic. Brulet claims Hanne gave her my address, but I've no recollection of having told her where I live.

Once she's finished talking about Vervloet, Brulet mentions Charlie. Apparently she and him were an item. She reckons there's a link between the two deaths, Charlie's and V's, but doesn't know what it might be.

I had a dreadful feeling something like this might happen. Just when I've made the decision to walk away and return to the fold, the bloody thing comes following me, snapping at my ankles. Now I won't be able to get rid of it. I was feeling bad enough even before the surprise appearance of Brulet, but now the sweating and the shaking worsens. Mertens' voice is in my head. 'So how do you know this woman and what exactly did you tell her?'

She knows too much for me to pretend I don't know anything and when she mentions the money and the map found beside Charlie, I find myself getting drawn in. She's heard that he might have started working for the Company just before his death, seduced by the money. I find this hard to believe. I certainly never came across him, but with the Company's level of secrecy, that means nothing.

It gets worse. The third man she mentions definitely does have a link with V. He's the man who wrote that fucking report on nuclear waste for God's sake! And now he's dead as well. I can't make sense of all this – need time to work it through.

I ask her about Vos. She seems to be expecting the question. How do I know about him? I explain, giving as little away as possible. Suddenly she's telling me about how he was assaulted when he was making investigations at Aalst Station. Maybe there's more to this old man than I'd thought. I try not to show I'm worried. Who's behind this?

It's a great relief when she leaves and I can creep back to my bed. But ten minutes later she's back! Car won't start, no buses this time of night, do I by any chance have a spare room? My first instinct is to refuse, but with this damn sickness bug I find I can't do it. Just about manage to find some bedding and leave her to it. Then I begin to worry. I know nothing about her. Will she start snooping around?

But, I'm dosed up to the eyeballs, can't move, can't get out of bed...

Fifteen

In the end, it was his mother who made all the necessary arrangements, which pleased Vos. His energy levels were up a little but still not sufficient for him to be able to tread the difficult pathway towards a successful reunion with Albert. Mr Wouters had come up trumps and suggested that they should all gather at his bungalow in Aarschot.

Helped by her daughter, Mrs Vos revived her dormant baking skills and busied herself preparing the room and the table. Harry and his brother Pieter arrived with Katerine acting as chauffeur. But there was no sign of Albert who'd insisted he could reach the gathering under his own steam. Conversation was a little stilted until Pieter started telling one of his stories. That seemed to break the ice.

Nobody recognised either the old Citroen DS that pulled up on the drive, or the elegant elderly woman who stepped out of it and proceeded to walk around the vehicle to open the front passenger door. Out stepped a dapperly dressed Albert. Vos thought he should have taken a photograph of the three of them – car included. He was even more nervous than he thought he'd be and now there was this lady, who he assumed must be his uncle's partner, Miriam, to add into the social mix.

But she seemed instantly at home, guiding Albert from guest to guest, with a word for everyone, though she was a newcomer to all. Mrs Vos held out a hand to greet Albert and suddenly there were tears in his eyes and she moved to hug him.

"How could I have been so stupid?" he said, wiping his eyes and blowing his nose with a freshly-pressed handkerchief. "All those years of shutting myself away! I should have known better." Mrs Vos said they'd been as bad as each other, sulking for decades like two thirteen year olds.

"What matters is that you're both here now," Miriam said, smiling.

Pieter wanted to know who Albert was. His uncle started to tell him about the two of them riding on a tractor on a farm long ago. Pieter suddenly remembered and continued the story. This surprised Vos, who had no recollection of the pair ever having met before. When the two of them wandered into the garden to continue the story, Vos took the opportunity to introduce himself to Miriam, telling her what a pleasure it was to meet at last. After asking him about his current state of health, she said she wanted to hear about his case. He assumed she meant Charlie and started to give her the basic details until she interrupted him. No, the man with the gun! What about the man with the gun? So Albert had told her about Demotte. Of course, he probably shared most things with her – maybe everything. Vos recounted the tale of the accidental meet-up in the hospital, of Demotte's account of his movements during 1944, of the impossibility of knowing for sure what had really happened. In a very matter-of-fact way, she told him that Albert had the firearm with him in his old shoulder holster. Vos knew he'd have to arrange for a discrete handover of the weapon.

Through the conservatory window, he watched his uncle talking animatedly to Pieter, who seemed transfixed. Albert seemed to have that effect on people these days. Vos thought with regret about all the encounters they'd never had over the decades, all the stories they wouldn't be able to tell because the events had never happened. He knew that kind of regret was pointless, but it didn't stop him. His mother was suddenly by his side asking him if he felt tired. He didn't like having to admit it. She joined the pair in the garden and Vos crossed his fingers that the siblings' first re-encounter would end amicably. As Pieter returned to the kitchen to refill his plate, Mrs Vos and her brother walked further down the garden, passing between the raspberry canes and the strawberry bed until they reached the fruit trees beyond. He put his hand on her shoulder and she returned the gesture.

Vos felt he should leave them to it. It was time for him to talk to his own brother.

+ + +

The day had taken its toll on him and he'd given in to the inevitable and gone to bed at eight in the evening. At four the following morning he felt suddenly wide awake. As far as he could tell, Katerine was still asleep and he made as little noise as possible, preparing an extremely early breakfast for himself.

At the party, he'd finally managed to corner Albert on his own and the handover of the gun had taken place, which meant he now had to decide what to do with it – hide it again in case he needed it as some kind of evidence or hand it over to the police, as he should have done originally.

As he put the gun back on the ledge in the chimney flue, he told himself that it was just a temporary use of the hiding place.

Deciding what to do with the new information Albert had given him was just as problematic. It completely contradicted Demotte's own version of events, but Vos was uncertain as to whether there was enough hard detail to warrant turning it over to the proper authorities, whoever they might be, the police or possibly a war crimes organisation, although he wasn't sure if such things still existed. It would be a huge step to take, particularly as, to borrow Albert's phrase, they'd be dealing with a whole spectrum of shades of truth and untruth.

And Demotte was an old and ailing man. What was the right thing to do?

Albert with his hand on his sister's shoulder – that's what Vos really wanted to think about. The afternoon had ended without any serious mishaps and even a promise of a future get together in Mons. Miriam had made quite an impression. Vos couldn't help thinking again about what might have been.

Sixteen

Edith's car had magically started first time the morning after her enforced stay at Maes' apartment. But the alleged failure of the car had provided a convenient and convincing excuse to justify her request to stay the night. And Maes hadn't suspected a thing. Once she'd heard him snoring, she felt she could risk starting her search.

He hadn't even taken the precaution of logging out of his computer, which surprised her. But she'd found nothing useful on the machine and had to stop herself getting distracted reading emails relating to his love life, of which there were many.

A search of desk drawers, illuminated by her head torch, had also revealed nothing of interest, with the exception of two pairs of frilly knickers, still in their wrappings. She wondered whether the discovery showed that he was just a very considerate boyfriend ready to help cover any partner emergency, or whether it might have been an indication of his own alternative choice of underwear.

When Maes had suddenly stopped snoring, she'd frozen and tried to work out where to hide. But it had restarted, even louder than before and she'd been able to resume her silent search. As the normal locations had produced nothing of interest she'd tried the abnormal. The kitchen cupboards were barren territory until she'd reached the larder unit. Inside one of the large boxes of breakfast cereal, she'd found two pages of handwritten notes. From a quick scan it looked like a summary of Maes' attempts to find out how Andries Vervloet had met his death. She took a photo of the notes with her phone, hoping the result would be of sufficient quality to enable her to read the script later.

She'd been up and about early the following morning and had peered into his bedroom. He'd been fast asleep and had looked really unwell. She'd felt guilty about leaving without thanking him but even more awkward about staying in the apartment any longer.

It was only afterwards, back with her grandma, that Edith realised how calm she'd felt whilst indulging in her own spot of espionage, which had been inspired by Vos' story about breaking into Andries' apartment. Maes' notes made it clear he suspected there was more to Vervloet's death than had been reported. Perhaps he'd been silenced because of something he'd uncovered?

The last line of his notes showed that Maes was worried about ending up with a similar fate. *No more on this, it's not worth it. Give M what he wants re the odd couple and back off. Don't want to experience an unwanted reunion with V!*

It was her grandma who pointed out that Edith and Vos must be the *odd couple*. But why would Maes have been investigating the pair of them?

Although she was under strict instructions from Katerine not to contact Vos for the time being, Edith felt he needed to know about Maes. Rather than ringing Vos and risk the call being intercepted by his carer, she decided to drive up to his place with a nice bunch of flowers and some fresh fruit to pay a strictly social call, which might just have some extra conversation tagged on the end of it.

Seventeen

Most people liked Ann Waarschoot's husband. They'd tell her how he always had time for a word, was considerate, calm and friendly. Except that he wasn't like that with her. She felt there was always that pressure, to look right, to be by his side when it mattered and to have the right views, although he hadn't been like that in the early days.

So she'd taken to going away, to escape the pressure she felt. There'd never been any kind of physical threat. It was more a feeling of being constantly watched. Each time she went away, she found it more and more difficult to return home to Lier.

He didn't know about the tiny studio in Mechelen, from where she now ran her photography business; a bolt hole which had just enough room for a sofa bed and a two-ring cooker. He seldom visited the city so there was little risk of accidentally bumping into him there.

She needed to pick up a few things from her home, so it was a flying visit. Her husband was a creature of habit. It was a golf morning and he left the house right on time. She watched from a distance in her hire car as he threw a set of golf clubs and a sports bag into the boot of his car and drove off. Parking on the driveway, she let herself in to the house, took a holdall from the landing cupboard and replenished her stock of clothes. There was room in the bag for a few of her favourite books and CDs and she picked up her post which was on the hall table. She was about to open the front door to leave when the landline rang and she hesitated, uncertain about whether to answer it. There was no likelihood her husband would return before mid-afternoon, so she had plenty of time. The number on the readout wasn't one she knew.

She didn't recognise the man's voice or his name but he said if she was Mrs Waarschoot, he'd like a word if possible. She told him to go ahead.

"I'm really pleased to have caught you. I got your number from a friend. I hope you don't mind me phoning. You see, I have a possible commission for you – photographic work – and I wondered if we could meet to discuss this, somewhere convenient for you, a café or a bar." He sounded genuine enough. She agreed to meet the following day in a café he suggested in Heist. It was only when she'd finished the call that she began to wonder which of her friends he'd spoken to and why they'd divulged her number to a stranger. But then they'd be meeting in a public place and if she didn't like the look of him, she could always leave.

Before the phone call had broken her concentration, she'd been about to leave the house. Now she felt she wanted to stay a little longer. It was odd. Even though she'd only been away for a matter of weeks, the house no longer felt like hers. In many ways it never had been, more of an office, museum and library for him, than a home for them both. The rambling old building contained hundreds of his books. She wandered into his 'study', as he called it. Black and white photographs – not her own, sadly – were displayed across one wall of the large room. A state-of-the-art computer was the only item on the large mahogany desk. Old files tied with pink ribbon were stacked on custom-made timber shelving. Current files, she knew, were locked away in the company office.

She ran her finger along the surface of the desk and blew the dust away. Without her attention, standards had clearly slipped.

The house felt musty and she longed to throw open all the windows. In the kitchen there was a row of empty wine bottles lined against one wall and a rack of full replacements waiting to be drafted into service on the opposite wall. The kitchen bin was full of takeaway cartons and boxes . Her husband had never had to cook for himself before and there was no reason to expect he'd do so now. On an impulse, she removed a bottle of Pinot Grigio from the fridge, opened it and took the wine and a glass upstairs. She waited for the bath to fill, undressed and sank into the warm water.

She could see the garden through the bathroom window and watched as the birds swooped from the silver birches to the low shrubs and back. A train flashed by the end of the garden. After two sips of wine she closed her eyes.

+ + +

Having had a good night's sleep, with none of his usual rambling dreams, Vos felt a little more energetic and told Katerine he was going to walk down to the coffee shop.

"I would have joined you, love, but I must finish this damned funding application and send it off." Secretly, he'd been hoping for such a response.

"Well we should go there sometime. It's called 'The Kat,'" he said, grinning.

Wearing his hat and sunglasses, he walked slowly into Heist. It took him nearly half an hour to reach the café and the longer he walked, the guiltier he'd felt about hiding what he was doing from Katerine.

There was a table free outside the café where he sipped his coffee and watched the passersby. His mental picture of Ann Waarschoot was of a woman in her early fifties, dark-haired, medium height and build, a little anxious. He was surprised when she appeared in front of him and matched his imagined description almost exactly. Had her husband described her? No, of course, there'd been that photograph – how could he have forgotten?

She didn't want a coffee, said she'd prefer a walk and set off, glancing over her shoulder every now and then.

"So you have a job for me," she said. "What kind of shoot will it be?"

Vos hadn't worked out quite when to tell her that there'd be no job. Would he get more out of her if he continued the fiction? He concluded that in this case, honesty was the best policy.

"I'm afraid I haven't been straight with you," he said, pulling his hat lower over his eyes to shade him from the glare of the sun. "There's no easy way of putting this but your husband has been worried about you and he's hired me to try and find out what's going on. I appreciate that you may not want to talk to me and would fully understand if you left now. But…" She'd stopped walking and was watching a group of school children passing by in a crocodile along the opposite pavement.

"What do you think of him – my husband, I mean?" Vos was caught out by the abruptness of her question and was unsure how candid he should be, but she continued talking before he could answer. "You see, they all like him. He presents a very good front, charming, helpful and supportive. If only he were like that with me."

They started walking again, passing the industrial estate where Vos had spent many years working in a factory that made bus parts. As they walked, he drained the last of the water from his bottle and returned it to his rucksack.

"What will he want you to do now you've found me?"

Vos was unsure about how direct to be with her. Should he mention her husband's suspicions straight away or wait and see how the conversation developed? He decided to play things low key.

"Well, he's concerned about you, wants to know you're OK and whether there's anything particular worrying you. I'm sure he's got your best interests at heart." Even as he made the comment, Vos wasn't convinced this was really the case.

Tiredness caught up with him suddenly and he knew he had to find somewhere to sit. There was a bench under the window in one of the gardens they were passing and he made a beeline for it, explaining to her that he needed a rest.

She looked concerned and was hesitant about following him into what was, after all, a private garden. He knocked on the front door and without waiting for a response, took a seat. The woman who opened the door looked annoyed until Vos said a few words to her and she disappeared, returning with a glass of water. Mrs Waarschoot took a seat next to him on the bench, waiting for him to recover.

He explained about his state of health as they walked onwards, then asked about her business, how long she'd had it for, how was it doing and did she run it from home?

"I used to, but that's another thing about Roland. He seems unable to let me get on with it and is always trying to interfere. He thinks I should build the business up, start employing an assistant or two. That isn't what I want. Once you take on staff you've got a responsibility to bring in the work to keep them earning. To escape his interference, I've moved the business out of the house into a little studio. He doesn't know about it. It's made a real difference for me."

So much for her husband's idea of a love nest, Vos thought. They'd walked full circle and returned to the café. Only one of the outside tables was free. Long, red-checked cloths almost masked the mix of wooden and metal tables, each decorated with a jam jar full of flowers. He went for a strawberry smoothie and she ordered two espressos, the first of which disappeared in seconds.

"It's typical, my husband hiring you to find out about me. We never were very good at just talking to each other. He's a lawyer, not very imaginative, used to following procedures and getting the detail right, doesn't really see the bigger picture. But there's no great mystery here. Perhaps you could tell him that I need more space. Mind you, that will make you sound more like a therapist than a private eye. What got you into this kind of work anyway?"

Vos told her how it had started, but kept it simple and didn't mention either the Charlie case or the people-smuggling.

"So, what kind of lawyer is your husband?"

"He's a property lawyer – always tied up with his work and his bloody pink ribbons. It's funny, here you are investigating me and I'm finding it relaxing talking to someone who knows virtually nothing about me or him." A passerby waved and recognising one of his neighbours, Vos waved back.

"Property lawyer, eh? I could do with one of those. My mother has just decided to sell her place. She can't really manage on her own any longer."

"No, he doesn't do that sort of property. With him it's all big stuff, redevelopment sites in the city or land for industrial development – not that he really tells me anything much about what he does. That's just it. He wants to know about everything I do, but it doesn't work in the other direction."

She finished her second espresso and looked across at Vos.

"So, what are you going to tell your client about what I'm up to? Do you have to give him a written report – *2:30pm, met subject in café. Established she now runs her business from a small studio. Told me she won't be returning home just yet and is trying to work out what kind of future she wants.* That's fine with me, as long as he doesn't know where my studio is. But then, you don't know anyway, do you, Mr Vos?"

He was surprised by how easy it felt chatting to her. He had all he needed to report back and, even though he hadn't asked her directly, was convinced she wasn't having an affair. There was no point in going any further. It would be up to the two of them to resolve their problems. It was on the tip of his tongue to ask about the 'old flame' that her friend had mentioned, but he held himself back.

He'd enjoyed his afternoon out, but was unprepared for Katerine's inquisition when he returned home. It turned out that the neighbour who'd greeted him at the cafe had spotted Katerine sunbathing in the garden on his return and had made reference to *her husband's lady friend*. Vos had to admit what he'd really been up to.

Katerine said she'd been pleased by the neighbour's reference to *her husband*.

Maes

Each time I try to escape the quagmire, I get sucked in deeper.

I should have guessed Mertens had installed cameras inside my place. He grilled me about Brulet and I couldn't work out how he knew. Simple answer – it was all on film!

I put Brulet up and she repays me by snooping around the apartment, going through all my personal stuff and taking those fucking photos of my notes. Of course I should have been much more careful and bloody suspicious of her. But the stuff I got from the pharmacy knocked me out as soon as I took it.

I had to tell Mertens the whole story and now I'm suspended, which means I'm probably finished. I wonder what they'll do to her and the old man. And on top of everything else, I can't seem to throw off this damn sickness. It's laid me low for days now.

So far there've been no repercussions for Hanne. Once I'm fit again, we won't use her place any more in case they've sneaked cameras in there as well. No sense in providing them with a free peepshow. A friend of mine's away working in the Gulf and I've got a key to his place. They might trace us there eventually but somehow I don't think they'll bother. They've got what they want and I'm no longer crossing the line. It's a weird feeling not working. I've no idea what to do with myself.

Maybe they won't get rid of me. After all I'm the best they've got. I go over and over it. Keeping a record was a big mistake. I got too cocky, reckoned they'd never find it because they'd have no reason to look in the first place.

I suppose there's nothing to stop me taking a holiday. Perhaps I can persuade Hanne to come with me.

< you should never have attacked him
< I got carried away
< you need to kiss and make up, we want him onside
< that's not my style
< well you'd better change your fucking style then

Eighteen

Roland Waarschoot found it increasingly difficult to understand his wife. Things had been much simpler in the early days, when she'd played the charming hostess, reliable and predictable. Even when she'd started nagging about setting up the photography business, it hadn't been too much of a distraction. But then things started to get out of hand. He put it down to the bad influence of her friends. Now he had no idea whether her business was still going. If it was, she was doing none of it from home.

Outwardly he projected an image of tolerance and understanding – we must let women these days find their own way forward. Behind this façade it was a different story. He was becoming more and more exasperated by her unexplained absences.

Although the investigator's report had stated that he'd come across no evidence of an affair, Waarschoot was still convinced there something was going on. Given how busy he was at work, he resented the distractions caused by his wife's activities and he wanted Vos to try again.

Access to the investigator was currently being controlled by the woman he'd met for a few brief and embarrassing moments when he'd made that pathetic attempt to pass himself off as a member of the local stroke support group.

Although he'd left a message with her, he wasn't confident that it would be passed on. There was also the question as to whether Vos would want to get involved in any further work.

+ + +

It was good to be able to drive again. The doctor had been pleased with Vos' progress, although it was difficult to be precise about what constituted progress. Most importantly there'd been no further episodes and his tiredness was beginning to lessen. And a visit from his other daughter, Josina, had really helped. She was always so positive that talking to her never failed to lift his spirits.

Recalling his conversation with Mrs Waarschoot, he'd checked on the internet for details of her husband's company and found it was called RW Legal. The name rang a bell, but he couldn't remember where he'd come across it. Katerine told him that Waarschoot himself had been on the phone concerned that his wife continued to be off the radar and still convinced that she was having an affair. At first, Vos resented this renewed contact, but when he reflected on what had actually happened, he realised he'd been a little too willing to take Mrs Waarschoot's word about a number of things. Maybe he needed to do his job more thoroughly and find out whether her monthly payments to Lambrecht were for a 'studio' or a 'love nest'.

Traffic was light on the drive to Mechelen and there were plenty of spaces when he reached the multi-storey. Passing the police station on his walk into the city centre brought back unwanted memories of the night he'd been held there under arrest, after he'd hit that awful man Daems. Hurrying on, he found the Lambrecht office next to a pleasant, tree-lined square.

The receptionist asked him to take a seat. After ten minutes he was growing restless. As usual the magazines held no interest for him and he'd already finished two plastic cups of water from the cooler in the corner. The young man who approached him looked barely old enough to have left school.

They sat in a small interview room, the windowsill lined with a range of well-tended potted plants. Violin music at a low volume drifted out through speakers high up on the wall – Vivaldi, Vos thought. It always seemed to be Vivaldi in this kind of place.

The youngster was very smartly dressed and didn't go in for the modern habit of not wearing a tie. He asked Vos what kind of property he was interested in.

"Something small, suitable for a studio. I'm an artist and I've outgrown my room at home. My wife keeps telling me there are too many canvases lying around. Makes it difficult to clean, you know. Do you have anything available that might fit the bill?"

The man, eager to please, said they'd recently let a couple of artisan workshop units and there seemed to be a growing demand for them. He'd check what else might be available and let him know. When Vos asked him which areas these two units were in, the young man took him across to a city map on the wall and pointed to the relevant streets, which were close together. He told Vos that it was likely that something else might crop up in the same area.

It was near enough to walk to. Vos felt he was getting back into his stride – literally, as he was having what he called a *good leg day*. Several buildings were under scaffolding and the whole area seemed to be buzzing. The first unit was occupied by a furniture restorer. The prices looked extortionate to Vos, but then it wasn't a market he was familiar with.

The second unit was the one. Judging by the framed photographs in the small display window, Ann Waarschoot was very talented, able to catch a quality of light in her pictures that made them appear almost like paintings. The unit was closed and there was no sign indicating anything as mundane as opening hours. The café on the opposite side of the road was the perfect location to be able to keep an eye on the unit and in any event it was time for a rest, the words *don't overdo it* ringing in his ears. He had been overdoing it, but at least he'd managed to stick, more or less, to the diet recommended by his doctor. There'd been a period of a week or so when he'd calorie-counted everything he'd eaten using his little guide and religiously written down details of each meal in his notebook. He'd become something of an expert on the subject and had to take care to avoid boring the pants off people with his new obsession.

Today, he felt, was a minor rule-breaking day and the small slice of chocolate cake disappeared slowly, teaspoonful by teaspoonful. He was pleased that the studio had turned out to be real and that he wouldn't now need to go searching for a love nest. He hadn't really expected Mrs W to show but, just as he was savouring the final mouthful of cake, she appeared on foot. At that moment his phone rang. It was Antoine wanting an update. Vos still hadn't got round to telling him about Poortmans' death or about T.I. and the network of companies they controlled and knew he couldn't delay it any longer. It took a while and he kept watch on the door to the studio across the street the whole time. Antoine said he was impressed with the progress made and yet again didn't seem to mind about the delay in information reaching him.

Vos paid up, crossed the street and pushed open the studio door. There were sounds of movement upstairs and he called out her name. Mrs Waarschoot made her way slowly down an open-tread timber staircase carrying two large ring-binders. She didn't seem particularly surprised that he'd found her base.

"I see you're back in action. I'll put the kettle on," she said, disappearing into a tiny kitchen area at the rear of the building and emerging minutes later with a cafetiere, cups and saucers on a tray. As there was no space available on the display table, Vos moved some of the photo albums to one side. "So how did you find my studio?" she asked.

He explained briefly, but was then in two minds whether to tell her directly about her husband's suspicions. However, the longer things went unsaid, the longer they'd fester.

"I was instructed to find your love nest." A wry smile crept over her face. "I suppose this place could be used for such a purpose but somehow I doubt it. What do you say?" She pushed the cafetiere plunger down, rather more forcefully than was required.

"That's typical of him. Not that I need to answer your question, but there's nothing going on here – or anywhere else. Sometimes I think it would be nice if there was. He might have picked up through the grapevine that an old friend contacted me recently. Hadn't heard from him for twenty years. But that's all he was and still is – a friend. We used to work together." Vos had no reason to think she was making this up. She seemed exasperated more than anything else. He couldn't see the marriage lasting much longer though.

He was caught in two minds again – whether to ask his next question or not. Their conversations so far had been pleasant and he didn't want to risk spoiling this. Still, needs must.

The realisation had come to him when he'd been taking his pills that morning. The second pill had literally been on the tip of his tongue, awaiting the water, when he'd suddenly remembered about RW Legal – Mr Waarschoot's firm – remembered where he'd seen reference to the name before. It was in Poortmans' report, the one he'd found in Vervloet's mailbox, *RWL?* pencilled in at the top of a couple of pages.

"You mentioned the other day that your husband works on large-scale property schemes. Well I have a new customer who's also in that field. He's involved with a company called Redline and I wondered whether they might be clients of your husband's firm." She hesitated before responding.

"I've certainly heard him mention the name, but whether they're clients or not, I wouldn't know. As I said to you before, he tells me very little about his affairs." He was relieved that she hadn't seemed to mind his question.

"OK, thanks. In that case, I might have a word with him."
They continued chatting for a while. He asked to see some of her
photographs and she showed him a series of pictures of the coast,
long sandy beaches. He was sure one of them was the beach near
De Haan where he'd found the body – the start of his involvement
in the people-smuggling case.

+ + +

The hoe made quick work of weeding between the rows. Ryck
knew he'd miss the garden, but with the demands of his course, he
wouldn't have a spare moment. And once the baby came, well…
He noticed his uncle's next-door neighbour keeping an eye on
him, under cover of pruning roses in her trim garden, secateurs
nimbly darting between thorns.

The Nissan pick-up which pulled up on the street was in
immaculate condition, in sharp contrast to Ryck's borrowed
Berlingo. The driver got out and walked over to the garden wall.

"Is Mr Vos in?"

"I'm Mr Vos. Can I help you?" Ryck, his foot up on the low
wall, was wary of the man. There was something else – a smell, an
aroma that he couldn't pin down.

"You're not the right age. I was told Mr Vos is an older man."
Leaning on his hoe, Ryck wondered again about the smell.

"Oh you must want my uncle. I'm afraid he's not in."

"Well I have some information for him about a case he's
working on. Could you ask him to give me a ring?" At first Ryck
had been just wary. Now he was wary but interested.

"You could tell me about it. I'm his assistant."

"I'd rather speak directly to him. Look, here's my number. Ask
him to call me."

Ryck took the piece of paper and watched the man get back
into his pick-up and drive off.

+ + +

"Hair very short, like an old crew cut, moustache neatly trimmed. I think he might be a drinker, eyes were red and you could see the blood vessels on his cheeks. But he had this odd smell. I couldn't quite place it. Something spicy I reckon."

As soon as he heard his nephew use the word spicy, Vos wondered how he could have forgotten such a distinctive detail about his attacker at Aalst station.

Vos rummaged in one of the kitchen cupboards, unscrewing the tops of spice jars, sniffing the contents and then replacing the tops – until he got to the cinnamon. After a quick sniff he held under Ryck's nose.

"That's it! That's the Spiceman!" Ryck said. "But who is he?"

"He's the man who attacked me."

"You're joking!" Ryck said. "What does he want? More aggression?"

Vos said he didn't think so, that he wouldn't have advertised himself in advance or given a phone number if that was the case. He tried the number, got through and arranged to see 'the Spiceman' later that evening. Ryck was all for staying on, in case the guest turned nasty. Vos reassured him that wouldn't be necessary, but he did ask his nephew for a favour. Once Ryck heard what was involved he agreed readily. It would be a bit like old times. After two bowls of his uncle's fish chowder, he departed in the Berlingo.

Just as he left, Edith arrived unannounced. Vos was worried. After all, the Spiceman had tailed her to Aalst and she'd witnessed his attack. How would she feel seeing him again?

"I'll be OK. In fact it'll give me a chance to ask him some questions. I agree with you that he'd hardly tell you in advance about coming here if he wanted to hit you again."

The Spiceman's timing was perfect – table cleared, washing up done, coffee in the pot. Vos filled three cups. Although he still

felt highly aggrieved about the assault, he didn't want this to get
in the way of finding out something new. He hoped he wouldn't
be provoked into losing his cool.

"My nephew tells me you have some information for me. I
presume it's about Charlie."

"I do have information about Charlie. But before we get to
that, I'm glad you're both here as I need to apologise, firstly to
you, young lady, for tailing you and secondly to you, Mr Vos, for
attacking you and stealing that key. I shouldn't have done what I
did. Let me explain what led up to it. I got to know Charlie not
long after you two split up," he said, looking at Edith. "That's why
I never came across you. Look – can we call him Rudy rather than
Charlie?"

Edith made it clear that they should use the name 'Charlie'.

"And while we're on the subject of names," Vos said, "how
about telling us yours?"

"It's Webers."

"And how did you find out my name and where I lived?"

"It wasn't difficult. Almost everyone leaves a trail these days.
Anyway, I liked Charlie. We did some stuff together. Do you
know about the Green Guards?" They both nodded. "We were
involved on the fringes for a while but then fell out with them.
Charlie started doing his own thing and when word got back to
the Guards they weren't happy. You'll know how short of money
he always was. In the end, it pissed him off so much he started to
look for work. When word got out that he'd started to freelance
for a land company, the Guards didn't like it – thought he'd sold
out."

"Charlie would never have done that." Edith's face reddened
as she spoke.

"Maybe he changed after you two split up. It's always hard
to know what anyone might do if pushed. Whatever, the Guards
wouldn't have taken kindly to someone they saw as a turncoat

and they'd have worried about being compromised by him – giving away trade secrets. After all he was involved with them for a short while."

Vos was all ears. This was the same kind of story both Poortmans and Antoine had been pushing. There might well be something in it. But he was worried about Edith's reaction. To hear someone else also claiming that Charlie had given up on his principles would be hard to take.

"What do you think happened to him in the end?" Vos asked.

"It took me a while to realise that Charlie wasn't around. He was often away for days or weeks at a time and I just assumed he'd gone off travelling. It was a real shock when I read about the body being found and saw the e-fit. I recognised him even though it wasn't one of their best. At first I assumed it must have been natural causes – there was nothing in the media suggesting otherwise. But then I started to wonder. I'd heard threats against him. Some of the Guards are real purists. Maybe somebody meant to teach him a lesson and it got out of hand. I didn't want to involve the police – don't trust them – so I decided to do some investigating myself to find out what he was up to over his final few weeks. You wouldn't have been aware, Edith, but that's when I came across you. I realised you were doing the same kind of thing. However I made the mistake of thinking you'd turned against your former boyfriend – because of the nature of the breakup, which an acquaintance of Charlie's told me about. So I jumped to the conclusion that you'd be trying to find evidence to expose him. Having tracked you down, I started following you and that took me to Aalst and the rest – well you already know about that."

"So why not just talk to us? Why attack us? Why assume we were on opposite sides?" Edith was having difficulty in controlling her temper.

"I know that now, but at the time, I got carried away. Charlie told me about this stash of documents he had about fracking, nuclear and chemical waste, some of them confidential. Said they were in a left luggage locker somewhere, didn't want them in his apartment. But I couldn't get him to tell me where. After his disappearance I got worried these papers might get into the wrong hands. I thought you two were the wrong hands. Couldn't believe my luck when I saw you both, with that key, at Aalst station, and I'm afraid I lost it. Turned out to be a false trail anyway. There was nothing of any interest in that damned locker."

Vos chuckled to himself. Far from being a consolation prize, Charlie's cryptic to-do list had perhaps been the real deal. But he was suspicious of this new, *oh so reasonable* version of the man who had nearly knocked him senseless.

"Have you been able to find out anything specific about whether the Guards had it in for Charlie?" Vos asked.

"Not so far. What about you two?"

Vos had expected this kind of question. Apart from claiming to be a friend of Charlie's, he couldn't work out where this man stood or who he might work for. But he could recognise a fishing expedition when he saw one.

"Nothing that's taken us any further forward." Vos was wary of revealing to Webers how much they knew.

"What do you know about the death of a man called Vervloet?" Edith asked, out of the blue. Webers seemed to be caught off guard by the question and it took him a moment to compose himself.

"Is that the man who was killed in a hit and run?" Edith nodded. "Well, only what I've seen in the media. What's that got to do with Charlie?" Vos tried but failed to send out a signal to Edith to keep her thoughts to herself.

"I'm convinced there's a link between his death and Charlie's. What do you say to that?"

When Webers said he'd not considered that possibility, Edith cut across his response.

"I've got a feeling you're not being straight with us. Surely after what you did, following me, assaulting Mr Vos, you need to build up some trust with us. It would help if you could open up and give us something we don't already have."

Vos realised his earlier caution had been unnecessary. She had the bit between her teeth. He watched Webers as he considered his response.

"It's a fair point you make. Unfortunately I don't know anything more about this man Vervloet. But with Charlie – it's different. I think I might get somewhere if I carry on nosing around the Guards and if I do pick up anything, you'll be the first to know. That's a promise. Maybe you could do the same for me."

When he signaled his agreement to this, Vos ignored the look of concern on Edith's face.

As soon as Webers left the house, Vos made a brief call. Edith was at him as soon as he'd finished.

"We're not really going to give that man anything, are we? I wouldn't trust him for a second."

Vos explained that he was interested in using Webers, not trusting him.

"OK I can go with that," Edith replied. "But, before I forget, I need to tell you about a man called Maes. I'd have mentioned him sooner, but with you being under Katerine's watchful eye, well I've held some things back."

Vos listened carefully to her story.

+ + +

The only other time he'd tailed a vehicle, he'd been on Daems' big BMW bike. He wished he still had the powerful machine, such a shame that he'd had no choice but to hand it back.

Still the Berlingo was inconspicuous and Webers wasn't flooring it. From the route he was taking, Ryck guessed they'd end up in Brussels. There were a few tricky moments when he was in danger of losing his man, but luck seemed to be on his side. The half hour spent waiting in the car park of a bar was frustrating but it was a relief that it hadn't been a lot longer. When Webers finally pulled up on the driveway of a detached house, Ryck reassessed the man – must have some money. He phoned his uncle to give him news of a successful mission.

Maes

I can't work it out. My suspension's been lifted and I'm back at work as if nothing's happened. I never did get that holiday!

From now on I'm going to play everything with a straight bat, as the English say.

When Mertens briefed me for this job in the Sambre valley he was in a better mood. The change in him surprised me. He told me Vervloet had been working in the area arranging for test drilling to be carried out. The reason given was that it was for a national geological survey. Apparently the owner wasn't bothered what it was for as he was being well paid for allowing access. In fact we arranged to test for shale gas and the results were very positive. Fracking's still banned in Belgium but the Company reckons that – as a result of some very persuasive lobbying – the position will change. My job now is to buy up the land on the quiet.

So I don't breathe a word about test drilling or fracking potential. He's been told I represent a company that wants to buy his land for 'horsiculture'. There's a lot of it about these days.

Over a beer we talk about valuations. There's been some work done already on this and it turns out we're in the same ballpark. He's more than OK with the cash bonus I offer on top – no questions asked. But there's something bothering him. We have another beer before he takes me across his field to a small river, shows me a ditch and tells me that's where the body was found by a local drunk. At first I don't have a clue what he's on about. Gradually it dawns on me. He's talking about the man known as Charlie. This is spooky – right here. Then he really stuns me by telling me that Charlie was doing the same kind of work as me, buying land from a local farmer. He won't tell me how he knows this.

It brings up all my previous doubts, just when I'd more or less buried them and it's all so confusing! From what I've heard, the guy was an out and out environmentalist. How could he have been doing the same as me and who was he doing it for?

And, much more worryingly, why did he end up dead?

Nineteen

Edith lay awake in her bed in the spare room at Harry Vos' place. She missed her work at the theatre. Acting got her out of herself, gave her the chance to forget about Charlie, the difficulty of finding another man since they'd split up and her chronic lack of money. 'Resting' was a pain and there was still no word about the next production. The repair work at the café was taking longer than expected so no work was available there either. Being financially dependent on her grandma was awful but, for the time being, she didn't have much choice about it.

The repeated claims about Charlie really upset her and she still refused to take them on board, despite the evidence pointing in that direction. Selling out to the opposition would have been totally alien to the Charlie she'd known.

At breakfast, she was pleased to see a sparkle back in Vos' eyes. He told her he'd just spoken to Bernard Antoine, but unfortunately, there was nothing new at the Charleroi end, where the security high alert was continuing. She wanted to know about the diagram in the notebook that was lying open on the kitchen table.

"Ah!" he said. "I'm glad you asked me that. At the top we've got Terra Incognita, the 'unknown land' that Kim's been investigating. We need to be careful about exposing anything directly to do with them. We'd risk upsetting some very powerful interests. Below T.I. there's the network of companies that Poortmans told you

179

and Katerine about. This stretches across a number of countries and seems to be involved in anything and everything to do with land. This tier includes Redline, known as the Company by insiders, which has Dutch origins and is registered in Aruba and GreenEarth which is registered in Luxembourg. Remember, they owned the site near Mol, the one referred to in Poortmans' report as having dodgy geological conditions. More coffee?" Vos refilled their cups. "Below this, there's a third tier, specialist service providers such as X-Tract who do geological surveys, and RW Legal, who I've only just found out about. I need to get more detail about their role."

Moving the milk jug and the sugar bowl to one side to create a bit more space, he pointed to the names written down on the next page of the notebook.

"We've got Vervloet who worked for the Company and he's dead. Charlie – more than one source claimed that he may have done some work for the Company – and he's also dead. Poortmans had been investigating the Company and he's dead."

"You need to add Maes' name to that list," Edith said. "He works for the Company and, so far, he's still alive." Vos wrote down the name. "What we don't know is how Webers fits into all this. Who's he working for?"

"Well at least we know his name and, thanks to Ryck, we know where he lives," Vos said.

"You know, his place is not so far from mine. No wonder he found it easy to follow me around. Did you get any feedback from your cousin after they circulated Webers' photo?" Vos told her it had drawn a blank. "Well, we need to find out more about him somehow. And how about seeing what else we can find out from Maes? Will you be OK to do that? I don't think he'd be too happy to speak to me again."

Vos agreed he'd talk to Maes. But before that, there was somebody else he wanted to visit.

+ + +

The care home wasn't the best. Staff were continually rushed, meals often lukewarm and cleaning poorly done. Despite a long working life, most of it spent down the mines, Demotte couldn't afford anything better. He hated the place and dreamed of escape. But there was nowhere he could escape to. He'd had to give up his rented bungalow, his savings had dwindled and his son had told him that living with him wouldn't be possible. All he had left were his fading memories, a few pieces of furniture that he'd been allowed to take into the home and a couple of old friends who dropped in to see him now and then.

He had what his doctor called a long term condition, one with a fancy name. All he knew was that breathing had got more and more difficult. And his increasingly unreliable memory didn't help matters. And following a recent fall, he'd been confined to a wheelchair which he hoped would only be temporary. Even with a support cushion it was still very uncomfortable. The only escape from the damn contraption was at bedtime.

Today was a little different from his usual Monday. Someone was coming to talk to him about the war. As soon as his visitor arrived Demotte knew that he'd seen him somewhere before. His guest sat on the only chair in the room, wooden and stiff-backed and handed over a bag of fruit, which was a nice gesture. But Demotte had recently gone off fruit completely. Something he didn't understand had happened to his tastebuds.

The gift of a small bottle of whiskey was much more to his liking and he propelled his chair slowly over the carpet to the chest, opened the top drawer and added the bottle to his collection of spirits. He usually managed to hide one somewhere within easy reach of his bed.

The visitor asked about the wheelchair and Demotte explained about his fall. Just as they were about to start their discussion, a care worker popped his head round the door to tell Demotte that the therapies woman had arrived in the lounge. He liked this woman. She always smelt wonderful. But he had a guest.

His deafness was getting worse and he'd missed what his visitor had said by way of introduction. Where had he seen him before? It was beginning to bug him. The man started to read from a sheet of paper, about 1944, Demotte's least favourite year.

"*Snow's been bad today. Looks like it'll get worse. We're nearly out of firewood. Those fucking snipers mean it'll be almost impossible to get any more. Seems comical now, thinking things would be better here. De Vries was the only one who knew the score and he's no longer with us. None of them trust me. Back there they'd got used to me. Of course I couldn't relax for a minute, but I knew the drill inside out. Sometimes had to do things which were wrong, but I didn't have any choice and, as I kept telling myself, it was all for the greater good. And from time to time I was able to get out a warning.*"

Demotte was amazed. These were his own words – words he'd written in that notebook all those years ago. But what was going on? The man wasn't reading from the notebook.

He tried to keep up with what his visitor was saying. It was a question about which unit he'd been in. He had to think hard. He'd never had this problem before. He'd always known, even if he'd never talked about the detail.

Suddenly it came to him. He'd seen this man when they'd both been at the hospital, recently, very recently and they'd talked about the war then as well. But how had he got hold of the words from the notebook and how had he managed to break the code?

Demotte recalled speaking to his son about the notebook. That was right – he'd asked him to find it. But his son had told him that he'd been unable to locate it. That's what he'd said anyway. There'd been something else as well, on the edge of his memory, but he was sure that if he really concentrated, he could bring it to mind. The man was still talking.

"…Vos, Harry Vos. I've come to apologise to you, Mr Demotte. You see it was me who found your notebook. Your son hired me to find it. You'll have the original now, but I have to confess, I made a photocopy of it. I shouldn't have done that without asking your permission. A friend of mine decoded it and that's how I'm able to read it out to you. But it's got me concerned, the things you were involved in back then. I felt I had to come and talk to you about it. That's why I'm here."

Demotte couldn't keep up. Why hadn't his son given him the notebook and who exactly was this man Vos? Some kind of investigator? He was worried.

"I've spoken to an uncle of mine," Vos said. "He's a bit of an expert on all this and was in the Ardennes at the same time as you. He told me that when he read your notebook, there were things that didn't quite add up. You might say it's none of our business, but with some of the action you were involved in, well it rang alarm bells. We didn't feel we could just ignore it."

Demotte was angry. Other people were always quick to judge and they didn't know the half of what had gone on then. It came to him suddenly, the realisation that the 'something else' he'd been trying to recall was his gun. How could he have forgotten about it and where was it now? He hated the thing, didn't know why he'd held onto it for all those years. Perhaps Vos had found it along with the notebook. He should tell this busybody all about what he'd done all those years ago. If he set the record straight, he'd feel better about it and he could put the man in his place.

Just as he tried to collect his thoughts, another care worker popped her head around the door and told him that his son had just arrived.

Twenty

It was another day of sunshine and bright blue skies. Katerine's crawl was impressive. Vos watched her as she swam length after length in the university's outdoor pool. His own swimming was limited to the occasional frolic in the sea. Pools were not his thing.

At first he'd thought that Demotte junior had been going to hit him when he'd arrived in his father's room, red-faced, puffed out cheeks, breathing heavily. Maybe that had been his intention, but one word from the father had brought him to a sudden, sullen standstill.

There'd been an awkward conversation with the son accusing Vos of exploiting his father, taking advantage of his vulnerability and copying his notebook without permission. Vos had been about to hold his hands up to all this when he was surprised by the old man coming to his defence. The old man had told his son to pipe down and to make sure he brought the original notebook with him on his next visit. A truce of sorts emerged. Ignoring his son's objections, Demotte senior had told Vos he'd like them to meet again. Nobody had mentioned the gun.

He finished the last of his coffee and watched Katerine towelling herself dry. He still couldn't believe his good fortune. She sat beside him and sipped her fruit juice, pulling a face because the drink had turned warm in the sun.

He'd had another pleasant conversation with his daughter – pleasant insofar as they'd stayed civil the whole time. The content of their discussion had been more difficult. She'd left her job 'by mutual agreement' as she put it. She hadn't gone into detail, but had been very pleased at the way her threat of legal action had turned the prospect of the sack into an enforced departure with a financial package. In the past this would have been the trigger for – well he didn't like to imagine how she'd have reacted. Now she talked of a sabbatical and maybe some consultancy work, before getting ready for the baby. Anders was fine with it all and they'd worked out that they'd be able to live off his income, at least for a year or so.

Once dried and dressed, Katerine took him to a new pop-up venue, part restaurant, part gallery, part off-the-wall nightclub, in Antwerp Zuid, housed in a disused apartment block, which was due for renovation. The beef-in-beer stew was cheap and very filling. Plastic tables and chairs were squeezed close together, the walls displayed the original 1970's wallpaper and rush matting covered the floor. Vos told her how pleasant it felt being out together and how he was looking forward to his first stay in her apartment since his illness.

She dropped him off there, before driving off to the university. The pile of mail behind the front door reminded him that Katerine had been away from the apartment for a while, keeping a beady eye on him. After a mid-afternoon nap he made his way to the local café where he found he had to explain his recent absence. He'd been missed as a new regular. When they heard about his illness they were very solicitous. It turned into a very pleasant afternoon.

Katerine arrived home earlier than expected to an empty house, poured herself a glass of wine and went through her mail. The glass slipped from her hand when she discovered the letter from Poortmans.

+ + +

"A lull in the firing, it's my turn to lug the latrine bucket uphill to the dung heap, a filthy job. Dysentery's spreading. Back in the cellar, no fuel left for the storm lanterns. Just dim candle light. Someone managed to cook spuds in the fire before we were told to put it out. We eat them cold and finish the last of the milk from this morning. The snow in the pails is melting slowly. There's no other source of water. We struggle to keep warm."

Vos' voice was slow and clear. Demotte had asked him to read some more extracts from the notebook.

"Three of us are sent out through the drifts, hard work, the sweat's soon dripping down inside our shirts, our hands still frozen inside thin gloves. We know there are mines and booby traps all over the place but we just have to trust to luck. In the torchlight we inspect the line, work out the best place for the explosives. Only a month ago I was doing this kind of job fifty kilometres away. I hope to fuck that there's none of them around here now. Maybe they're all dead. The line goes to Roche."

It wasn't the first time Vos had read a reference to Roche. But this time, it triggered a dreadful memory, a vision of a country road, he and his father driving towards Roche for a walking holiday, a vehicle coming straight at them, that awful descent through the trees, his father's lifeless body.

Unable to continue reading, Vos slumped in his seat and tried to hold back the tears. Demotte looked worried but didn't move.

Vos had very rarely spoken about the accident, the vehicle that hadn't stopped, his utter despair, and it was all he could do to hold himself together in the cramped room. After saying a few brief words about his dreadful memories of that day, he picked up the notebook and continued reading, keen to distract himself.

"On our way back we find a dead calf by a shell hole. Ronny is all for dragging it back to the cellar but I tell him it'll likely be poisoned – white phosphorous. We leave it there. I think about

*nothing but food as we stumble through the snow, up to our thighs
in places."*

Demotte signalled for Vos to stop reading. The words were
getting to him and he needed a break. They both needed a break.
The wheelchair made slow progress across the carpet to his spirit
store in the chest of drawers. His hands were insufficient on their
own to propel the chair forwards and he used his feet to gain a bit
more momentum. Vos thought perhaps he should help the man,
but remained seated. A shaft of sunlight kept catching his eye and
he asked if it was OK if he partly drew the curtains.

"Tell me, what really happened back then?" Vos said, keen to
move things along. "As I said before, my uncle couldn't work it
out. If I'm honest he said the part about you being in the resistance
didn't ring true. He had you down as maybe on the other side."

Vos knew he was taking a risk coming out with this. Albert
had been all for denouncing Demotte and starting the ball rolling
to get him investigated for war crimes. Vos had held his uncle
back, told him to wait until there'd been chance to talk directly
with the man. After all, the notebook was far from clear. There
were things described which crossed red lines, but until he knew
more about the 'why', Vos was reluctant to make a judgement.
And he felt guilty because he'd had no right to read the notebook
in the first place.

The old man didn't respond, but held out the whiskey bottle.
Vos reluctantly accepted the offer. With some food inside him it
would have been fine, but he'd had nothing to eat since breakfast.
He took a sip, placed the glass on a small table beside his chair
and waited for Demotte to answer his question.

"Young people like you don't have any idea about what went
on then. These days there's all the talk of the Geneva Convention
and war crimes as if there were clear boundaries. When it's kill
or be killed you don't see those limits in the same way. It's clear
to me that you and your uncle aren't going to let this drop so

I'm going to tell you some things I've never told anyone. I was a typical lad, liked to get pissed in the evening, when I had the money for it, and find a woman. It was bloody awful working in the mine and accidents were frequent. Back then I'd no political views, thought it was all nonsense. Some of my workmates were different – union this and union that. I didn't agree with them at all, but they were good friends. When they told me they were off to join the resistance early in '44, I thought they were mad. But I missed them and after a while I joined up as well. Once it got known that my French was as good as my Flemish, the high-ups asked me to go undercover and infiltrate one of the Walloon collaborator splinter groups, find out what they were up to and report back in whatever way was possible. I still don't know why I agreed. It was more or less a death sentence but as you can see I'm still here." Vos noticed a slight smile on the old man's face. He took another sip from his glass and asked his host to continue.

"Turned out I was good at it – the undercover bit I mean, a natural actor, not easily thrown, usually ready with a suitable answer to an unsuitable question. But I had to prove myself, so, yes, I did things which I'm not proud of so I could get right in there amongst them and find out what I needed to find out. There were things I wouldn't do, where I had to draw a line, which led to some real confrontations but I did enough to keep them happy. In the notebook I was careful what I wrote – that's what will have confused your uncle. I wanted to write down enough to remind me what had happened but not so much that I'd be shot if it was discovered. By late '44 it was getting impossible to keep going and one day I just went AWOL from the unit. A week later I was back with my old resistance squad. But I felt like an outcast. Nobody trusted me, not even the bastards who'd got the benefit of all the operational detail I'd managed to send them, risking my life in the process, I might add. They said they thought I'd gone too far, but it had never been their necks on the line. There wasn't much paperwork about what I'd been doing. What there was, they destroyed. They didn't want to be implicated. But at least they didn't cut my throat. There you are. That's my story. You can tell that interfering uncle of yours all about it and then ask him what he'd have done in the same circumstances."

The old man drained his glass, poured another and waved the bottle in front of Vos who shook his head. His drink was still almost untouched.

This wasn't what Vos had expected. Demotte was right. He really had no idea. He'd have to phone Albert and put him in the picture.

Twenty One

Katerine had explained to Vos about Poortmans' letter from beyond the grave. Forwarded by a colleague, it had sat in her mailbox for days.

The report was a gem. Poortmans might have been a complete maverick but he was a meticulous researcher and must have spent an age painstakingly trawling through records to unearth Redline's activities, most of them unethical and some of them illegal.

Vos couldn't work out why the man had taken such risks. From what Katerine had told him, Poortmans hadn't bothered with even the most elementary security precautions. Sending such documents through the post was a big risk in itself and he'd been so open about his activity. They now had to consider how best to use the information.

Vos found it strange to be back in the Sambre valley, back at the site where Charlie's body had been found. A return trip was an idea he'd had for a while, clutching at straws in all likelihood, but he hoped there might be a chance of coming across something that could have been missed in all the previous searches, including his own. He poked about in the undergrowth, walked backwards and forwards along the riverbank and examined the ditch in the hope of discovering some small elusive item. But there was nothing.

Antoine had given him the name and address of the local farmer, the one who Yannick the drunk had stumbled across in his confused state, just after finding Charlie's body. The police had interviewed the farmer, but he hadn't been able to tell them much. His farm was on the other side of the river. Vos walked over the fields back to his car, checked his map to locate the nearest bridge and drove slowly down a narrow lane, before crossing the river and turning onto an identical-looking lane on the other bank.

The land looked in poor condition and the farm buildings were crumbling. Vos could see a rusting Panhard, raised on bricks, in a tumbledown shed and an old Fiat Punto parked on rough ground close to the front door. There was no response to his repeated knocking and he was about to turn away and walk back to his car when he was startled by a voice shouting out. Glancing up, he saw it was coming from an upstairs window, the caller a man in his fifties with a long straggly beard.

"What do you want?" The voice was neither hostile nor friendly.

"I've come to talk about Charlie. You were there when his body was found, weren't you?" The man disappeared. Vos was unsure whether that was it, or whether he might reappear. Eventually the front door opened and the man emerged wearing a pair of long johns, wellington boots and a flat cap. "Have you got five minutes?" Vos asked him.

"Well I'm here, aren't I? Who are you?"

Vos introduced himself as the father of Charlie's girlfriend.

"She was really cut up about his death. The police don't seem to have got anywhere finding out how he died, so I'm doing a bit of digging around myself."

"In that case, what do you want to know?" Vos thought the farmer had turned the frost down a degree or two.

"I've been working on this for a while now and have a feeling that Charlie's death was tied up somehow with environmental issues. He had this concern, you know, about how land was being misused for things like nuclear waste storage sites and fracking."

Vos noticed how he'd suddenly got the man's full attention. "Does that ring a bell with you?"

The farmer beckoned to Vos to follow him, not into the house, but to an adjacent barn where two camping chairs and a small table were set up next to a stack of hay bales.

"Sit yourself down, Mr Vos. I often spend time out here – prefer it to the house really, fewer ghosts. Now, you look like a man I can trust. I've never told anyone about this and I'll deny it if you breathe a word. That day, when the drunkard found the body, was very strange. He turned up here, badgering me to get the police out. In the end it was his face that convinced me – he looked terrified! I'll never forget it. But I want to tell you about something that happened a few months before that. I had a visit from someone wanting to buy my land – this place, can you believe it? It's hard making a living round here. He offered me cash, a lot of cash, said it was a deposit. But I had to promise to say nothing to anyone about the deal. Of course I bit his hand off and pocketed the money. Then I heard nothing more. No paperwork, nothing about completing the sale. When the body was discovered I read all the stuff in the papers. I couldn't be certain, but I reckoned he was more than likely the man I'd done the deal with. Well that left me with a dilemma! Should I let the police know about my suspicions or keep quiet? I didn't want to have to pay back the deposit money. In fact I'd already spent it – bank chasing me about the bloody overdraft. So I kept quiet. From the timings I read about, I reckon he must have died just after he saw me. I have to say, I think he was a newcomer to the game, offered me far too much but I wasn't going to tell him that. Don't forget now, I don't want you saying a word about this to anyone else."

Vos tried not to let it show how important this information was to him – yet another piece of evidence showing that, for whatever reason, Charlie had switched sides. As he watched the farmer walk back towards the rundown farmhouse he had a thought.

"Just a minute," Vos called out. The man turned. "Before I called here I was down by the river on the other bank. To tell you the truth, I was looking for something – Charlie's phone. Didn't find it. Seems odd it's never turned up. My daughter told me he never went anywhere without it. I don't suppose you can remember if he had it with him that day?"

"He did. Made a call in fact but I couldn't hear who he was talking to." The farmer hesitated. "Look, it's been bugging me ever since they found him. I've got it – his phone, I mean." Vos was astounded. "He must have dropped it without realising. By the time I came across it, I had no way of contacting him and didn't want to tell the police. I was worried that everything would come out and I'd have to pay the money back. So I held on to it. I'll get it for you. It'll be a weight off my mind.

Maes

The last few days have been quiet, which is a real relief. I'm just getting on with the job and hoping there'll be no more nasty surprises. I asked Mertens if there was any chance of another trip to England and he said he'd think about it, which was encouraging. But there's something odd about the way he's been treating me recently, like I'm on some sort of probation.

I'm sitting in my comfy leather armchair, feet up on the stool, halfway through a DVD from a Scandi-noir box set, defences down. The doorbell rings and I'm on edge straight away. Unexpected visitors here are rare.

Through the peephole I can see it's one half of the odd couple, not the girl this time, but Vos, the old man. She must have given him my address.

Shit! With mikes and cameras in here, I don't want him coming in. But I do want to talk to him. Once outside, I put my finger to my lips and beckon to him to follow me, leading the way to the Oude Zwaan. Only when we are seated at the very back of the bar do I let him start speaking.

He tells me he wants my help. I know I should get up and leave straight away. But deep down I know it's too late for me to continue playing the loyal operative. My boats are already burned. For some reason Mertens is still hanging on to me, but that reason will have nothing to do with my interests and everything to do with his. So I remain sitting where I am and listen to Vos.

He's been doing his homework. There's a list of organisations in his notebook, one of which is Redline and a diagram he's drawn which shows how these link together. It looks surprisingly accurate – not that I know all the detail. When the waiter arrives at our table we order two glasses of Troubadour.

The diagram is just the starter. The main course is the phone he pulls out of his jacket pocket. After a few moments fiddling with it he passes it over, telling me it's a text from Vervloet. This is fucking weird! But who's the recipient. Whose phone is this and how come Vos has got hold of it?

It's about a site in the Sambre valley, very close to where I've just been. I'm already completely thrown and then Vos tells me that it's Charlie's phone. All the questions rush in to my head at once, jostling to be first in the queue.

Vos asks me what I make of the text. The problem is it's short and cryptic and could be read in more than one way. What's clear is that for some reason Charlie was involved in buying land down there. He was getting information from Vervloet, under the radar presumably, otherwise, surely, he would have disappeared at the same time as Charlie. Or maybe other people knew about it, but didn't let on.

I've got a very bad feeling about this. If Charlie was working for us, then who would have wanted to shut him up? Whoever it was, did the same person make sure that Vervloet was also silenced, once they were aware of his complicity? Could a group like the Green Guards be behind what happened to the pair of them? They'd have seen Charlie as a traitor and, from what I've heard, some of them are mad enough to do something extreme.

Vos talks in a quiet, methodical way, dropping his voice when he refers to anything particularly sensitive. He seems genuine enough but is he really doing all this just out of curiosity?

As I'm thinking this, Vos pulls a photo from his inside jacket pocket and asks me if I recognise the man. I'm too slow in disguising my reaction and before I know it I'm admitting that I've seen the guy with my boss. I regret it as soon as it's out of my mouth.

He asks me about the boss – what he's called and where he's based – but I clam up. I've already told him too much.

Twenty Two

When Vos had shown Edith the texts on Charlie's phone, she'd admitted that they'd blown a large hole in her carefully constructed view of her former boyfriend. Perhaps she'd been kidding herself for too long about what he was really like.

Unfortunately there was very little other history on the phone. Perhaps Charlie had deleted messages as he went along, or maybe he'd only had it a short while. Vos knew the phone should really already have been in police hands. It was a vital piece of evidence and one of their techies would be able to check whether there were other messages that could be retrieved. But he'd been reluctant to give the phone up and held onto it as if it were a talisman.

He'd wanted to push further about Webers, but knew Maes was in a difficult position, cautious, conflicted in his stance, giving away some pieces of information and guarding others. This was no surprise. He had a lot to lose.

So he and Edith decided to see what more they could find out from the man himself. Just in case his aggression might surface again, they arranged to meet him in a public place.

+ + +

The evening sun flickered through the trees as they drove south to Brussels. Vos cursed because his sunglasses were sitting where he'd left them on the kitchen table and adjusted the sun visor to give his eyes some protection.

The park was full of parents watching their shrieking offspring at play and teenagers kicking footballs around. Webers was already there, seated on a large ornamental bench, in a quieter area. Vos and Edith sat down on a low brick wall facing the bench.

"There've been some developments since we last met, which have changed our view." Vos paused to sip from a bottle of water. "For reasons we don't yet understand, it looks like Charlie started doing some work for a company called Redline. You know of them?" Webers said he did. "Vervloet sent him details of a site and the odd thing about it is that it's right next to where his body was found." Vos paused to give time for this information to sink in. "We think somebody in the Guards found out about this, saw it as a betrayal of the cause, a risk to the organisation and decided to take action."

"I think you may be right," Webers said. "Last time we met, I said I'd do some snooping around. There are a couple of Guards I've had my eye on. Nothing definite yet, but I reckon they might have decided to silence Charlie before things got really out of hand."

"So, who are these guys? Do you have enough to get the police involved?" Vos said in a low voice.

"Not yet but it shouldn't be long. Being only on the fringes of the organisation, I've got to be careful. If I move too quickly I'll lose all access – or something worse will happen to me."

"So how long is this going to take? Maybe we should be involved in this," Edith asked, suddenly animated.

"I can't say exactly yet but you need to leave it with me. I know my way around the Guards whereas you two would be starting from scratch. And it could be dangerous."

A football hit the bench and Vos rose to throw it back to a group of lads who were having a kick-about nearby. He knew

Webers was right. It wouldn't be sensible for him and Edith to go blundering around trying to get information out of the Guards.

"And you still think Vervloet's death was just a hit and run?" Vos asked.

"I haven't come across anything that leads me to think otherwise."

From the very limited information they'd got from Webers so far, Vos was convinced that he was just stringing them along. They'd need to try another approach.

< what have they worked out?
< fuck all
< did they buy your line about the Guards?
< hook, line and sinker

Twenty Three

It was time to hand over Charlie's phone to Antoine. He was impressed that Vos had managed to trace the phone and said he'd arrange for a local detective to come and pick it up. When Vos told him about the discussion with Webers and the Green Guards angle, his cousin said it wasn't his area of expertise, but he'd talk to a colleague who was more clued up on environmental stuff.

Antoine sounded less than pleased when Vos revealed that he'd been working with Edith. He tried to explain to his cousin about the promise he'd made to her not to reveal either her existence or Charlie's real identity. But he failed to make a convincing case.

"You should have told me Harry. Although our resources are stretched we might have been able to move things on more quickly. Still, we're not going to fall out over it."

Vos was relieved but totally unprepared for Antoine's next comment.

"With these recent developments, we're going to have to step up the official investigation and I'm afraid you'll be off the case. I know it's not what you want to hear, but there it is."

Perhaps he should have anticipated this response, but it didn't stop him feeling bitterly disappointed. He'd be out in the cold just at the point when he felt he could have made real progress.

Now the professionals would take over and claim all the credit.

+ + +

But this was not what happened.

The phone contained no other secrets. The police found out it had been purchased only shortly before Charlie's death. Vos had seen everything there was to see. And enquiries about possible Green Guard involvement in his death got nowhere.

Edith made a brief statement through a lawyer, but refused all interviews. The tabloids had a field day when his real name was revealed. They trumpeted their foresight in christening him Charlie and commented on how uncanny real life and death could be. One paper went so far as to claim there was something in the stars that had predetermined it all.

Vos submitted details to the police about Redline's activities, hoping this would lead to a full enquiry, but once the lawyers took hold of the process, accusations of illegal activity were kicked into the long grass. The Company issued a brief statement which confirmed that one of their freelancers had died in a hit and run accident. They'd expressed their condolences to his family and made a financial settlement. They had no knowledge of the man who'd been found dead in the Sambre valley and stated that he'd never been contracted by the company to carry out work for them.

With the lack of further progress on the case, media interest died down as quickly as it had been rekindled.

+ + +

Vos was fed up kicking his heels. At least the hiatus had meant he'd had time to get an agent sorted out for the sale of his mother's house. Interest in it had so far been limited. There'd been time to spend in the garden and he'd enjoyed a sociable night out with Zyg and his friends around selected bars in Antwerp. Katerine had taken him on a couple of trips to the coast. But his mind was always half on unfinished business.

He decided not to tell Antoine that he was putting himself back on the case.

The gaping hole in the investigation was that they still didn't know the cause of Charlie's death.

As his mother and Mr Wouters had gone away to Amsterdam, Barto was with him for the weekend. It was their second walk of the day, down Lostraat, past the football ground and left onto Tiendestraat. When he answered the call on his mobile he was surprised to hear that it was Kris, the tattooist in Mons.

Vos let the dog off the lead, watched him bound across the playing fields and listened as Kris told him about a conversation he'd just had, one about Charlie, albeit under his nickname Rudy. It turned out that he'd visited another tattooist, one in Brussels. Vos knew he had to follow it up and would start with a visit to the Mons parlour.

Walking back through the town, he wandered slowly through the flea market, Barto stopping at virtually every stall to sniff and explore. Most of the stallholders commented approvingly on the dog, asked his name and offered him a treat. One or two shooed him away, anxious to protect their merchandise.

Back at the house, Vos started his preparations for the evening meal, laid the table and, mindful of the need to try and control his alcohol intake, poured himself his sole glass of wine of the evening, a chilled sauvignon. His visit the previous day to see old Demotte had turned out much better than he'd expected. Barto had been popular with the residents and several had asked if he could come again.

When Vos made his confession about the gun, Demotte had surprised him. Far from being annoyed about the non-appearance of the firearm, Demotte had thanked him for getting rid of a problem. Despite some misgivings, he'd kept the gun all the years since the war. Then it had finally dawned on him that it was a just a reminder of part of his past he should forget about, so Vos had done him a favour.

Vos wished he really had handed the gun over during the firearms amnesty, instead of just pretending he had. Now he had no need to hold onto the gun as potential evidence, he'd have to find some other way of getting rid of it.

Katerine arrived in good spirits, fresh from a day out with her best friend.

"What did you two get up to then?" Vos asked her, as he poured her a glass of wine.

"This is going to surprise you. We played tennis! She brought along a spare racquet for me and we spent an hour on the public courts. It was wonderful but I'm very rusty and I'm going to pay for it tomorrow."

"I didn't know you could play tennis," Vos said. "You've never mentioned it before."

"Well, there are a few things I haven't told you. You'll find out over time, my dear."

The mackerel salad went down well. They ate sitting at a fold-up table on the patio, watching birds roosting in a nearby willow tree. When Vos told her about the call from the tattooist, she said she'd come with him on the trip to Mons. Edith wouldn't be making the journey as she'd finally been able to restart her job in the café.

Lying side by side in bed in the late evening, Katerine's head on his chest, Vos reflected on how fortunate he'd been to make that first phone call to her, the one that had started off the whole people-smuggling investigation. He'd just picked out her name and number from a university list and remembered thinking that there'd be little chance of her returning his call.

She kissed him on the ear and whispered something he didn't quite catch. Only when she repeated her question did it become clear.

"*Will you marry me, Mr Vos?*" He was completely lost for words. It wasn't that he'd never contemplated the idea, but he'd never dreamed that *she* might ask *him*. There was a sudden vision of him and his wife Margriet walking alongside a Venetian canal, a vaporetto creating waves as it sped by. It was the best holiday they'd ever had and neither of them had wanted it to end. What would she think? What would his mother say – and his children? He told himself to stop thinking this way. The woman he loved was waiting patiently, or so he hoped, for his reply. But he dithered, unable to decide whether ultimately it would be a good thing or a bad thing for their relationship.

"Would it be alright if I thought about it, love?" Even as he uttered the words he knew how they would come across. She told him that of course it would be OK, but he could tell that she was disappointed that he was unable to make a decision right away. Although neither of them moved, it felt to him as if his words had opened up a gulf between them.

+ + +

In the end he drove to Mons on his own. Katerine suddenly discovered she had an appointment at the university, one she couldn't miss. She was pleasant enough but rather distant.

He hadn't slept at all, tossing and turning most of the night. He needed someone to talk to, but didn't know who. Once he'd cleared Brussels he began to feel better and decided to try and put the big question to one side, at least until the return journey. There was no need to spoil the whole day going round and round in circles.

Parking close to the bell tower in Mons, he made his way through the narrow streets of the old town to the tattoo parlour. Kris was expecting him. Vos waited while he finished off a flowered pattern on a young woman's leg, puzzling yet again why anyone would want to undergo such torture.

A young man entered the shop and waited on the opposite side of the parlour, flicking through screens on his phone. Nobody said a word until Kris was finished and the woman had left.

"This is Lennert," Kris said. "He's my apprentice." Vos wondered if this was like an old apprenticeship, studying at night class, taking several years to complete and with a qualification waiting at the end of it all. Somehow he doubted it.

"Lennert. Tell Mr Vos what you told me." Kris was quite abrupt in his manner.

"OK, but first I don't want any of this getting back to Brouwers, the geezer who runs the parlour where I used to work in Brussels." Vos nodded his assent even though he had no intention of treating any information as confidential, if it turned out to be useful in pursuing the case. "Well, as I told Kris, I was supposed to be an apprentice in this parlour, but Brouwers never taught me anything. That's why I left." The young man stopped talking for a moment to blow his nose noisily into a tissue. "Anyway, this customer came in one day, with a mate in tow. He used the name Rudy with us but I'm certain now it was Charlie. It was a removal job, the last but one session. At first he said he didn't need an anaesthetic, he'd done all the other sessions without one. There's some customers like that, reckon they're macho. But his mate reminded him that he'd moaned like mad about the pain, after the previous session. So Rudy agreed he'd have the jab and filled in the form we used to give consent and record any allergies. He has the injection, the boss does the necessary for the removal and that's that." Vos wondered where this story was going and how much useful information he'd get in the end from the lad. Lennert continued.

"A couple of weeks later he's back, with his mate in tow again, for the final session. Only this time, it didn't go well at all. Not

long after he'd had the anaesthetic, he started reacting, flushed
up, sweating like a pig, eyes streaming, said he felt faint and sick.
What was strange was that he hadn't reacted like that the first
time. Made me think perhaps the boss hadn't used the same stuff
in the second jab. Still, whatever the reason for the reaction, the
thing is to get the customer to hospital pretty damn quick. The
boss told Rudy he'd call an ambulance. At this point Rudy's mate
jumps up and says – no point in phoning for an ambulance, might
have to wait for ages. He'd take him to the hospital straightaway in
his car. So that's what happened."

This was just the kind of information Vos had hoped for, but
suspected he'd never get. As Lennert talked, he scribbled down
notes in the file that was balanced on his knee.

"How come you didn't say anything about all this earlier?
It must have happened months ago." Vos tried not to sound
critical. After all, what the lad had just given him was a valuable
new lead.

"I thought you might ask me that. The thing is, I quit not long
afterwards, told the boss where he could stuff his job and went
off travelling, something I'd wanted to do for ages. So I missed
all the publicity about Charlie. It was only the other day I saw his
mugshot on TV and put two and two together."

"In some cases," Kris said, "an allergic reaction can be fatal if
not treated. If that's what happened to Charlie or Rudy, whatever
he's called, there are two things I don't understand – firstly why
he wasn't sorted out at the hospital and secondly why there's been
nothing in the media about an allergic reaction being the cause
of death."

Vos said he'd need to check what had happened at the hospital
and check again with the police about the detail in the autopsy
report, particularly anything to do with toxicological side of it.
As he jotted down some additional notes in his file, it fell off his
knee and the papers scattered across the parlour floor. Lennert

helped him to gather them up. He stopped suddenly when he came across a photo.

"That's him," he said.

"Who? Vos asked.

"The man who said he'd take Rudy to the hospital," Lennert said.

"Are you sure?" Vos asked, dumbfounded.

"Certain. I'm good on faces."

Vos stared at the photo of Webers. At last, something concrete linking him to Charlie. Maybe he was a step nearer to finding out how Charlie had died. Vos could hardly contain himself.

"I don't suppose you can remember when this happened – I mean the actual day. I'll need that if I'm to get anywhere at the hospital."

Lennert surprised him again. Sure he could remember. It had been his birthday.

+ + +

It was only a short drive to his uncle's house. Albert appeared to have aged even in the short time since they'd met up at Mr Wouters house. Some of his sprightliness had gone. It was still warm enough to sit in the garden where they drank some of Miriam's wonderful homemade lemonade from tall, elegant glasses. She herself was away visiting friends, which was a disappointment to Vos, as he really wanted to see her again and get to know her a little better.

Albert was clearly tired and Vos told him he'd be on his way. As he was leaving he mentioned Katerine's proposal. It just came out. He hadn't planned it. His uncle perked up immediately and said he very much liked the young lady and wouldn't have hesitated for a moment if he'd been in Vos' position.

As he drove back to Brussels, Vos wondered how he could possibly have been so stupid.

Maes

I have to make a decision – keep it all to myself and hope nobody finds out, or tell Mertens what Vos told me. In the end I realise I haven't much choice if I'm to have any chance of hanging on to my job.

So I dress it up and tell him that I contacted Vos to see what useful information I could get out of him. Mertens is incandescent when he hears that Vervloet must have somehow arranged for Charlie to carry out some work for the Company. So I was right. Vervloet must have kept it all completely under the radar.

The photo Vos gave me is burning a hole in my pocket. When I show it to Mertens, his mood worsens – if that's possible. I make the mistake of asking who the man is and what connection he has with us and I'm told to mind my own fucking business. Then I think he realises he's gone over the top.

It's harder to cope with what happens next though, as he starts to confide in me. It's never happened before and it's a strange feeling seeing another side to a man one you've never glimpsed before – a bit like the dark side of the moon.

It turns out the man in the photo is called Webers and has some connection with the Green Guards. I know how they operate, always trying to get dirt on us (though they don't know the half of it), always at the front of any demo, spouting off about damage to the environment and always more than ready to talk to the right kind of media. When the boss says he suspects the Guards were involved in Charlie's death it confirms my suspicions.

Mertens tells me he pays this guy Webers to get information about the opposition. Well it does make sense to know what they're up to.

I test out this new mood of his by asking him about Vervloet's death. At first he trots out the same old party line – hit and run – but then he adds that he wouldn't be surprised to find out the

Guards were behind that death as well. So I ask him straight up. Why doesn't the Company go to the police with whatever evidence it has? In response, he just shrugs, says nothing he has is conclusive.

As I'm leaving, he tells me to continue keeping tabs on Vos and his sidekick and report to him immediately anything new comes up.

I wonder about his real motivations. I'm already badly compromised and this could just make things worse. If I'm not careful I'll be stitched up. All Mertens' instructions are verbal. It would be his word against mine if it came to it and I know who'd win that particular battle.

Twenty Four

Lennert's revelations had left Vos buzzing. The RO was frustratingly busy and the traffic was no better once he turned off to head for the tattoo parlour. He was itching to get back to Katerine to give her the good news, but before he could do that, there was a tattooist to grill and a hospital visit to make. He left the N8 and hit a maze of side roads. It took him a while to find the right street.

This time he posed as Rudy's uncle. Brouwers, the tattooist, didn't want to talk and at first denied Rudy had ever been a customer. Vos lowered his voice and made it clear that either they had an immediate conversation or he'd be calling the police. The tattooist told his assistant to take over and ushered Vos into an office at the back of the parlour. In the cramped space, the two of them only inches apart, Vos felt vulnerable.

Getting straight to the point, he asked about the tattoo removal job carried out on his 'nephew'. Had there been a problem? The question was met with a blunt denial. Vos pressed on, told him he knew all about the adverse reaction to the anaesthetic. No further denial.

"Look I'm sorry about what happened to the lad, but I'm not a mind reader. I ask them to write down on the form about any allergies they've got and they don't. Then they get a reaction and I have to sort it out. I got him the ambulance and after that it was all down to the hospital."

"Except there was no ambulance, was there? This man took him in his car, didn't he?" Vos held up the photo of Webers.

"I don't know why you're coming out with such a pack of lies. I've never seen that man before."

"And did you even check to see if he got sorted out at the hospital? Of course you fucking didn't. Professional negligence I'd call it." Vos could smell the tattoist's breath. His bare arms were covered in elaborate multi-coloured designs. Momentarily distracted, Vos wondered whether it was possible to tattoo yourself. But, when his throat was grabbed, he realised he'd let his guard down and put himself in unnecessary danger.

"I did what I had to do. I've got nothing more to say. Stop hassling me and let me get on with my job."

As Brouwers shoved him out onto the street, Vos risked a final question.

"Which hospital would he have been taken to?"

"The nearest fucking one of course – St Theresa's."

+ + +

Having checked the location on his phone, he drove to the hospital and speculated on what the sequence of events might have been. Webers knew Charlie was having tattoo removal work done and went with him to the parlour. Did he persuade him to have an anaesthetic and if so, why? It all went OK on the first appointment. Did the tattooist use a different drug at the second session, one that Charlie was allergic to? Why would he have done that? And when Webers took Charlie off to hospital in his own car – what happened next?

The hospital car park was full. He hovered, waiting for a space to become free, his frustration mounting. It boiled over at reception when his request for information about Rudy was refused. The nurse stuck to her guns. He wasn't a police officer, couldn't prove he was a close relative and didn't even know the young man's surname. The matter was confidential. She wouldn't even confirm whether someone named Rudy had been admitted on the day in question.

Back in the car park, he phoned Antoine. His cousin gave him a mild reprimand for putting himself back on the case without informing him, but promised to find out whether Charlie had been admitted at St Theresa's or any other hospital.

Vos explained about Webers' involvement. Was there sufficient evidence to warrant some questioning by the police?

He was pleased when Antoine agreed to his proposal.

+ + +

Nearing home, the only place he could find flowers was at a garage. He knew this was supposed to be a no-no, but they didn't look too bad and at least there'd been some water in the bottom of the black plastic bucket. One final detour before returning home and a text to Katerine to say he was on his way. It was a while since he'd been to his wife's grave. Somebody had cleared away the old flowers, for which he was grateful. He arranged the replacements in the two vases which he filled from the cemetery tap. It wasn't his usual kind of discussion with Margriet, just a bit of communing and he felt the better for it.

Katerine was annoyed. Pans were slammed onto the stove and crockery clattered onto the table. When she served up, the food was dolloped onto his plate. They ate in silence until Vos pulled a small box from his pocket and gave it to her.

"I know we don't need to get engaged, but I thought you might appreciate this. It was my grandmother's." Katerine looked taken aback. The lid of the box was stiff and she took care opening it. Watching her face as she removed the ring, he knew he'd done the right thing.

Albert had insisted he take it and put it to good use.

+ + +

They had breakfast in bed. He'd prepared the meal dressed in pyjamas and dressing gown and had made two trips with a tray to convey all the goodies to the bedroom. It was mid-morning before they were up and dressed. When he told her he'd be going out, she fussed around him, anxious that he shouldn't overdo it. He stressed that this time it was only a trip to Lier and she gave him permission.

If he'd been honest with her, he'd have admitted that he was overdoing things and would have liked nothing better than to have stayed around the house and garden. But for the first time he felt he was making real progress and didn't want to risk losing momentum.

RW Legal's office was in an imposing early nineteenth century building in a leafy suburb of Lier. Roland Waarschoot didn't look at all pleased to see him.

"I don't deal with personal matters whilst I'm at work," he snapped. "And you don't even have an appointment. Still, now you're here you might as well update me. What have you found out?" The two men were still standing and Vos realised that he wasn't going to be offered a seat.

"I'm not actually here about your wife, although I can tell you that your fears of an affair are groundless. No – I'm here about another case of mine. It's a business matter and I thought *you* might be able to help *me*. I understand a company called Redline is a client of yours." To give him his due, he thought Waarschoot remained remarkably calm.

"I won't ask you how you came across that particular piece of information, but yes I do carry out some business for them. I can't imagine what interest you have in the company. Perhaps you could come to the point." Icily polite.

"That sounds like a good idea," Vos said. "I recently spoke to a man who is a Redline operative. I now need to speak to his boss, the man who instructs operatives locally. I couldn't persuade my contact to reveal either the name of his boss or where he's based. So I'm hoping you might be able to help me." Still calmness personified, Waarschoot told him that would be out of the question, a simple matter of a lawyer's commitment to client confidentiality.

"I understand your position which I think is admirable. However I think your loyalty may be misplaced. I've recently found out rather a lot about the less savoury aspects of Redline's activities. So far they've managed to avoid exposure but that's about to change. I don't know to what extent you're aware of what they get up to, but you may want to consider distancing yourself from them. All I ask in return for this valuable briefing is a name and a location. Do you think you could help me out?"

Vos paused. He could imagine Waarschoot making the assessment – loss of fees versus loss of reputation. Eventually he responded.

"The man you want is called Mertens and his office is in Antwerp. Here, copy this address down. I sincerely hope I'll never see you again, Mr Vos."

+ + +

He drove on to Antwerp, trying to forget his promise to Katerine that the day involved only a short trip to Lier. But with the chance to confront Mertens, he knew he couldn't stop.

Redline's office was located in one of the fine streets of the Het Zuid area, cheek by jowl with the fashion houses. The high price of property in the district was an indication of the profitability of the business. It took him an age to find somewhere to park and a further fifteen minutes to walk back to the office. There was no sign on the wall to indicate the name of the firm. The receptionist was decidedly frosty, but then Vos didn't look at all like a typical client. When she told him that no one by the name of Mertens worked in the building he interrupted her.

"Please just mention my name and tell him I'd like to talk about Mr Webers." One phone call later and he was escorted upstairs to an interview room. As the coffee pot was warm, he poured himself a cup and sat on an ornately carved chair at a highly polished table, leaning across to smell a large vase of roses.

Mertens was an imposing figure, tall, tanned and without a gram of spare flesh. He sat down opposite Vos and sipped cautiously from a glass containing a pink liquid.

"How can I help you?"

"I've come to talk about a man called Webers. You know him?" Mertens nodded. It was all going rather well, Vos thought. Mertens had agreed to see him, was polite and didn't deny he knew Webers. But he guessed Mertens was the kind of operator who'd have you in a trap whilst still smiling. Probably a good chess player, adept at thinking several moves ahead. "Well I'm not sure if you've heard, but he's been taken in for questioning by the police. I understand it's in connection with the circumstances surrounding the death of the man known as Charlie. You know who I mean. " Mertens nodded again, put down his glass and fiddled with the knot of his tie.

"Look Mr Vos. I know exactly why you're here. You have an idea – maybe it's more of an obsession – that my company is up to no good. You're going to tell me some unpleasant things about Mr Webers. Let me clarify the position for you and save us both wasting our time. Occasionally we pay him to provide us with information about the environmental opposition. All completely above board. What else he might get up to is none of our business. If he's been taken in for questioning by the police – well that's not a great surprise. His sort likes to live on the edge. Probably gets a thrill from it."

Vos wriggled in his seat which, despite appearances, was far from comfortable. When he reached to take another sip from his coffee cup he realised that it was empty and put it down hurriedly, feeling rather foolish. Mertens reached across the table, removed the cup and saucer, took clean replacements from a glazed wall unit, filled the cup and put the crockery back onto a coaster. All his movements were smooth and assured. Vos was about to respond but Mertens held up his hand.

"I haven't quite finished. I've no doubt that you want to ask me more about this Charlie character. This fanciful idea is floating about that he was working for us when he died. Nothing could be further from the truth. I'm sorry about his death but it has absolutely nothing to do with Redline. If you must continue your investigations than I suggest you look in the direction of the Green Guards for answers. Do I make myself clear?"

Vos was disarmed. Mertens had been ahead of him. He guessed he'd get no further, but felt he had to mention Vervloet. The smile on Mertens' face was one of condescension.

"As our press release said, Mr Vos, we were very sorry about Andries Vervloet's death, particularly as he was working for us when it occurred. Hit and run accidents are distressing because they can leave many questions unanswered. However that's what it was – an accident. The problem with well-meaning amateurs such as yourself, is that they get obsessed. They have neither the detachment nor the professional skills to make the right kind of assessments. It's far too easy for people in that frame of mind to jump to completely the wrong conclusions. My advice to you is to go home, enjoy your retirement and leave any further investigations to the proper authorities. After all you wouldn't want to be accused of harassment – would you?"

A uniformed security man entered the room at the exact moment Mertens finished talking and Vos wondered how such perfect synchronisation worked. He rose to his feet and went to shake his host's hand.

"You have a fine way with words. Regarding Webers though, I've got a feeling he plays a rather bigger role for Redline than the one you outlined. What's more, I think he had some involvement in Charlie's death, maybe not the one who pulled the trigger – or should I say stuck the needle in – but implicated nevertheless. I'll consider your advice about retirement, but it will need to be deferred at least until I've had chance to put together a few more pieces of the jigsaw. Once that's done I can present my report to Chief Inspector Bernard Antoine."

Twenty Five

The doctor had taken his blood pressure which was fine and a blood sample which would be sent for analysis. His weight was down, which was a pleasant surprise and he forced himself not to lie when asked about his weekly intake of alcohol. The doctor told him that there was scope for some further reduction in that area.

"And how are you feeling generally, Harry?" Vos told his doctor that he still felt tired quite frequently, just as he had before the mini-stroke. "Well that's not uncommon. Three things I always emphasise to patients in your position. Keep taking the pills. You'll be on them for life now. Stick to your diet – including keeping an eye on the alcohol intake – and make sure you get regular exercise."

Having sat and listened to these instructions, Vos felt free to ask his question. Although Kris the tattooist had told him about adverse drug reactions he wanted to get the view of a medic. The doctor was used to Vos' sudden switches of focus. For once he had a few spare moments and felt he could indulge his patient by listening to the brief summary of the circumstances that had led to the death of the man called Charlie. He remembered reading about him in his newspaper. When Vos had finished, the doctor paused before replying, hands steepled on the desk. He talked a little about the background to adverse reactions, before saying that in his view, it was probable that Charlie's problems had resulted from an allergy. However unless something had gone seriously wrong, he would have been stabilised at hospital.

+ + +

Being able to get back to work in the café was a great help to Edith. The day to day normality of serving coffees, snacks and lunches was pleasantly reassuring. There'd also been word from the theatre company that a new production was about to get underway and they wanted her involved.

But she still had some time to spend on the investigation and was pleased that after a period when things had stalled, the pace was hotting up again. She was heartbroken to learn from Vos that, after his reaction to the anaesthetic, Charlie hadn't been admitted to any hospital. She couldn't bear to think about the kind of death he must have experienced.

Vos had told her about Lennert and his crucial evidence. As he'd have been one of the last people to have seen Charlie alive, she felt she wanted to meet him. Having persuaded Kris to give her the number for Lennert's mobile, she had a long conversation with him and they agreed to meet in her café. Something clicked between them. He was keen to find out whether there might be evidence in the tattoo parlour showing some kind of link between Brouwers, his former boss and Webers. It seemed unlikely that what had happened was all down to chance.

A text Edith had just received from Vos informed her that Webers had been taken in by the police for questioning. She saw an opportunity and hatched a two-part plan with Lennert over their third cup of coffee. Edith said she'd be doing it for Charlie. Lennert told her that motivated him too, but he'd also be sticking it to his ex-boss.

After a diversion via Lennert's bedsit to pick up his tools, they made their way by bus to the tattoo parlour. Edith had decided to leave her car at home, fearing it might be picked up on CCTV. Lennert was nervous. His career to date had been somewhat chequered and he knew he'd have some explaining to do if he were to be picked up by the police with tools in his rucksack. As he'd hoped, getting into the parlour was straightforward. The rear door off a narrow alleyway had a simple lock which delayed him only for a few moments and the door was unbolted on the inside. The beeping of the alarm system sent Edith into a panic, but he went calmly to the control panel, entered a four digit code and the noise stopped abruptly.

"I knew he wouldn't have got round to changing the number since I walked out. He doesn't know the first thing about anything electronic." Lennert looked pleased with himself.

Gloved up, they crept around the parlour, penlights held low and entered the cramped, disorganised office. Edith made sure they had a system for searching for any documentation that referred to Rudy. Although they found no reference to him in the paperwork stored in a cardboard box, his name was there in the appointments book for the two relevant dates. A computer screen glowed in the darkness. Stuck under the small desk, Edith found a password on a post-it note which got her into the machine.

Scrolling quickly through the internet search history, she came across a link to a medical site. Clicking on this, details about adverse drug reactions appeared. Lennert explained what these were and she printed off copies of the relevant pages, without quite knowing how she'd be able to use them. On the off-chance she tried the same password on the email system and smiled as it let her in. People were so careless with their security! She scrolled back through emails in the inbox to the time around the dates of Charlie's two appointments. There were plenty of mundane details relating to appointments and supplies but nothing of interest to her. Webers must have been careful not to put anything in writing. She should have assumed that.

Lennert watched over her shoulder as she worked away and she could feel his breath on her cheek. It felt pleasant. Switching to the sent box, she found an email to a finance company informing them that his outstanding debt would be cleared within their seven day deadline. That was more like it. Another print off. Wondering where else within the office they could search, she glanced up to the pinboard above the desk which was covered in photos of tattoo designs and a rash of curling, yellow, post-it notes. Scanning them quickly she had to stifle a shout of 'yes!' when she saw the name Webers on one of the scribbled notes. Underneath his name, someone – presumably Brouwers – had scribbled a phone number and the words 'check total debts'. She knew that by itself, this didn't prove anything but put together with other evidence it might prove useful. Having taken a photocopy, she placed the note carefully back in position on the board. They were finished in the parlour.

It took two buses to get to Webers' house. On the journey she reassured Lennert that Webers really was being held by the police for questioning, so it was the ideal time to break into his place.

"Do you know if anybody else lives with him?" Lennert asked, as they surveyed the darkened, detached house from the opposite side of the street. Edith shook her head. "We'll just have to take a chance then."

They were relieved when there was no response to the front door bell. Lennert put his tools to good use again, but this second break-in was much more time-consuming. It was a warm evening and the tension just made the sweating worse, his thin shirt sticking to his back, his hands in danger of dropping the delicate tools. At least the thick garden hedging meant they wouldn't be seen from the street. Edith started to wonder about the sense of what they were doing. Webers might be a nasty piece of work, but breaking into his house was still a crime. Once she heard the satisfying sound of the barrel turning, she relaxed a little and they slipped inside the front door. To their great relief, the alarm control box just to the right of the door remained silent. Maybe Webers had been whisked out of the house so quickly by the police that he'd not had time to set it.

They both collapsed onto the sofa in the back living room.

"I don't think I could go through that again," Edith said. "Right, let's get to work."

"I hope he doesn't get an early release," Lennert said, instantly regretting his off-the-cuff comment when he saw Edith's face fall. "Not that it's going to happen. We'll be long gone by the time he's out."

Webers' place was in stark contrast to the disorganisation of the tattoo parlour, neat, tidy, almost spartan. There was no sign of a computer or a smartphone and very little in the way of paperwork, apart from a file containing a few household bills, one of which was for a phone. Edith scanned it quickly, all the time dreading the thought that some friend or relative of Webers, or worse still the man himself, might suddenly walk through the front door.

Charlie's number didn't appear on either bill. Then she kicked herself, opened her rucksack and retrieved the piece of paper where she'd written down the number of the phone Charlie had been using shortly before his death. There was a single call to that number on Webers' bill. Looking over her shoulder, Lennert whispered loudly that the call had been made a couple of days before Charlie's last appointment at the tattoo parlour.

"There's a call to the parlour as well," he added. Edith took a photo of the bill. Just before she replaced the papers she noticed a copy of a bank statement and took a photo of that as well for good measure.

Shelves in the front living room contained a surprising number of books. Edith hadn't expected Webers to be a reader. The red and white spine of one of the books caught her attention. She could remember a very similar one sitting on a shelf in Charlie's apartment. When she pulled it out she knew immediately it was one of his notebooks.

Later, in the sanctuary of the Café D'Anvers, as they drank to the success of their partnership, Edith flicked through the notebook.

"Webers must have taken this from Charlie's apartment or maybe there was something in the locker at Aalst station after all. It's all written in Marollien so Webers might have got nothing from it."

"What?" Lennert asked. She realised he had no idea what she was talking about and filled him in on the background, continuing to turn the pages of the book as she spoke.

"This is so brilliant. I can't wait to tell Harry about it," she said. "But I need to get my grandma to translate this for me."

"What?" Lennert asked again. She explained.

"So what are you going to do with the stuff we've found?"

"Well we probably won't be able to use most of it directly, because we've nicked it. But it can point us in the right direction. Charlie's notebook is a different matter. I'll claim I found it hidden in his apartment. There'll be no point in Webers trying to contradict this because then he'd have to explain how it came to be in his possession. So, I'm pretty certain we'll be able to use whatever we find in the notebook as direct evidence."

It felt good when she texted Vos to let him know what they'd discovered. It was another step forward in her efforts to nail Webers for what she was convinced he'd done to Charlie.

After they'd both finally calmed down, Lennert escorted Edith back home by bus and kissed her as they parted.

< so the lawyer got you out?

< very impressive, but there were big gaps in their evidence anyway

< anything serious to worry about?

< nothing that can't be sorted

< don't get complacent – he's worked it out

< has he got proof?

< no, he's full of bluster, but he could be dangerous

Maes

We're in the Oude Zwaan again. Vos builds up to things slowly, before telling me he tracked down Mertens. I panic until he reassures me that my name wasn't mentioned at all. The real shock is when he tells me Webers was taken in by the police for questioning about Charlie's death. Unfortunately a combination of insufficient evidence and Weber's fancy lawyer meant they couldn't hold him for long.

Vos goes on to talk about his two theories. Number one: Webers was involved in Charlie's death acting for the Green Guards. Number two: Webers was involved in Charlie's death acting for us – the Company.

He knows he's not going to get any further by trying to talk to Mertens again and asks me about Company records, whether they might be a route into finding out more about Webers. I tell him it's not a normal firm. Records are kept to a minimum and are tightly controlled. So there's a practical difficulty of knowing where to look. Operatives like me aren't based in an office. We're strictly self-employed and work from home, car or café – wherever's convenient. I tell Vos that the only way to mount an internal search would be to get into Mertens' office.

My mind is suddenly so focused on this possibility that I almost miss what Vos is saying. I've been expecting him to ask me to do something – he's had that look. But I'm wrong. He's giving me advice, telling me to go away, leave the country until it's safe to return. He's so insistent I promise him I'll disappear.

And when I tell him this, I really mean it.

+ + +

I even pack my bag. But I can't do it, can't just leave everything up in the air. If Mertens has any evidence, maybe I'm the only one who can find it.

I've only been to his office a couple of times before – reprimands after I'd fucked up jobs. Well that's the way he saw it anyway. I don't know the girl on reception but she seems nice enough. She looks at the rarely-used pass hanging round my neck and tells me I'll need to wait for the boss to return as he's just popped out to get something to eat. I haven't really got a plan. Should I just confront him or try and be more subtle about it? The waiting area is spacious, drinks machine in one corner, usual coffee table magazines on display, low reception desk and a room behind this where I can hear a copier churning away. Inner double doors leading to the office area are pass-controlled but I don't have the right kind of pass.

The copier's suddenly silent and the girl disappears. A man emerges through the inner double doors, struggling with a pile of files which threatens to topple and I'm quickly there by his side holding the door as he walks through, thanks me and disappears through the automatic exit doors. This is my chance. All the office doors in the inner sanctum are identical apart from their number and I'm struggling to remember Mertens'. Left along the corridor then first right, I seem to recall. The water cooler is a help. I remember there was one next to his office. The door isn't locked. It's all neat and tidy inside. He won't be out for long and I don't want to be here when he returns. Then I see it – his mobile, on the swivel chair behind his desk. Must have slipped out of his trouser pocket. I grab it and leave the office. Out in reception, there's nobody about. Through the half open door I can see the girl struggling with the innards of the copier. I tell her I can't wait any longer, will call back tomorrow, though I'm not sure she hears me.

Sitting in the taxi as I scroll through Mertens' phone, it feels almost like he's watching me.

I think I've hit the jackpot.

< find the phone first, then him
< this is getting out of hand
< just do it

Twenty Six

It was a two-boiled-egg day, a treat, with wholemeal toast, coffee, apple juice and Ravel on the radio. As Vos picked up his paper, the doorbell rang. It was a delivery man with a package to sign for. Vos scrawled an illegible signature on the electronic device that was placed under his nose and took the jiffy bag.

He called out to Edith, who was visiting so that they could plan their next steps, telling her that breakfast was on the table.

Swallowing a mouthful of slightly runny egg, he opened the bag and stared first at the mobile phone and then at the handwritten note.

This is Mertens' phone! Hope you find some of the messages useful. Must dash. M.

So he hadn't taken Vos' advice and left the country. He'd taken a huge risk to get hold of Mertens' phone and would now be in even greater danger. Vos didn't want there to be yet another victim. But the phone itself! Maybe it could help them tie the case up. He called out to Edith again. Her bleary-eyed look disappeared in an instant when she read the note.

They sat listening to the disembodied voices and scrolled through the texts, realising very quickly how valuable the information was. Vos slipped Mertens' phone into his pocket and pulled out his own. It was completely flat! He cursed himself for not having charged it overnight and asked Edith if she could tell Antoine about the package and its contents. Edith nodded, said she also needed to phone her grandma who hadn't been well and disappeared into the sitting room to make the calls.

Vos was in need of more coffee. As he waited for it to brew, the doorbell rang again. He swore, hauled himself up from the kitchen chair and went to answer the summons.

The fist knocked him off his feet. Webers loomed over him before hauling him up and propelling him into the kitchen. His face was so contorted that it was difficult for Vos to work out what he was saying. The gist of it was clear enough though – he'd come for the phone. But how had he known its whereabouts? Had he already dealt with Maes? The thought sickened him. As the note and the jiffy bag were still on the kitchen table, Vos was unable to pretend he hadn't received the phone. Webers slapped him hard across the face, demanding he hand it over.

"You'll see more of my fists unless you give me the damn thing right now!" Vos was at a loss to work out what to do next. Edith must have heard the commotion but perhaps was, very sensibly, hiding in the sitting room. Taking on Webers on his own would be very difficult. His head hurt and he just wanted to lie down.

Suddenly Webers looked away over Vos' shoulder and his face changed instantly – dominance replaced by complete distraction.

Vos turned. Edith was standing in the doorway, both hands grasping Demotte's gun tightly.

"I should put that down, young lady. You'll only end up hurting yourself!" Webers started to move towards Edith. She told him to stay where he was or he'd regret it. He sneered in response and kept moving forwards.

The gun flashed. The sound was deafening.

Maes

I'd asked the taxi to wait for me, a block away, whilst I was in Mertens' office. Afterwards, it dropped me off in the city centre. I mailed the phone to Vos – easy to find his address via the internet – then sent him a warning text.

I'd already decided to take his advice and had my passport and a small holdall with me. An immediate holiday, somewhere far away, was required. It was a long shot but I decided to phone Hanne to ask her to come with me. It wasn't until we started speaking that it dawned on me. Mertens would put his attack dog to work and if Webers was unable to find me, he'd go for Hanne. I warned her about this and in the next breath told her about my emergency holiday plans. She was up for it!

The following two hours seemed like an age, drinking coffee after coffee at the airport, keeping one eye open for Webers with the other desperately willing Hanne to come into view.

When she finally arrived, she was in tears. Webers had gone to her apartment, caught her just as she was leaving and grilled her until she broke down. She had no choice but to tell him I'd mailed the phone, special delivery. But she'd no idea about the package's destination as I hadn't told her. Webers had left in a rage.

Hanne had the good sense to take an indirect route out to the airport. Our flight wasn't busy, check-in was mercifully quick and we were both so relieved when the plane eventually took off.

Twenty Seven

Webers froze. He was still standing, but looked shaken and confused. Having guessed what had happened, Vos took his opportunity in an instant, caught Webers with a left hook and watched as he slumped to the floor. His old boxing skills were still there.

Vos and Edith stood staring at each other for a moment, open-mouthed.

"I can't hear a damn thing," Vos said, shouting. "How did you know about the gun?" She said she'd tell him later. He looked down at Webers' prone form. "He's not going to move for a bit, so we've got a little time to sort things out. Wipe your prints off the gun, just in case they find it. Wrap it up in a tea towel from the drawer there and put that in a plastic bag. We won't return it to the chimney flue. Storage amongst the potatoes would be a better bet – the ones growing outside, not the ones in the veg rack. Luckily, my ever-nosy neighbour has gone out – I saw her leave a bit ago – so she won't have heard anything and won't be there to watch you while you carry out a quick bit of gardening. Once you've buried the gun, which we won't mention again, I'll call the police and an ambulance."

When Edith returned to the kitchen, Vos made the call and they sat waiting for the emergency services to arrive.

"How come you know how to shoot a gun? You handled it very professionally. No wonder Webers looked terrified. And where on earth did you get that blank cartridge from?"

"Ah, so you guessed! I've got my father to thank for teaching me how to shoot. We used to go hunting in the woods outside Paris. As for the blank – I had one in my bag, a 5-in-1! It was just lucky that the 1910 was one of the compatible calibres."

"Sorry, you've completely lost me there."

"Look, perhaps we'd better leave explanations until later. It's hard enough for me to hear what you're saying. The important thing is, because the blanks were crimped, there was no discharge. Just a flash and a very loud noise. So we've got a good chance of getting away with denying the existence of a gun. Talk about being professional though. The way you floored Webers was very impressive. How about a coffee?"

They sat in silence, sipping occasionally from their mugs, Vos fearing the worst for Maes. He didn't want to have to read about yet another death.

+ + +

Blue lights everywhere, Weber, conscious again, carted off to hospital for a precautionary check-up, Vos and a police inspector sitting at the kitchen table.

At least it wasn't the annoying brat who'd interviewed him at Mechelen police station the last time he'd knocked a man unconscious. This guy was a lot older – and wiser too, Vos hoped. It took him a while to tell the whole story, Webers, Charlie, Vervloet, fracking, nuclear waste. The only thing he omitted from his story was any reference to the gun. Edith was being interviewed separately in the sitting room. Vos felt confident she'd stick to their agreed script. He was equally sure that sooner or later the accusations from Webers would start flying.

The inspector left the room telling Vos he had to make some phone calls. When he returned, his earlier politeness had disappeared. Despite his strong objections, Vos was handcuffed and told that he and Edith would be taken to Antwerp for further questioning.

+ + +

Vos recognised Chief Inspector Dirken straight away, thought he looked incongruous, dressed in checked trousers and a pale yellow shirt and assumed he must have come straight from the golf course, dragged in to the investigation on his day off perhaps, unlikely to be in a good mood.

"I thought I'd made it perfectly clear to you, Vos, that there would be serious consequences if you repeated unsubstantiated claims about links to nuclear waste in this case. But it looks even more serious for you now, given Mr Webers' statement that you pulled a gun on him."

Although he was expecting the accusation to be made at some point, Vos had to make it look and sound as if he was genuinely appalled by Dirken's words.

"What on earth are you talking about? What gun?" The plastic cuffs dug into his wrists painfully.

"Webers has been interviewed and stated clearly that you pulled a gun on him, just before you knocked him unconscious. How do you explain that?"

"He's making it up, trying to cast himself as some sort of victim when there's clear evidence of his involvement in the deaths of at least two people. As I've already told your inspector, there's more evidence on the phone of a man called Mertens who works for Redline. He used Webers to do his dirty work and that included arranging for both Charlie and Vervloet to be killed. You need to be concentrating on that. Webers is trying to distract you. Look, please phone Chief Inspector Bernard Antoine in Charleroi. He'll confirm everything I've said."

"You mean your cousin. Yes I'm sure he'd confirm it all, but you may well have been feeding him a line. Whether there's any truth in what you've been telling him and what you're telling us now...we'll have to wait and see. Don't forget, Vos, Webers has been interviewed previously about your claims and subsequently released."

"But that was before the evidence revealed on Mertens' phone. That's what you need to consider now!"

Dirken scratched his chin, reached into his pocket and pulled out a red golf tee, studying it carefully as if it were a source of inspiration.

"But it's not just the gun, is it? Your record includes another recent assault, a previous conviction and time spent inside. I have to say it doesn't look good for you."

Vos hoped things wouldn't get any worse. But then his conviction for assault had been in the 1960's, although for some reason it was still on the books. And his arrest for an assault on Daems, only a few months previously, had eventually been proved to be self-defence. And Antoine would back him up, surely.

+ + +

It was the early hours of the morning before they were released. By then, the police had examined the messages on Mertens' phone and realised Webers was implicated up to his neck. Ryck arrived at the police station, to act as taxi driver. He wanted to know everything. Vos was exhausted, but gave him an edited summary, whilst Edith dozed on the back seat.

"So he claimed you had a gun? I can't believe it!"

"Nonsense, of course," Vos said wearily. It was very hard to keep up this pretence. He wanted to tell his nephew the full story, but felt it was essential to maintain the cover-up consistently. That way, nobody could blurt out the truth inadvertently if the police should come round asking awkward questions.

Despite all the worrying and confusing events of the previous day and the early morning, Vos couldn't help but feel amused by Webers' claim that it was him who'd been the one to pull the gun – not Edith. Perhaps admitting that he'd been brought down by a woman didn't square with Webers' macho self-image.

Katerine was on the doorstep to usher them in. Taking one look at Vos, she knew all the questions buzzing around her head would have to wait until the morning.

+ + +

5:00 am. Wide awake. Vos realised that his phone was where he'd left it the previous day, plugged in for recharge.

Two texts from Maes. The first warned him about Webers, which would have been very useful had he only opened it yesterday. The second produced a huge sigh of relief.

Out of the country, heading for the sun, back when it's safe. Thanks for the advice. I just took a while to act on it! M.

+ + +

Edith was up well before Vos. By the time he arrived in the kitchen to tuck into the scrambled eggs ready and waiting on his plate, she was just finishing telling Katerine her account of the previous night's events. This pleased him as it meant he wouldn't have to go through the story himself. But, as he finished the eggs, he was taken aback by Katerine's question.

"Did you know the police came here to search for a gun? It was dreadful. Is there anything you'd like to tell me?" Without glancing at Edith, Vos made a quick decision. If there was one person who had to know the unexpurgated version of the story, it was Katerine, particularly as he'd said nothing to her about

holding onto the gun for all those weeks. The police search would
have been a real shock for her.

During his combined explanation and confession, he was
impressed by Katerine's calmness. He put it down at least in part
to Edith's continued presence.

"Don't tell me where you've hidden it, I don't want to know,"
she said when he'd finished. "But please tell me you're going to get
rid of it for good." He agreed immediately, but added, somewhat
in self-defence, that a combination of the weapon and Edith's
quick thinking had saved him from a proper beating at the hands
of Webers, so it wasn't all bad. "Edith told me about the blank.
Did you know?"

"Well I guessed when the damn thing went off and Webers
was still standing that it was probably a blank. But you'll have
to enlighten me, Edith. How come you walk around with one of
those things in your bag?"

"Well, you know I'm an actor. We use them on stage. The play
we're doing at present is a whodunit, and a gun is fired in Act One
Scene One. Because I'm the only one who knows anything about
firearms, I'm the one who gets to look after the blanks. The pistol's
kept elsewhere so it's perfectly safe."

"And what was that you said about a 5-in-1 or something?"

She explained that such blanks could be compatible with a
range of different calibers. She'd been lucky that it had fitted the
old wartime 1910.

"But how did you know about the gun and where it was
hidden? That's another thing that amazed me," Vos said.

"Well – I have a confession to make, Harry. If you remember
I was staying here when you returned from your uncle's welcome
party. You took a plastic bag out of your rucksack and disappeared
into the sitting room. It was all a bit furtive and I'm sorry to say
spying on you was the only way I could satisfy my curiosity.
The door was partly open and I was able to see you taking out

the gun. The difficulty you had in reaching the hiding place in the chimney flue made it clear to me exactly where it was and I double-checked this a while later. I certainly wouldn't have found it otherwise. I hope you can forgive me."

"Given what you saved me from, I think that might be possible," Vos said smiling broadly.

"That must have taken real nerve, Edith," Katerine added. "How can we ever thank you enough?"

"Well I have to admit," Edith replied. "I got a lot of pleasure firing that gun at Webers. It was a little bit of revenge for what he did to Charlie."

Twenty Eight

Little Sun bounced up and down on Vos' good knee. The living room in Magda's house was full of toddler things, a series of trip hazards, he couldn't help thinking with his old union hat on.

He was reeling from a volley of nursing facts and figures that Ryck had been throwing in his direction. Once that particular running commentary ended, he started on the latest details about Magda's pregnancy. At the end of these two monologues, there was only a brief pause, before his questions started.

"Tell me about Charlie. Everyone I know is hooked on the story," he said, as he refilled his glass with fruit juice

"That stuff won't last long, the speed you're drinking it at. It doesn't grow on trees you know!" Vos wondered at first why so many people seemed to take such vicarious pleasure in other people's misfortunes, not to mention their deaths. But then, wasn't he just as guilty of that? "You're right about Charlie. There's been no end of interest. Did you know there'd been a second autopsy?" Ryck said he'd seen something about it on TV. "Well they did another toxicological analysis and the details showed that cause of death was most likely to have been the kind of adverse drug reaction that you told me about. The suspicion is that Brouwers, the tattooist, deliberately used a substance he knew Charlie was allergic to."

"So why wasn't this highlighted by the first autopsy?" Ryck asked.

"Well the body had been exposed to the elements for months – all that rain and the ground was waterlogged – so the signs of a reaction were much less pronounced than they'd normally be. Perhaps it wasn't surprising that they were missed first time around. "

"And what about Webers? How did you work out that he was carrying out dirty work for Redline?"

"Well I was a bit blind to that at first and had him down as being a Green Guard. But the more I found out, the more it seemed to make sense that he might have been hired to do various jobs for the Company. We only got proof of it when we read messages on Mertens' phone, the one that Maes liberated. Sorry, are you familiar with those names? They both worked for Redline."

"Yes, I remember. Will the police be able to nail Webers then?"

"I'm confident they will, not least because of incriminating evidence on his own phone. Several other things tie him in to Charlie's death: Lennert's testimony about what went on in the tattoo parlour, some of the information he and Edith found on their break-ins at the parlour and Webers' house and then there's two lots of CCTV footage – firstly of Webers bundling Charlie into the back of a car outside the tattoo parlour and secondly from another camera, which showed Webers in the front passenger seat and another man driving them out of the city. I think I told you before, that when the police checked, they found that Charlie hadn't been admitted to any hospital, so that again points the finger at Webers because he'd told them in the parlour that's what he'd do. Lack of treatment led directly to Charlie's death. Any chance of some of that fruit juice for me by the way, before it's all gone?"

"It must have taken some nerve for Edith and her guy to carry out those break-ins. What else did they find?" Ryck said filling a glass and handing it to his uncle.

"Thanks. Yes – they took some real risks. I'd no idea what they were up to. Most of the stuff they found can't be used as direct evidence, because of how it was obtained. But it's been really helpful in building up the bigger picture. It's different with Charlie's notebook. They told the police that they found it hidden away in Charlie's apartment, which means the evidence it contains can be used. But – keep this to yourself, Ryck – the truth is they found it when they broke into Webers' house. The notebook tells us a lot. Charlie wrote a fair bit about Webers. They seem to have got quite close. Through their friendship, Webers found out what Charlie had really been up to."

"And what had he been up to?"

"The detail was all in Charlie's notebook and it was a real surprise! He worked out a way of undermining Redline by playing them at their own game. His pal Vervloet told him about the Company's plans for a fracking site. Redline were in the process of arranging test drillings there. This wasn't public knowledge – it was all hush hush. Along comes Charlie armed with this inside information and he goes and makes an offer to buy one of the farms, one which was crucial to the viability of Redline's plan. Used money his dad had left him – which was much more than Edith or anyone else knew about – and he also had plans for some kind of crowdfunding to do the same thing again. It was a complete spanner in their works and that's why Redline decided he had to go, for fear that their fracking plans would unravel. Mertens told Webers to cook up a plan to get rid of Charlie before everything got out of hand. Oh! Hang on a minute, I think this little one needs changing."

Vos handed Sun over to Ryck for the nappy-changing routine and waited until both were settled, before continuing his story.

"There were two parts to Webers' plan. The first was to discredit Charlie by putting the story about that he'd sold out and gone to work for Redline. He knew this would infuriate some of the Green Guards and he could then put it about that they were the ones responsible for Charlie's death. The second part of the plan was to make arrangements to get rid of him. Webers knew Charlie needed two final tattoo removal sessions and he used their friendship to persuade him not only to go to Brouwers' tattoo parlour for these sessions but also to have an anaesthetic. Now, here's the thing. The police discovered from details on Webers' phone and some information found in the parlour, that Brouwers had done a number of fixer jobs for Webers over the years. So Webers had a hold over him. Not only that, but he knew the tattooist was up to his ears in debt and they came to a deal – all his debts would be cleared in return for him arranging some kind of mishap with the anaesthetic used on Charlie. Brouwers used an appropriate jab for the first session, but for the final one he used an anaesthetic he knew from the consent form that Charlie would be allergic to."

"So Brouwers is the one directly responsible for Charlie's death, but Webers and Mertens are guilty of setting it all up?"

"Exactly! Now it just needs to be proved in court."

"That's an awful lot to take in, Uncle," Ryck said. "Are you OK to carry on for a bit longer? I don't want you getting too tired." Vos said he'd be alright for a short while.

"So how did Charlie's body get to the Sambre valley?"

"It's my view, shared by the police, that Webers and the other guy in the car must have driven out to the river near Charleroi and dumped his body there. It would have taken two men to carry him from the nearest vehicle track to the riverside. So it's no wonder there wasn't a trace of Charlie on the CCTV cameras around Charleroi station. He never went near the place. Perhaps the train ticket in Charlie's pocket was put there by Webers in order to confuse any police enquiry"

"But I don't follow," Ryck said. "Why would they want to leave his body in that particular place by the river?"

"That puzzled us all for a while, but it makes sense when you think it through. Like I said before, Webers wanted to make it look like some extremists in the Green Guards killed him because he'd sold out to the Company. What better place to leave him, than slap bang in the middle of the intended Redline fracking site?"

"And what are the police working on now?"

"Getting more evidence basically – checking CCTV footage, trawling through bank accounts, phone records and the like. From what Bernard told me, it's just a matter of time before they get enough on both Webers and Mertens. Edith was particularly interested in a text which referred to Webers hacking her phone. No wonder he was able turn up at Aalst station at exactly the right time to rob me of the locker key. He knew from a message on her phone where, when and why we'd be meeting. Look, I'm sorry, Ryck, I need to put my feet up for a bit. Katerine will be dropping in here soon to pick me up. You could always try grilling her if you've got any more questions."

+ + +

It turned into a bit of a family gathering. Katherine arrived at the house at the same time as Magda's father, Zyg. She decided not to rouse Harry but let him sleep on for a while. She caught up with news of Magda's pregnancy then listened as Zyg told his granddaughter one of his stories. As they sat around the table eating sandwiches and cakes, Ryck asked Katerine if she'd mind filling him in on one or two bits of the case that he'd not yet heard about.

"Certainly Ryck, particularly if it means there'll be less for Harry to have to tell you. Where are the gaps?"

"Well, I think I'm up to speed as far as Charlie's concerned, but I wanted to ask about Vervloet and the other man whose name escapes me."

"You mean Poortmans?" He nodded. "OK, Andries Vervloet first. It looks like Webers was in the car that killed him – either as the driver or a passenger. There was a woman who witnessed two men at the scene just after he died. Since then, she'd been away on a cruise for weeks, but on her return she was able to identify one of the men as Webers. You might already have heard that Vervloet and Charlie were schoolmates. They'd lost touch and then met up again through some environmental organisation. It wasn't the Green Guards – another smaller outfit whose name I forget. Over time, Andries had got more and more disillusioned with the work he was doing for Redline and wanted to expose their methods. Not only did he leak information to Charlie about the fracking site in the Sambre valley, but he fed confidential information about the Company to Poortmans who was a university researcher. Redline didn't find out about all this until after Charlie's body was discovered. Webers heard a rumour through the Guards' grapevine about what Vervloet had been up to. That's when they bugged his apartment and picked up on his links with Poortmans. Mertens decided he was a loose cannon, too much of a danger and the hit and run followed."

"And what happened to Poortmans? Wasn't he the one whose car crashed into a bridge?"

"That's right. No evidence has been found to link his death to Redline. I told Harry that I had personal experience of Poortmans' awful driving, so his death may just have been a dreadful accident."

"Thanks Katerine. I think that's all – well, apart from Edith. Is she back home now?" Katerine was beginning to realise just how relentless Ryck's questioning could be.

"After Charlie's funeral, she was finally able to get away – took herself off to India. I think her grandma treated her to the holiday. Goodness knows she needed a break after all she'd been through. And it looks like there's something happening between her and the young tattooist Lennert. Is that your lot, Ryck?"

"One final question – I promise! What's Harry decided to do with Barto? Is he going to keep him?"

"I'm pleased to say he is. The doctor told Harry he needs to have regular exercise. But you know what he's like. He'll usually find something else to do. But with Barto there's no choice and he'll have to walk him twice a day. Your grandma and Jan will still be able to have him on loan now and then and they're fine with that."

Stretched out on a sunlounger in the tiny back garden, Katerine thought about the things she hadn't told Ryck. It had been on the tip of her tongue say something about her and Harry. But as she was keen for things to be small scale and low key, she didn't want to tell anyone about a wedding they weren't going to be invited to.

And there'd been no mention of the gun either. It had been very promptly removed from its temporary hiding place in amongst the potato tubers and made the journey to Albert's house. Now it was on display in a local museum. When he made the donation, Albert told them he'd held on to the firearm ever since the war but had decided he no longer wanted the responsibility of having it in his house.

Vos had said he thought it was exactly what Demotte senior would have wanted – had he been consulted about the matter.

The sound of a wind chime filtered through from an adjacent garden and mingled with the distant shrieks and shouts of children playing. Katerine thought about Kim who was working two days a week – some kind of consultancy which paid megabucks. Despite risking her career to provide information about Terra Incognita, nothing had happened to the company since the detail had been passed on to Dirken. They were probably untouchable – too well connected. Responsibility for problems arising within their empire would be blamed on individuals who'd gone off the rails, nothing to do with the network – the classic 'bad apple' defence.

Still, at least Redline would be taking the hit.

On a Greek island

The two witnesses were the owners of the bride and groom's three-storey wooden holiday house.

It was a brief ceremony. Vos was far too hot in his tweed jacket, one he'd bought on a holiday in Scotland many years ago. Katerine wore a light, floaty, long blue dress she'd spotted in the local market two days previously, a small spray of flowers pinned to her hair. They had a wedding breakfast of freshly caught fish and freshly picked fruit.

Afterwards, the bus took them from Skopelos Town to the beach at Panormos where they swam together, he slow and ponderous, she cutting through the clear water effortlessly.

In the beachside taverna, they sat sipping drinks at a table in the shade of a fig tree.

"So, no regrets, Mrs Vos?" he said, in his best teasing voice.

"Oh no! I'm still Katerine Verlinden to you and the rest of the world."

"I meant, any regrets about coming here without any of our friends or relatives?" She paused and looked out across the bay before answering.

"None at all. I've never told you this. I was sort of ashamed about it – not that I should have been. Years ago when I was just a young woman, I was due to be married." Vos looked incredulous. "We had this big ceremony planned, over a hundred guests, posh reception we couldn't afford, the works. And he got cold feet two days before the big day. At least it wasn't at the altar! So this," she said, spreading her arms out, "is perfect."

He stood up and put his arms around her, kissing the top of her head.

"You poor thing! Why didn't you tell me before now?"

"Like I said, love, I was embarrassed by the whole thing. I said I'd never get married after that, but luckily I changed my mind." She looked up and kissed him.

"You know, I could live here," Vos said, gazing at the tiny ripples on the shoreline.

"Could you?"

"No, not really! But maybe one of us could sell up and we could invest in that olive hut in the trees over there, our very own holiday retreat."

"Now you're talking," she said, closing her eyes.

Acknowledgments

Thanks to Emma, my editor and John, Paul, Andrew and Virginia, my readers.

Thanks to all at the Yorkshire Writers' Lunch group for their encouragement and support.

By the same author

DARKSTONE

DARKSTONE

DAVE RIGBY

Ellis Landsman, a forester living in the Scottish Outlands in the 2020's is shocked to find a wolf in his forest uncovering the body of a young woman.

He rescues the body and makes the long snow-covered journey to Glasgow to report the death and hand the body over to the Brigade, the semi-militaristic security force that has replaced the police.

But Ellis doesn't trust the Brigade to investigate the death and decides to try and find out for himself who the woman is, how she died and how she came to be buried on his land.

But all is not as it seems as Ellis struggles to track down the young woman's killer…

SHORELINE

A HARRY VOS INVESTIGATION

DAVE RIGBY

Harry Vos, a retired man in his 60s and a part-time private investigator, is shocked to find a body washed up on a beach on the Belgian coast.

Unable to get a signal on his phone he hurries to a local bar to contact the police.

On his return he discovers that the body has disappeared and finds he has some explaining to do once the police arrive.

They regard him as a time-waster.

Harry decides to try and find out what has happened and his investigation leads him into the murky and dangerous waters of people-smuggling.